CHANCE ENCOUNTER

OTHER BOOKS AND BOOKS ON CASSETTE
BY JENNIE HANSEN:

Run Away Home

Journey Home

Coming Home

When Tomorrow Comes

Macady

Some Sweet Day

All I Hold Dear

The River Path

CHANCE ENCOUNTER

• • • • • • • • • • • • • • • • • • • •

A Novel

JENNIE HANSEN

Covenant Communications, Inc.

Covenant

Published by Covenant Communications, Inc.
American Fork, Utah

Printed in the United States of America
First Printing: August 2000

07 06 05 04 03 02 01 00 10 9 8 7 6 5 4 3 2 1

ISBN 1-57734-671-8

For all those who have a special place in their hearts for Christmas and children, and especially for my grandchildren who remind me of the simple joys of the season. This is for you, Christopher, David, and Nathan Robinson, Spencer Sperry, and Mckayla Anderson. God bless you always.

PROLOGUE

The car lurched crazily, and there was no mistaking the rhythmic thump that met her ears. A flat tire! That was all she needed. Kendra slowed the car and brought it to the edge of the road. She didn't immediately shut off the engine. She let it run, keeping the heater pumping warm air into the car while she considered her options. If she were Cameron or Katy, she could pick up a car phone and summon a husband to come to the rescue. The windshield wipers mocked her contemplation. She wasn't her sisters and there were no options—or husband. The tire was flat, and rain or no rain, there was no one to change it but her.

"Over the ground lies a mantle of white . . ." Kendra frowned, and with an angry snap turned off the radio. She was sick to death of Christmas carols, and she didn't need any reminder that she should be grateful it was only raining, not yet snowing. She wasn't in the mood to be grateful.

Pulling her coat closer around her, she checked the buttons to make certain they were all fastened. Too bad she wasn't wearing her thick ski parka, but the forecast had said milder temperatures than normal. And she was on her way to southern California. Besides, Katy would consider her parka hopeless, swiftly donate it to some charity, and replace it with something terribly chic and terribly expensive. Kendra had left the parka hanging in the back of her closet, waiting for her return.

The coat she wore was a soft cream-color with a rich, chocolate lining that had caught her eye on her lunch hour a few days ago, and she'd thought it perfect for this trip. Impulsively she'd bought it. She didn't usually give in to impulse, but the coat had seemed so right. Her sisters entertained lavishly and she didn't want them to be ashamed of her. It was bad enough they pitied her.

Before stepping out of the car, she looked both ways up and down the highway. There was no help in sight. Of course, she wasn't the helpless sort of woman who needed assistance changing a tire, she reminded herself as she popped the trunk, then stepped outside the car. She shivered in the cold, wet air as she retrieved the jack and necessary tools.

It took longer to loosen the lug nuts than to actually change the tire. She was perspiring in spite of the drizzling cold rain by the time she finished. Giving the wrench a final twist, she glared at the small tire. It just seemed so stupid to go to all that work to put on a tire that would only take her forty or fifty miles, then have to be changed again.

As she put away the tools, she noticed a dark smear on her coat, and the hem sagged where she'd gotten it wet, kneeling to push the tire into place. Her shoulders slumped. That was all she needed—to arrive at her sister's house looking like a drowned rat!

Once back in the car, she turned up the heater full blast and stripped off her coat, setting it on the floor in front of the heating vent on the passenger side to dry. Perhaps it would look better once it was dry again. Her silk shirt and tailored slacks weren't much protection from the cold, she thought as she surveyed the mud spatters on the wet fabric. The knee-soaked pants were probably ruined—along with any hope of arriving at Katy's home looking chic and successful. Shivering in spite of the heater, she dug through the suitcase she'd left on the back seat until she found a dry pair of jeans and a sweater. She almost hadn't brought the jeans. They lacked a designer label and would cause Katy to wrinkle her nose in disdain. After only a moment's hesitation, she decided the steamed-over windows and the continuing rain provided an adequate privacy screen. Wiggling to avoid the steering wheel, she quickly changed.

Feeling drier, if still not warm, she changed the heater to defrost, trying to clear her windshield, and wiped the side windows until she could see her mirrors. The car lurched slowly as she pulled back onto the highway to begin the slow bumpy trek to the next town. She hoped there would be a service station where she could get the tire fixed. She might have to stay the night, she thought gloomily. Just what she needed, a night alone in some small Nevada town she'd never heard of! That should contribute to making this the most miserable Christmas ever!

She knew she shouldn't have delayed starting this trip. Ordinarily she would be excited over seeing her sisters and playing with their children. But this year she had a touch of Scrooge fever. Each Christmas seemed to get harder, and this one was shaping up to be the worst yet.

She'd tried to get out of making the trip this year, but her sisters had insisted that families should be together for Christmas. That was easy for them to say; they both had husbands and children of their own. With the Church's emphasis on marriage and families, she'd comforted herself for years with the belief that her turn would come. But with the passage of her thirty-fifth birthday last month something seemed to die in her heart, and she dreaded the coming of another Christmas surrounded by her sisters' families. They would be kind to her. They loved her and she loved them, but it was hard to avoid wondering why God had been so much more generous with His blessings to her sisters than to her.

Kendra had offered to cancel her vacation and stay at the office to work in someone else's place, but the ones who didn't have plans wanted the overtime, and the ones who did, had already made arrangements a long time ago to have their positions covered. Without an excuse to stay in Salt Lake, and lacking the will to disappoint her sisters, she was once more traveling to California to ooh and ah over their beautifully decorated homes, sit through their boring, but perfect dinner parties, and admire their adorable children. Kendra sighed inwardly. Indulging in a "Why did I get stuck with two Martha Stewarts for sisters?" pity party would get her nowhere. Her sisters were wonderful young women, and it wasn't their fault she wasn't more like them.

A dark cluster of trees loomed on the horizon, and Kendra breathed a sigh of relief as she passed a sign that said Darcy, 2 mi. Thank goodness, there was a town up ahead. It wasn't yet five o'clock, so with a little luck, she still might be able to get the tire fixed and be on her way before dark.

CHAPTER 1

The sudden silence brought Vicki's head up. No! Not now! That old washing machine couldn't quit on her now. It was less than a week until Christmas, and with Guy out of work, there was no money for repairs.

"Look, Mom!" Becca held up an advertisement from the local paper. "Decker's has a toy village with Santa. Can we go see the dolls tonight? It says they have the new Sports Barbie." There was a wistfulness to the girl's voice that clearly spelled out her hope that the doll would miraculously find its way beneath their Christmas tree in a few days' time.

"Do they gots trains? Choo-choo-choo!" Five-year-old David doubled up his fists and with his arms bent at the elbows, mimicking the piston action of the wheels on an old-style locomotive, began chugging around the kitchen.

"Go play outside," Vicki snapped, peevishly flipping her long blond hair away from her damp face. She couldn't stand one more word about Sports Barbies or trains. There wasn't enough money to put a decent meal on the table for Christmas, let alone purchase expensive toys. She wished there were some way to just make Christmas go away.

"In the rain?" David asked, obviously half hoping she meant her impulsive order.

"Rain? No, of course not." Vicki wiped a lingering hand across her face, pressing the spot beside her eye where a headache had started. Of course, she hadn't meant to send the children out in the rain. "Just . . . go in the other room to play. I've got to get the clothes out of the washer and hang them up." The dryer had dried its last load months ago. The clothes she washed these days had to be hung from the shower rod in the bathroom, on an olden wooden rack she'd found in the garage when they'd moved in, or draped over kitchen chairs.

"I'll help," Becca volunteered. She skipped over to the washer to peer inside. She started to reach inside, then turned questioning eyes toward her mother. "It's still full of water," she observed solemnly.

"I know." Vicki knew her voice sounded defeated. "It broke again."

"Can Daddy fix it?" Becca's eyes mirrored the discouragement her mother felt. The holiday excitement that had radiated from her face moments ago faded.

"I hope so," Vicki responded, but she didn't fool her daughter. She knew it wasn't likely the washer could be repaired. It was nearly twenty years old and had come to them secondhand. Guy told her the last time he'd repaired the washer that it was worn out, and even if he had the money for parts, it wasn't worth fixing. She watched Becca walk back across the room to pick up the flyer. Without even glancing at it one last time, she folded it in fourths, and dropped it in the trash can. Becca was mature for her age and knew better than to expect an expensive doll for Christmas, but it hurt Vicki to see her daughter's hopes dashed this way.

"Hey!" David shouted. "I want to look at the trains."

"Trains cost too much money," Becca informed him in that superior manner only an older sister can muster. "Daddy doesn't have a job, so he doesn't have any money."

"I'm going to ask Santa Claus, not Daddy," David defended his wish.

"What's this you're not going to ask Daddy?" came a voice from the doorway.

"Daddy!" David ran to meet his father, who promptly scooped him up in one arm, making him giggle as he brushed the little boy's cheek with his own cheek, tickling him with his five o'clock shadow. "Becca says I can't have a train. But I've been really good, and I'm going to ask Santa Claus."

Vicki's eyes met Guy's over David's head, and she saw the discouragement there. "No luck?" she mouthed. Her husband shook his head, but then his expression brightened.

"I helped old Mr. Mosely down at Mosely's Market unload a couple of pallets of fresh produce for his store. Mosely said he couldn't pay me cash, but he gave me a ham and this bag of potatoes and oranges and things like that."

Vicki tried to smile. At least she wouldn't have to serve her family Christmas dinner with whatever she could put together from their meager supply of bottled fruits and vegetables in the basement. Guy had worked for these few groceries, but somehow it still felt like charity. The ward Relief Society president had given a lesson a couple of weeks ago on the blessings of giving and had quoted the familiar scripture in the thirty-fifth verse of Acts chapter 20. *It is more blessed to give than to receive.* She'd certainly like to be able to be on the giving end rather than the receiving. Giving might be full of blessings, but receiving was just plain hard. She took the bag from Guy and began removing items to place in the refrigerator.

"I stopped at the post office to pick up the mail, too. There's a letter from your dad," Guy told her.

"Probably a Christmas card. He's not up to much more than that these days." Thinking of her father added to her melancholy. She wished she could help him, but the distance was too great and they had no money. They wouldn't even be sending him a gift this year. He'd broken his hip several months ago and his recovery had been painfully slow. Lately it seemed that it had become increasingly difficult for him to write as well. The children would be disappointed when he didn't send them packages for Christmas this year. But he really couldn't get around well enough to go shopping or to haul packages to the post office. Vicki suspected his long convalescence had pretty near stripped his savings account and that he didn't have the financial means to buy gifts anyway.

She reached for the envelope and slipped her fingernail beneath the flap slowly sliding it across the seal. To her astonishment out fluttered a fifty-dollar bill. Becca scooped it up before Vicki could bend to retrieve it.

"It's money," the little girl gasped with resurrected excitement. "Can we go to Decker's?"

"I don't think so." Vicki tried to temper what she knew would be disappointing for her daughter to hear. "Grandpa sent that money so we could get something we all need for a Christmas present." It was money her father couldn't afford to give away, she thought guiltily. Even so, it was easier to accept money from him than the groceries Mr. Mosely had given them or the hand-me-down clothes Mrs. Robertson sent over last week for the kids.

"I want a Sports Barbie," Becca stated her case.

"I want a train!" David's eyes shone.

"Guy, the washer broke down today. Fifty dollars is enough for a down payment . . ." She let her words trail off. She didn't want to see the disappointment on her children's faces. She didn't have to see them to know they'd consider a washing machine a poor Christmas present.

Guy's shoulders slumped and he looked like the burden was too much for just a moment, then he straightened his shoulders and smiled. "Let's go into the living room. There's a story I want to tell you. It's all about the very first Christmas." With an arm around Vicki, he led the way.

• • • • •

Kendra hunched her shoulders and drew deeper inside her coat while taking a step closer to the plate glass window, as if its brightly lit display would offer her a little warmth. She should go inside, out of the rain, but she really wasn't in the mood for Christmas shopping. The man at the garage had said an hour and suggested she wait across the street at Decker's Department Store. She'd nodded absently and crossed the street, but now that she was here she felt reluctant to go inside. She wanted to be on her way.

She wondered why she was so anxious to be on her way when she wasn't all that anxious to arrive at her destination. Sure she looked forward to seeing her sisters, but she'd stayed with Cameron and Kurt last Christmas and felt like a useless fifth wheel, and she didn't expect it would be any better this year at Katy and Bob's home. Kendra had alternated Christmases with her sisters since they'd both married several years ago. There had been a time when she'd dreamed of a husband and children of her own, and she'd imagined how they'd spend holidays together wrapped in love and warmth, doing all those things families do to build traditions and share with one another.

Too much work and worry had ended her dreams. For a time the dreams had kept her going, and though she couldn't say exactly when they had ended, eventually reality had intruded. Kendra knew she wasn't pretty or outgoing; in fact, most people saw her as shy. Even before her mother died, leaving two young sisters for her oldest daughter to raise and put through school, Kendra had known she wasn't like other girls. Boys—and later, men—didn't give her a second look. Perhaps they would have noticed her more if she'd been able to dress better, but she could never spend money for clothing and social activities when every penny was needed to care for her sisters.

Now at thirty-five, she didn't suppose she would ever marry. She should be grateful her sisters and their families loved her and invited her to share their happiness, but Christmas always left her a little depressed, wondering what might have been.

She didn't really regret anything she'd done for her sisters. They'd grown up to be lovely young women, and she was proud of them and all their accomplishments. They'd married likable men with good professional expectations. It was just Christmas. Something about the holiday always left her feeling like an outsider. She had a good job, and she liked her apartment. She had friends, and she wasn't the only single sister in her ward. It was just the incessant holiday cheer, the constant barrage of Christmas carols, and too much rich food that left her feeling she was missing something. Then there were the memories. Christmas always made her remember how it had been when she was really small and Daddy was alive, before Mama became ill. Daddy never seemed to mind that she preferred jeans to dresses and sports to tea parties.

A gust of wind blew a spray of rainwater in her face, causing her to shiver. She was being childish; she still had presents to buy for her nephew and nieces, and little time left in which to finish her shopping. Instead of standing here feeling sorry for herself and getting soaking wet, she should be thankful her flat tire occurred near this peaceful little town, rather than far out in the desert she'd just crossed, or on the mountain road she'd soon be following. She'd only had to travel about twenty miles on her car's spare "doughnut." With Christmas less than a week away, standing here in the rain was sheer foolishness.

"Whooo! Whooo!"

Startled, Kendra glanced around for the source of the sound. Practically at her elbow stood a small boy with his face pressed against the department store window. He turned, and their eyes met. A sparkle of mischief lurked in his eyes' deep blue depths, and a broad grin spread across his face, revealing a dimple in each cheek. A mop of blond curls sparkled with rain mist where his hood had been pushed back. He looked not much older than Katy's four-year-old Bobby.

"I like the red one best!" the small boy announced enthusiastically.

"The red one?" She was startled into a response.

"See!" He pointed at the window with one chubby hand. A mitten dangled from a cord hanging out of the sleeve of his too-small coat.

She looked to where he was pointing. For the first time, she noticed that the window where she'd huddled for a small respite from the cold rain housed a miniature ceramic village with two electric trains racing through tunnels, crossing bridges, and hurrying in endless circles through the town. One train engine was black, and the other red. A fleeting memory of herself as a small girl, peering into a toyshop window to watch the trains, rose in her mind. She smiled, thinking of the little tomboy she'd been, and how she'd dreamed of having an electric train of her own.

The memory dimmed. There had been no money for trains, and even if there had been, her mother wouldn't have given her a train. Her mother's tastes ran more to dolls with real hair and satin dresses, dolls that looked just like Katy and Cameron had looked when they were little girls.

If Daddy were alive, he would understand about the train, she'd consoled herself each Christmas when she'd found the inevitable doll under the tree. In time, she'd accepted that Daddy was gone, and there never would be a train.

No, she wouldn't think about that. And she'd gotten past comparing her tall, gangly shape and short brown hair to her sisters' golden curls and doll-like features a long time ago. God had blessed her with good health, a sound mind, and the ability to work hard, and for that she should be grateful.

"Do you think Santa Claus will bring me a train like that?" The boy scrunched up his face and studied hers, as though he expected she had all of the answers to life's difficult questions.

"I don't know," she answered honestly. "You should ask your mom or dad about that." Where were the child's parents anyway? Hadn't he been taught not to speak to strangers? "Are your parents inside the store?" she asked, supposing she should find the store manager or someone with some kind of authority to take charge of the child and see him reunited with his family. What kind of parents allowed a child to roam around alone in the rain, anyway?

"Mom's looking at washing machines, and Dad is watching football on a great big TV." His disgusted sigh brought a smile to her lips. "She said Becca and me could wait in the toy department, but Becca just wants to look at girl stuff, and I couldn't see the trains really good. They're better out here."

Again Kendra stifled a nostalgic smile. She'd hated shopping with her mother and little sisters, and she'd worried her mother more than once by disappearing to follow up some interest of her own. After her mother's death, she'd taken on the responsibility of raising her sisters and had gained a greater sympathy for her mother's concern. A child who strayed from a parent's sight was no small matter. She needed to stop dawdling and get this young man back to his family.

"They're really neat trains, but you know it's raining awfully hard out here, and your parents are probably worried about you. Let's go find them," she smiled encouragingly. The boy glanced guiltily toward the door.

"Mom's going to be mad." He thrust out his chin and tried to look defiant. He seemed to consider for a few minutes, then he asked, "Are you a stranger?"

She hid a smile; he had been warned not to speak to strangers. "Your parents don't know me," she spoke carefully, not wanting to frighten him. "My name is Kendra Emerson, and I'd like to meet your mom and dad. Do you think you could take me to them?"

"Okay." His broad smile returned, and he announced proudly, "My name is David William Rolando."

"I'm very glad to meet you, David." She smiled back at him.

"Why's it have to rain so much? It's 'bout Christmas, so it should be snowing, not raining."

"You're right," she agreed, and reached for his small hand. "But this rain is so cold, I think it will probably turn into snow before long." She hoped she'd be across the Sierras before snow became a serious problem.

"Bye, train." David turned for one last look at the little red engine. Just as he turned back toward Kendra, the huge window shattered in a noisy explosion. Shards of glass flew through the air, and without conscious thought, she grabbed the child and pulled him close, sheltering his small body with her own from the flying glass.

CHAPTER 2

Before she could gather her wits about her or check the boy for injuries, a thick arm settled around her throat and tugged her hard against a form she could not see. Something hard pressed against the side of her head. She started to scream, but when a harsh voice ordered her to keep quiet, she did as she was told.

Through the driving rain, she made out the shape of another man a few feet away, facing her and the man who held her. He held a drawn weapon and wore a uniform. She felt a moment's relief until she recognized that there was nothing he could do to help her. Over the thundering fear in her ears and the pounding rain, she knew he spoke, but she couldn't make out the words.

"No," the man behind her snarled in her ear. "She's insurance." He dragged her a few steps toward the curb where a van waited. With growing horror, she understood that she had become a hostage. The man holding her planned to take her with him, but she wouldn't go; she'd fight him. She began to struggle. If he planned to shoot her, she'd rather it happened here in a public area where she had some chance of getting help rather than allow herself to be dragged to some place where she would be completely at his mercy. Jabbing an elbow backward, she heard a heavy grunt, followed by a tightening of the arm across her throat. A wave of dizziness blurred her vision.

"Hold still or the kid gets it," the voice snarled in her ear, and she froze. A whimper reached her ears, and she remembered the small boy huddled against her. Instinctively her arms tightened around him. Fear for her own safety slipped to a secondary position in her mind as she grappled for a means to get the child safely back to the store.

"Let the kid go." This time she understood the officer who stood helplessly such a short distance away. His feet were braced far apart, and his rigid stance spoke of his determination. Was it her imagination or did she detect a note of fear in his voice? Scared or not, she recognized strength in his voice, too, and knew the officer was willing to barter his own life for hers and that of the child.

"No way." The man shuffled a few more steps toward the van, dragging Kendra and David with him.

"Please let him go," she whispered harshly in spite of the pressure against her throat. She released her grip, hoping the child would run to safety. Instead two arms reached out of the van to drag him inside. She was abruptly shoved in behind him, staggering and falling as the van lurched into motion. She lost her balance and fell to the floor. A sharp pain radiated from her elbow and she suspected she'd have bruises. Tires squealed and the van fish-tailed as it tore down the street. She heard two loud pops and cringed. Belatedly she realized her captor had fired two shots, but the officer hadn't returned fire. Why hadn't he shot out the tires or done something? Had he been hit? Logic won out over threatening hysteria. The officer hadn't returned fire for a reason. She understood; she might be willing to die rather than submit to being a helpless captive, but she could do nothing that might endanger the boy, and neither could the officer left behind in the rain.

"Shut that kid up!"

Through a red haze she heard David's hysterical screams. "You're mean! I hate you! I want my mom!"

Blindly she reached for the child and pulled him onto her lap. She cuddled him close and whispered words of encouragement, making promises she doubted she could keep. The van careened around a corner, and she felt herself flying toward the opposite side of the van. Her head struck the metal side, and instinctively she used her arms to protect the child from a similar fate. Fearing he'd start to cry again, drawing their captors' anger, she ignored the pain and drew herself to a sitting position once more where she could hold him. Bracing her back and feet the best she could to keep the two of them from flying at the next sudden corner, she mouthed words of assurance in the little boy's ear. Instead of crying, he sat upright and announced, "Mom said I have to wear a seat belt ALWAYS!"

"Sh-h." She pulled him back onto her lap. "There aren't enough seat belts for us," she whispered. "See, there are only two seats and two seat belts." Both seats were occupied. From one, the driver hunched over the steering wheel, peering through the intermittent swipes of wiper blades, while the other man seemed to have his eyes glued to the large mirror just beyond his window. The second man turned to glare at them, his eyes dark and menacing through the holes in his ski mask, then he turned his back on them and resumed his preoccupation with the side mirror.

Heaving a sigh of relief that David's outburst hadn't brought swift retaliation, she tried to make David and herself more comfortable, but she soon learned there was nothing comfortable about the hard metal floor of a van racing down wet streets and lurching around corners at frightening speeds.

"I want my mommy," David whimpered.

"I know you do," she whispered. "And I'm sure she wants her David back where he belongs, but we have to be really quiet now so those men won't be angry with us."

"They're bad! And mean!" His body trembled with indignation, and she hugged him, again trying to soothe him. She wished she could see him better. Even in the dark rear of the van, she knew he was crying from the soft snuffling noises he made, but at least it wasn't the loud panicky cry of earlier. Eventually he lay still, and she suspected he'd cried himself to sleep.

She knew by the hum of the tires and a lessening of tilting around corners that they had reached the highway. Once or twice she picked out the sound of a siren, but it never seemed to draw closer. She tried to determine the direction they were moving, but the absence of windows in the back of the van, and her inability to see beyond the windshield wipers from her position on the floor, left her confused. She had no idea where they were or even how far they were from the town where she'd stopped to have a tire repaired. She considered trying to escape, but she'd seen enough of the front console to know the van had power locks on its doors. Besides, she couldn't risk the child's life by jumping with him from a moving van.

She studied the backs of the men's heads and realized both wore ski masks. She took that as a good sign. If they were taking precautions to ensure she couldn't identify them, they must plan to let David and her go eventually, she thought.

A sudden swerve sent her sliding across the floor again, and this time she knew they'd left the highway and were now climbing. The road was rougher, if they were even on a road. The way the vehicle jolted about, it occurred to her to be thankful the men hadn't tied her hands or feet. If they had, she'd be helplessly flung back and forth against the floor and sides of the van. She listened for the wail of the siren, but she never heard it again.

She'd often felt a helpless frustration as she struggled to raise two teenage sisters and felt her own plans and dreams slip away, but she'd never experienced this kind of physical helplessness. She recalled every personal safety class or lecture she'd ever attended, but nothing she'd learned seemed to fit this occasion. Her mind dredged up a long-ago Laurel adviser who had cautioned the young women in her class to be found in holy places and to choose their companions wisely.

For a moment anger flared, then abated as quickly as it had come. It would be useless and unfair to rail against God because she'd had no part in choosing to be in the place where this horrible experience occurred, nor the company she now found herself in. Prayer and study had taught her that her teacher hadn't been talking simply about places and circumstances so much as the condition of a person's heart. As long as she kept herself spiritually clean and close to God, wherever she found herself could be a holy place. And what better companion could she choose than an innocent child? Her heart softened as she recalled that long-ago lesson. She bowed her head and began to pray with all the fervency she'd once put into seeking His help as she struggled to raise her orphaned sisters.

The sound of David sniffling in his sleep focused her attention on him. What if he had been alone when those men needed a hostage? Warmth stole silently into her heart. Her flat tire hadn't been without purpose. The Lord had seen David's need and sent her to help him. She didn't know what she could possibly do, but she felt filled with a fierce determination, like Nephi, to go and do whatever the Lord asked.

At last the van slowed its mad race, and the two men in front exchanged high fives and began to converse excitedly. She assumed they were congratulating themselves for losing the police car that had been following them. Several times she heard the rattle of planks beneath the van's tires and thought they must be crossing a creek or river. The men continued to ignore their two captives, and Kendra did nothing to remind them of their presence, but her mind was busy formulating and discarding one escape plan after another.

Eventually the van left the rough road and lurched its way across uneven ground. She had no sense of how much time had passed. David awoke and huddled closer to her. He didn't speak or cry, and she wondered if he was frightened or cold. Of course he was cold and scared! The van's heater didn't reach this far back, and if she was scared silly, the child had to be absolutely petrified with fear.

She could tell the men were running the heater, and she wished more of its warmth penetrated to where she and little David huddled. They were both wet, which only added to their discomfort. The rain had dampened their pants and plastered their hair against their heads. Inactivity had further lowered her body temperature.

Trying to take her mind off the cold, she speculated where her purse might be. It held a cotton scarf and an extra pair of gloves in addition to some cash and credit cards. Surreptitiously she searched the area around her with one hand, and finally concluded she must have dropped it on the street in front of the shattered window. For a moment she wondered if she'd ever see it again, and if it were gone how she would pay for her tire repair. Or was she worrying about a moot point? Refusing to speculate on what the future held in store for her, she reached into her coat pocket and found a package of tissues. Pulling out several, she attempted to pat David's hair and face a little dryer. Beyond looking after the little boy the best she could, she could only put their fate in God's hands.

CHAPTER 3

The van lurched to a stop and the hum of the engine died away. Kendra braced herself for what was to come. Instinctively her arm tightened around David, and she drew him into the curve of her body. She held her breath, waiting.

"He's not here!" A voice exploded from the front seat, followed by a string of curses.

"Relax. He'll be here," the driver spoke, and she watched as they both peered through the rain-streaked windshield. "It's not time yet. He won't be expecting us this early."

The first man drummed his fingers against the dashboard in an irritating tattoo, and neither man spoke for several minutes. David squirmed in her lap, and she placed a finger across his lips, praying he'd remain quiet.

"What about them?" asked the man who had dragged her to the van, and Kendra saw him jerk his head toward the back of the cargo space, where she crouched with David in her arms. She swallowed convulsively with fright while straining to hear the other man's answer.

"Dunno." The driver seemed unconcerned.

"Well, do we still need them? We don't, do we? Maybe we ought to take care of 'em now," the other man hammered the point.

Kendra's heartbeat accelerated wildly.

"Better wait." The driver didn't elaborate, and a sudden tap on the window beside him sent the other man clutching for his gun. He waved it toward the window, then back toward the hostages.

"Put that thing away," the driver snapped. "Kelly's here."

"It's about time," the man grumbled, but he put away the gun, much to Kendra's relief. The driver rolled down his window and spoke to someone outside, but she couldn't see the new man's face or hear the words they exchanged. After a few minutes both men climbed out of the van, and Kendra wondered if this might be their chance to escape. Still holding David, she inched forward to where she could see three men swathed in rain slickers standing together near a sports utility. They appeared to be arguing. She shuddered, wondering if they were arguing about David's and her fate.

Stealthily she reached forward to see if the keys had been left in the ignition. They hadn't, but she really hadn't expected to be so lucky. Perhaps they could escape out the door on the side away from the men. Setting David on the floor, she cautioned him to be quiet, then scrambled over the center console before pulling him after her. With one arm around the little boy, she reached for the door handle and gently squeezed.

An ear-splitting blast from the horn ripped through the silence. Lights flashed and the horn continued its din. Power locks! She'd noted the van was a late model; she should have considered the possibility of an intruder alarm. Frantically she shoved at the door, but it refused to yield.

In seconds the door opened from the outside, and a hand fastened around Kendra's arm, jerking her out onto the muddy ground. David tumbled after her. He clutched her side and buried his face in her coat. She held him to her and glared back at the three men who stood over them. The two masked faces looked grotesque with eyes burning back at her through black-rimmed holes. Shockingly the third figure was the most frightening. He wore no identity-hiding mask and his smoothly shaved face was actually quite handsome. Dark curls clung damply to his forehead, and his pale blue eyes conveyed an emptiness as though he were soulless. She couldn't prevent the shiver that shook her body in a quick convulsive shudder.

"Want me to take care of 'em?" the man who had captured them growled a little too eagerly while the toe of his boot nudged her side.

"I don't want anything to do with a murder charge," the driver of the van made his view clear. "We've got the money and a foolproof escape plan, but they'll never stop chasing us if we kill the woman and her kid."

"No problem," the new man spoke smoothly. "We won't have to do a thing. Unload the stuff from the van, and put it in the Cherokee." He turned his attention to the two figures huddled on the ground and spoke almost pleasantly, "You might as well start walking; we won't stop you."

Kendra wasn't sure she could trust the man to keep his word. Her instincts read something cold and hard behind his words; nevertheless, she struggled to a standing position. With a touch of defiance, she reached back down for David and lifted his small body into her arms. The man stepped back, and, with a mockingly gallant gesture, motioned her to walk away.

Slowly, hesitantly, she started walking. Her shoulders stiffened and she expected an attack from behind, but she refused to look back.

Avoiding the muddy track the van had followed to reach this remote point, she kept her feet on the dried grass at its side. Rain pelted her face and wet strands of hair clung to her cheeks. At last she stopped just beyond the first curve in the trail to set David on his feet. She pulled his hood over his head and fastened the tie beneath his chin, then crouched down to tug his mittens over his cold little hands. Once more she wished for her waterproof parka with its thick lined hood.

An explosion rent the air and she whirled about to face the way they'd come. As smoke and flames leaped from the van, the sport utility headed up a little-used road toward the desert, gradually disappearing from sight. The child's hands clutched at her coat, and she reached for him, hugging him tightly while her mind struggled to assimilate this new factor. Slowly it made an awful kind of sense. The thieves, or robbers, or whatever they were, had probably stolen the van, but when it was of no further use to them, they had gotten rid of it. The vehicle they were now driving was undoubtedly one the police wouldn't be looking for.

She and David were also of no further use to them, but not wanting to kill them outright, the men had turned them loose to wander in this desolate area of rocks and brush until they succumbed to the wet and cold, far from where the men had exchanged vehicles. Blowing up the van had served a second purpose as well; it ensured that the former hostages could not take shelter there. The men obviously weren't concerned about anyone seeing or hearing the explosion, so they must be a long way from any habitation.

Kendra glared through the rain-slashed night until the flames died, then slowly her shoulders straightened. She wasn't beaten yet. It wasn't the first time she'd attempted the impossible. She'd cooked and cleaned house while caring for her sisters so her mother could hold down a job, then she'd nursed her mother through that last terrible illness, and when her mother died, she'd given up her own plans for college and a life of her own to raise her sisters and put them through school. When they no longer needed her, she'd gone to night school to complete her own much-delayed education. She wasn't a quitter. With God's help she'd somehow get David back to his parents.

Turning back to the tracks the van must have followed, she took David's hand and began to walk. Their shoes made crunching sounds with each step. The mud was freezing and the falling rain felt like shards of glass striking her face.

"It's snowing!" In spite of their precarious situation, or perhaps because he was too young to understand the danger they faced, David greeted the change from rain to snow with enthusiasm. Kendra struggled to hide her dismay and the added fear that the snow would soon start sticking to the ground, thus obliterating the tracks she'd hoped to follow.

Without slowing her steps, she closed her eyes and once more breathed a hasty prayer. "Please, Father," she beseeched. "Help us find our way back to the road."

"Are we lost?" David asked, concern darkening his face.

"Sort of," she hedged.

"Does Heavenly Father know where we are?" David sought assurance.

"Heavenly Father always knows where we are." She attempted to grant him that assurance.

"Then let's ask him." His face brightened.

"Yes, I think we should," she agreed, then put out her hand to stop him as he began to kneel. "I think He'll understand if we stand. I don't think He wants us to get any wetter by kneeling in this mud."

"Okay," he grinned before folding his arms and beginning to speak.

"Heavenly Father, we're lost. Please help us get home for Christmas. Thank you. Name of . . ." He closed his simple prayer and tears sprang to her eyes as she witnessed his simple faith. Determination swelled in her breast. She wouldn't let him or her Savior down.

"Are we going home now?" David asked.

"Yes." She hoped it wasn't a lie.

"Good," David bounced as he walked. He seemed to have completely dismissed from his mind their capture and had no inkling of the danger they still faced. "I asked Santa Claus to bring me a sled and a red train, so I gotta be at my house for Christmas."

CHAPTER 4

Chase splayed both hands against the open hood of his truck and stared at the mass of wires and metal. He'd done everything he could think of, but still the engine wouldn't start. Once more he reviewed the possibilities, while deep down he suspected the truck had died of old age and too much hard work. He'd bought it second-hand fifteen years ago, and he couldn't complain. It had served him well, but he wished the timing were a little better. He didn't relish a five-mile hike back to his place in this bitter, cold rain.

With one hand he adjusted the angle of his hat to keep the rain from running down his neck. He should get started. Instead he reached under the hood once more to jiggle a small wire, then he picked up the wrench he'd left sitting on top of the carburetor. After a few more adjustments, he stepped back and tilted his Stetson once more. That was when he noticed the rain had turned to snow. A fine layer coated the sagebrush and dusted the road. If the truck didn't start this time, he'd better start hiking.

He'd been foolish going into town today. He usually stocked up on supplies well before all the Christmas hoopla started. He'd gotten busy this month and forgotten how close the holiday was. Today's trip into town had certainly refreshed his memory. Tinsel garlands were wrapped around every post, and were swagged across the street between the bank and Decker's department store. Strings of red and green lights were wound through the garlands. Between the decorations and the rain, Darcy's few stop lights had been hard to see. The feed store, of all places, had one of those little silver fake trees in the front office, all covered with blinking white lights. A sound system, set up in front of the town offices, blared out Christmas carols, stirring up memories better left forgotten. The windows of Carla's Café, where he'd stopped for lunch, had been painted with Christmas murals, and even the elderly busybody Elliot sisters had teetered over to his table to wish him a merry Christmas.

He stepped toward the cab of his truck and some flicker of motion in the distance caught his eye. He stood still, peering into the falling snow and wondered if he'd imagined the movement. It was probably just a coyote. It could even be one of his neighbor's steers that had been missed in last fall's roundup. He opened the door and ducked his head, then stopped again. His eyes watered as he strained to see past the falling snow. Whatever was out there was still there, and coming closer. It was too big for a coyote, and something told him it wasn't livestock either. As he watched, the shape dissolved into two forms. The smaller one fell, and the larger bent to pick it up. That's when he knew. The shapes coming toward him were human.

He started to run, his boots slipping and sliding in the snow. As he narrowed the distance between himself and the approaching figures, he became certain the snow-covered forms were a woman and a child. The woman crumpled in a heap and didn't move for agonizingly long seconds, then just as he reached them she moved her legs and slowly dragged herself upright. Shock slowed his steps. For a minute he thought he was seeing an angel emerging from the snow. He blinked his eyes and the angel became a flesh and blood woman wearing a white coat, just a shade darker than the snow. The child clasped her tightly around the neck, and she staggered as she regained her feet.

"Here!" He reached for the child, but her grip tightened around the tiny form. Other than to increase her hold on the child, she seemed unaware Chase was even present. He'd have to get them inside his truck, then figure out a way to get them warm. "It's not far to my truck," he attempted to urge them on. She looked at him blankly, then began to sink toward the ground, again as though her legs had forgotten their usual function.

One big hand reached out to halt her downward motion. He looked at her, then squinted through the falling snow toward his truck. He guessed he didn't have much choice if she couldn't make it as far as the truck on her own. Most folks would consider her tall, but she didn't come to more than his shoulder, and she didn't look to have much meat on her bones. Sweeping her up in his arms, he checked to make certain the kid was tightly wedged between her body and his as he started walking as fast as his slick-soled boots would allow.

As he hurried toward the small amount of shelter the truck offered, he wondered what the two were doing out here alone. If they'd had car trouble, they should have stayed with their vehicle and waited for help. From the looks of the woman, they were greenhorns and had no idea how much trouble a person could find himself in by getting off the main roads. Nor how much trouble they'd be causing him.

It appeared they'd been out in the storm for some time. He suspected they were both soaked clean through, and he recognized the feel of wet denim turning stiff as it froze. The main road, which didn't amount to much, was a good twenty miles away, and the interstate another forty. They were five miles from his ranch; a river and nearly fifteen miles separated him from his closest neighbor. Even if he could get his truck started, there was no way he could take them back to town. The roads were already in bad shape from the rain; covered with snow they'd be impassable. As cold and wet as these two appeared to be, he'd have to get them to the closest shelter where they could get out of their wet clothes and get warm. Unfortunately that would be his house.

Long strides carried them quickly to the truck. He shoved the woman across the bench seat, then climbed in behind her, before slamming his own door shut. The sound seemed to rouse her a bit, and she looked around in obvious confusion. She turned to look at him, and he recognized fear in her eyes. That annoyed him. His face wasn't a pleasant sight, but it shouldn't scare her more than the storm outside had. A few scars wouldn't hurt anybody. But he knew from experience that most women seemed to think his scars represented some kind of danger to them.

"I'm not going to hurt you," he growled. "I'm trying to save your life."

She didn't say anything, and he wondered what to do next. She and the kid were cold, really cold. Even if he could get the truck started, they'd be to his house before the sorry heater kicked out any heat. What they needed was something to hold in the pitifully small amount of heat left in their bodies now. He remembered that sometimes he kept a horse blanket in the truck. He turned to dig behind the seat and felt a surge of triumph when his fingers grasped the edge of the blanket. It hadn't been used for a month, not since he'd boarded his mare with the vet as a safety precaution until her colt arrived. The dogs might have sat on it a time or two, but it could be worse.

Regretting that it wasn't clean, he quickly placed the rough blanket around the two shaking figures. Dust and animal hair clung to it, and it smelled pretty bad, but it was all he had. He caught the kid peeking over the woman's shoulder at him. He had a hunch he wasn't just shy or cold. The little guy had the same glint of fear in his eyes that he'd glimpsed in the mother's eyes, but he sensed the boy was tough, and that nothing kept him down for long. Something told him the woman had her share of courage, too. Startled by the instant sense of kinship to the two, he busied himself tucking the blanket more securely around them.

"Are you one of the bad guys?" The kid's question proved him right where the kid was concerned, even as it startled him.

"David," the woman whispered in a futile attempt to shush the boy. So the woman was more aware than she'd let on.

"It's okay," Chase answered, looking directly at her for what seemed a long time as he tried to convey silent assurance that he hadn't taken offense, then he turned to the boy. "I don't think I'm a bad guy, but we've got a bad problem here. You two are wet and cold, and my truck has been acting up. I'm not sure it will start."

The boy continued to stare, wide-eyed, at him. "The bad guys' truck 'sploded! It made a big fire!"

Chase didn't know what to make of the kid's words. He turned questioning eyes to the woman, but she didn't say anything. She huddled inside the blanket and appeared almost asleep. She didn't have a hat or gloves, and her coat didn't look as though it were waterproof like the kid's. It was the pretty kind of coat city ladies wore to their offices. Its pale color seemed to accentuate the woman's paleness. Her skin appeared stretched taut, and a tinge of blue ringed her mouth. She was an attractive woman, even with her wet hair plastered against her head and her face devoid of any makeup that might have once lent her a little color. Her skin looked soft and sort of delicate, like it would bruise easily. And her eyes were a soft gray that just missed being blue. Thick dark lashes, owing nothing to cosmetics, made a striking contrast where they formed little half moons above her pale cheeks. Catching himself up short, he wondered what had come over him. It had been a long time since he'd noticed such personal details about a woman. Of course, it had been a long time since he'd been this close to a woman. Even this self-conscious awareness couldn't keep him from staring at her.

He couldn't say what it was about her that fascinated him, but as he watched her face, something fierce gripped his heart. He had to save this woman and her little boy. He hadn't been able to save his own wife and baby, but perhaps God was giving him a second chance.

Startled by his own mental comparison, he smashed one booted foot against the clutch, jiggled the gearshift, and reached with frozen fingers for the ignition key. He didn't expect much, so he nearly killed the engine when it suddenly rumbled to life. "Thank you," he whispered with a quick upward glance as the truck began to move.

But it sure didn't move very fast. Any slower, in fact, and the truck would probably just stop.

CHAPTER 5

"Go on home, Guy." There was sympathy in the sheriff's eyes. "Get Vicki and Becca to bed. They're completely done in. There's nothing you can do here. We'll call you as soon as we hear anything."

"There must be something I can do," Guy protested. "I can't just do nothing."

"Look, son." The sheriff rose to his feet, and walked around the desk to place a hand on his shoulder. "There's an APB out for that van all across Nevada and the surrounding states. Someone's going to spot them."

"But what if they're in the back country. You said your officers lost the van on the highway. They probably turned off some place. I could drive around . . ."

"No, those men are armed. A confrontation could . . . Anyway I have officers combing every back road in the county, but with this rain there are a lot of bridges washed out and a lot of gullies running like rivers. We'll find them, and you can rest assured, I've got the best negotiator in the state flying up here to talk to them, once they're located. You just take Vicki and that little girl on home." The sheriff glanced pointedly to where Vicki and Becca huddled together on a bench.

Guy looked at his wife and daughter and knew the sheriff was right. Becca had cried herself to sleep, and Vicki looked so miserable he knew he needed to get them home. His heart broke to see Vicki looking so beaten and defeated. But how could he possibly comfort her? There would be no comfort until David was found. Guilt swamped him. It was his fault. Vicki said she didn't blame him, but he blamed himself. If he had stayed in Denver where he had a good job, he would have been able to support his family the way he should, and they wouldn't have gone out on such a stormy night to try to replace a washing machine he should have replaced years ago.

While Vicki studied the different washers, he should have been watching the kids, instead of assuming they'd stay in the toy department. He still couldn't figure why David had gone outside in the rain.

Slowly he walked across the room. After a moment's hesitation, he sank down on one knee before his wife and reached for her hand.

"Vicki, the sheriff says we should go home. Becca should be in bed." He waited for a response, and after a slight hesitation she raised her head to simply nod her agreement.

When he stood, Becca was in his arms, her head pressed against his shoulder. Vicki led the way. He paused at the door before following her out to look back at the sheriff.

"I'll call," the sheriff promised. His eyes were full of sadness and not much hope.

The drive home passed in a blur and Guy's heart sank as he noticed the rain had thickened to a thick, mushy sleet. Too many awful scenes flashed through his mind. The way that van had squealed around the corner, he feared the driver would wreck it on the slick roads. The abductor had shot one man; what might he do to a child?

Pulling into the shelter of his carport felt unreal, as though he'd gotten there without any awareness of the trip between the sheriff's office and his family's home. Everything around him appeared in a time warp, like one of those old black and white movies that were sometimes shown late at night on TV. Seeing Becca slumped on the back seat reminded him the nightmare was all too real. He reached for her while Vicki opened the door to the house.

Becca awoke when he placed her on her bed. "David?" she mumbled sleepily. "Is David home?"

"No, love. Not yet." Vicki smoothed her daughter's hair with one hand.

"Do you think those men will hurt him?" Becca turned frightened eyes toward her father.

Guy didn't know how to answer her. When the plate window had exploded, he like everyone else in the store, had hurried to the front to see what had happened. He'd arrived in time to see a body sprawled on the sidewalk and an arm reach from inside a van parked at the curb to pull David inside. Another man with a gun shoved a woman in behind David. No one in town seemed to know who the woman might be.

Becca had been one of the first to peer through the broken window. She'd told the sheriff a man had hurt the woman's neck, but the woman still tried to protect David. Becca had seen the security guard shot and heard his scream as he fell. Anguish squeezed his heart. Wasn't it nightmare enough to have his son abducted, but must his daughter live with the memory of that shooting?

"I don't know what they will do," he admitted truthfully. Becca was smart; she'd know if he lied, and she already knew David was in serious trouble. She knew, too, that the men who had stolen David were capable of destroying anyone who got in their way. Those men had not only stolen his son, but had stolen a piece of his daughter's innocence as well.

"Let's ask Heavenly Father to help him get away from those bad men." Becca climbed off the bed and reached for her parents' hands. Her eyes were pleading. He should have realized she needed the comfort of prayer. For that matter, so did he and Vicki.

Guy wondered if he could pray when his heart was so full of grief and anger. Clumsily he knelt beside his daughter's narrow bed. Six hands clasped together as much for mutual support as in supplication. He struggled to find the words, then, strengthened by the love communicated through the hands of his wife and daughter, he began to pray. Stumbling at first, he pleaded with his Heavenly Father to protect his son and bring him safely back home.

Gradually a measure of peace filled his heart. God was a father, too. He understood.

CHAPTER 6

The windshield wipers left a lot to be desired, and the truck wheezed and spluttered, nearly dying a couple of times before they reached the bridge. It slid sideways frequently on the snow and lurched in bone-jarring jolts across deep ruts. Chase glanced over at the woman and noticed she wasn't really asleep. One hand gripped the arm rest on the door beside her, and her lips moved like she might be praying. Praying struck him as a good thing to do about now. She appeared more alert a few minutes later, and he saw her search for a seat belt, only to give up in defeat when it penetrated her consciousness that it was wedged too deeply behind the seat for her numb fingers to extract. No one but the dogs ever used that seat, and he wouldn't know how to go about convincing a dog to wear a seat belt, so the thing had slipped farther and farther down the crack behind the seat. The woman wrapped herself halfway around the boy as though preparing to come between him and any sudden danger. Seeing her protective gesture hurt a bit. It was as though she expected him to hurt the boy.

He slowed, if going slower were really possible without stopping, as they approached the bridge. Rattling across the plank bridge had never concerned him in the past. In the fifteen years he'd lived on the isolated ranch, he hadn't given much thought to the bridge. It was the only access to the road that led to town from his ranch, except for the sheep bridge, and a person couldn't take a vehicle across that. The planks were sturdy for the most part, but the bridge was old and a few of them probably needed to be replaced. That was the trouble with bridges; they needed constant upkeep. The guard rails were in good shape, though.

In the spring, bridges occasionally washed out in this high desert country if the snow melted too fast higher up, but this was winter. Still, as he studied the bridge, he could see where water lapped at the planks more so than in any spring runoff since he'd bought the ranch.

The river wasn't usually deep or terribly swift. In fact, calling the stream "a river" had always seemed like an exaggeration to Chase. It passed on one side of his land, but did little to irrigate the dry land it passed through, since it ran at the bottom of a gully cut deeply through rock. For the river to be high enough to even touch the underside of the bridge, there had to be a massive blockage further downstream. Not even two weeks of steady rain, by itself, would leave the river this high. The only explanation was some kind of dam preventing the water from escaping to the desert floor.

In the morning he'd head downriver to see if there might be something he could do. Right now he had to get across the rain-swollen gully. The woman and kid needed dry clothes and a fire to warm them, and they needed it soon. They were already half frozen, and judging by how quickly his windshield was icing up, it was getting colder. It struck him that his passengers were exhibiting signs of early hypothermia, and hypothermia could be nasty business. If he were alone, he'd leave the truck and hike across the bridge, sparing the stressed timbers the weight of the vehicle, but the woman and child were in no shape to hike across the slippery bridge then walk another mile to his house. Further exposure to the cold could cost them their lives. He had to gamble that they would make it across.

Carefully he eased the truck onto the bridge. Ice made the planks slippery, and each time the engine spluttered, he held his breath. Snow capped the posts of the railing, and ice turned the steel cables between the posts into glittering strands like some society woman's fancy diamond necklace. Glimpses of angry, black water swirling on either side were visible through the sharply slanting snow. As Chase reached the center point of the bridge, he felt a slight lessening of the strain that bowed his shoulders, just knowing they were halfway across.

The faint sense of relief was short-lived. A jolt to the bridge made the truck lurch dangerously toward the water and sent sweat pouring down his face. It also re-upped the stakes. Something, a block of ice, a tree trunk, perhaps a boulder had struck the pilings beneath the bridge a dangerous blow. An ominous crack like the breaking up of ice on a mountain lake sounded above the truck's engine, and Chase felt the bridge sway. Some element of self-preservation urged him to gun the engine, to get across as fast as the truck would go, but a quieter, deeper voice whispered to remain steady to avoid sliding on the icy planks. He'd learned the hard way over many years to listen to that quiet voice.

Slowly the truck inched forward. Chase concentrated every bit of his attention on driving. He didn't spare even a moment to glance at his passengers, but some inner sense told him the woman understood the gravity of the situation, and he experienced an uncanny oneness with her. Scarcely breathing, she made no audible sound at all; still, some undefined instinct told him she shared his fear. A mental picture of the woman's mouth moving silently a few minutes earlier flashed through his mind, and he knew she was praying. Without conscious thought, he added his silent prayer to hers and felt a lessening of his fear.

With just a few feet left, he felt more than heard a rumbling beneath them and carefully pressed the accelerator, urging a fraction more speed from the tired engine. It responded in what seemed like slow motion, but at last the tires crunched across gravel, and he knew they'd made it to safety. Feeling too numb to speak, he quietly shifted gears and continued on toward the house still a mile away.

• • • • •

Kendra hunched down beneath the smelly blanket their rescuer had wrapped around David and herself. *Would this nightmare ever end?* she wondered wearily. She didn't care if it did reek of dirt and horses and something else; it felt like a little bit of heaven. She didn't know where she was or where they were going, but at least she wasn't still stumbling through the snow in the dark trying to carry a child who had gone from thirty or forty pounds to at least a hundred, as she walked.

David was a good child, and he filled her with a maternal longing she'd believed long vanquished. She thought of the small boy curled in her lap and experienced a wave of tenderness. He'd walked until he couldn't take another step, and he hadn't fussed or complained. She owed him a lot; she would probably have given up long before the cowboy found them if the little boy hadn't given her a reason to keep going. She was glad he'd fallen asleep before they'd come to that bridge, though. She trembled, remembering. She had been terrified, then had experienced a strange calmness as though a power beyond the rickety bridge held them safely above the black water she'd glimpsed, twisting and foaming beneath them, until the truck had lurched from the icy planks to a muddy track leading up a hill.

The cowboy didn't seem upset. He hadn't looked to the right or left, even when she thought the bridge was breaking apart; he'd just focused straight ahead and drove this battered old heap at the same slow, steady speed until he reached the other side. He didn't even pause, or look back, when they reached solid ground; he just continued on his way.

A smidgen of heat escaped the decrepit heater, and an involuntary shudder swept through her thoroughly chilled body, but her mind seemed to be functioning again. She glanced at the man beside her and noticed for the first time the old, thick scar tissue covering one side of his face from cheekbone to jaw. He'd been hurt badly once a long time ago, she speculated. To her inexperienced eyes the scar looked like the remnant of a severe burn. The scar didn't repulse her, only cause a strange sadness akin to wishing she'd been there to ease his pain.

She scoffed at the whimsical thought. The situation she found herself in was causing her to become melodramatic. She'd had little experience with men. They usually made her feel tongue-tied and nervous, but she didn't feel that way now. He was a big man, and she'd always been particularly wary of large men. Somehow, this one affected her differently. Not since that first moment when she'd found herself face to face with a stranger had she been nervous or afraid. In fact, just the opposite seemed to be true. Some instinct told her she could safely place her own and David's safety in his hands.

She wondered how old he might be. At first she'd thought of him as old, but he wasn't. He probably wasn't more than a few years older than herself. Noticing his hands gripping the steering wheel, she could see they had been burned, too. The pain must have been nearly unbearable. She'd always believed a person could tell a lot about another person by his or her hands. She studied the scar tissue on the backs of his capable-looking hands and knew that though the scars were old, the grease on them and several deep scratches were new, and that these things didn't detract from the man's strength nor his willingness to do whatever needed to be done.

The truck hiccoughed and the engine sputtered and nearly died, then it seemed to right itself and stagger on. She expected the cowboy would say something, but he didn't. Somehow the truck suited their rescuer, she thought. They're both battered and scarred, but when they are needed, they come through.

She was being fanciful, she chided herself. She didn't know anything about the cowboy, so how could she assume she could count on him? She couldn't answer her own question, but something deep inside, in a place she'd almost forgotten, assured her she wasn't wrong.

At last the truck stopped, and the engine either died or was shut off. She struggled to see out the window, but all she could see was whiteness. The door beside her opened and the cowboy reached inside to take the sleeping child from her arms. She felt bereft for just a moment without the boy's weight, then she slid out to follow the man and boy up a narrow walk to the front door. The walkway was built of heavy planks of lumber, much like the bridge. Just remembering the bridge caused her to wince.

He didn't knock or reach for a key, but simply turned the knob, pushed open the door, and walked inside. Still following, Kendra stepped through the door right behind him into a large room with pine paneling on the walls and a massive lava rock fireplace filling one end. Near the fireplace were a sofa and a couple of deep comfortable chairs. There was a definite masculine air about the room, but she imagined that once a fire burned in the fireplace, it would be warm and cozy. She noted the complete absence of any feminine touches or a light left burning, which seemed to indicate the man lived here alone.

He stood still for a minute as though puzzling what to do with the burden he carried. A strange expression flitted across his face as he looked down at the sleeping child, then he nodded his head toward an archway she could see at the other side of the large room.

"Bathroom's that way," he spoke. "Don't worry about hot water. There's plenty. You'll find a robe hanging behind the door and sweats in the bottom drawer. Help yourself."

"But David—"

"I'll take care of him. I've got a deep utility sink just off the kitchen where I can give him a bath and get him into something warm and dry."

"But I—"

"Don't argue. Just go climb in that tub. But don't go to sleep, or you'll have company in about thirty minutes." He turned away, and she stared after him in astonishment. She wasn't sure whether his words were a threat—or if the cowboy actually had a sense of humor.

CHAPTER 7

Twenty minutes later she glanced at her watch which she'd left on the vanity beside the tub and decided she'd better force herself to get out of the water. David might be frightened if he couldn't find her, and she didn't want to take the chance that her cowboy rescuer was serious about coming after her if she dallied. A stray imp of temptation whispered, "wait and see," bringing a blush to her freshly scrubbed skin. She must be more tired than she thought.

She scrambled to her feet and reached for a thick navy blue towel, determined to wipe out any personal thoughts concerning her rescuer.

The cowboy's bathroom was nothing like she had expected. She wasn't sure what she had expected; she just knew it wasn't this. There wasn't a piece of plain white ceramic in sight. Talk about a custom job! The tub was huge and round, looking suspiciously like a tin horse trough with the added luxury of water jets, the lavatory continued the theme, and the toilet at first glance resembled a turn-of-the-century outhouse except that at the push of a button, it flushed.

She found fleece sweats right where she'd been told to look. They were many sizes too big, but by rolling up the sleeves and legs and cinching up the drawstring waist, they'd do. This was certainly a case of beggars not being choosers. When she added the thick robe, she felt ready to face the world—or at least, one rugged cowboy and one small, scared boy. Her thoughts sobered as she thought of David. The ordeal they'd been through seemed unreal. At the same time she couldn't quite grasp that they were alive and the ordeal was over.

Stepping out into the hall, she came face to face with the cowboy. He'd removed his heavy coat, but still wore a thick fleece-lined vest over a red and black flannel shirt. His boots were gone, and she noticed a small hole in the toe of one of his gray socks. He was tall, even without the boots, probably several inches over six feet, and big—as the seams of his shirt stretched across his wide shoulders attested. In spite of the scarring on his face, he was a disturbingly handsome man. She was struck by how worn and tired he looked, and felt guilty for taking care of her needs first while he saw to David. Disturbed by her awareness of their rescuer as a man, she quickly looked away.

Before she could ask about the boy, he pointed to an open door further down the hall as though he'd read her mind. She hoped he hadn't read *all* her thoughts.

"He's asleep. He scarcely woke when I bathed him. I think he's all right, just right worn out." He paused, looking slightly uncomfortable, before going on. "Do you mind sharing a room with your son? I've only got two bedrooms, but the sofa makes out into a bed if you'd rather sleep there."

"No, I don't mind sharing. He might be frightened if he wakes up alone," Kendra quickly agreed to the suggestion, without bothering to correct his misconception of her relationship to David.

"All right. If you're hungry, help yourself to anything in the kitchen. You'll probably be asleep before I get out of the tub." He turned away and she reached out, touching his arm to stop him a moment longer. A small shock ran through her hand, and she quickly withdrew it. It left her feeling warm and excited, a little nervous, and much too aware of the hard muscles she had briefly touched.

"Mr. . . ?" She paused awkwardly.

"That's right." He smiled a brief, lopsided grin that caused her breath to catch unexpectedly. "We never got around to introducing ourselves. My name is Chase Kirkham, the sole owner of the Krazy K sheep ranch."

"Sheep?"

He laughed. "I suppose you thought I was just another cowboy." His eyes sparkled with teasing amusement for a few seconds before his features resumed their usual somber appearance. She smiled self-consciously and knew she wouldn't admit to him that she had done just that. She'd grown up with a fascination for the West and the men who were bigger than life as they conquered rustlers and grizzlies and fended off Indian attacks. She'd dreamed of the kind of man who roped and rode and called a woman "ma'am." She supposed that because he had rescued her and because of the way he dressed, stress had turned him into the imaginary cowboy of her youthful dreams.

Looking up—and it was nice to actually look up at a man—her eyes quickly reaffirmed what she'd noticed a few minutes earlier. He was a very attractive man. When this was all over and she was safely back in her little apartment, she would probably continue to think of him as "the cowboy."

"I'm Kendra Emerson, CPA, with Mason and Fitch in Salt Lake City." She spoke quickly with her customary efficiency, hoping to cover the momentary lapse from her usual crisp way of dealing with men, especially those who were strangers.

"And Mr. Emerson? Is he an accountant, too?" Chase leaned forward, giving her the impression he was more than a little interested in her answer. She experienced a strange urge to lean forward, too, toward him. For some reason it pleased her to learn he was interested enough to ask if she were married.

"There is no Mr. Emerson. I'm not married." She felt just a little breathless and a bit like the flirty college girl, she'd never had time to be. Chase glanced toward the open bedroom door down the hall, and she remembered he'd referred to David as her son. She felt a flush creep up the side of her neck and hurried to explain. "David isn't my son. We were both looking at the same display in a store window in some little town—I don't even remember the name of the place!" Her voice started to rise as the terror returned to her. "There was a robbery, and two men used us as hostages. When they didn't need us anymore, they left us . . . I need a telephone. May I use your phone?"

Chase wasn't sure he was getting the story right, but he didn't like what he was hearing. The woman and kid had been through a much worse ordeal than he had suspected. No wonder they both looked scared to death when they saw him. He'd chalked their reaction up to the wide patch of scar tissue that covered most of one side of his face; it bothered some people. It kind of pleased him to realize her reaction to seeing him for the first time had nothing to do with his scarred face.

"I don't have a telephone," he apologized, sensing she was emerging from some kind of shock with an awareness that the authorities needed to be notified that she and the child were safe. She seemed appalled that she had forgotten for even so short a time.

"David's parents must be going out of their minds. We have to get him back to town." She literally wrung her hands as she spoke, and he felt an unfamiliar urge to put his arms around her and tell her everything would be just fine. Stunned at how close he'd come to acting on that impulse, he backed up a step.

"There's nothing we can do tonight," he spoke softly so as not to upset her any more. "The bridge has probably washed away by now, and my old truck wouldn't make the sixty miles in this storm anyway."

"Oh, those poor people," she moaned.

"Go on. Get to bed," he urged. "You can tell me all the details in the morning, and we'll work something out." Exactly what they'd work out, he didn't know. As far as he could tell, they were well and truly trapped. He'd avoided people for fifteen years as much as he could, although it wasn't because he was some kind of hermit. He didn't dislike people. He dreaded their pity and hated the times when someone saw his scar and was afraid, or worse, asked about the fire. He could certainly offer this woman and child a safe, dry haven on a night like this. He'd seen neither fear nor pity in her eyes. Of course she was still pretty much in some kind of shock and might not have taken a really good look at him. For the first time in fifteen years, he found himself pleased to have company.

Minutes later in hot water up to his chin, he felt a stab of guilt. He didn't begrudge his unexpected guests his hospitality. In fact, he was almost glad there was no way to return them to town tonight, or probably even tomorrow. He remembered the feel of the boy's small body held in his arms and the way the child had clung to him as he lowered him into the sink full of warm water. It was a good feeling. He'd never dressed a child before, yet he'd felt comfortable pulling an old shirt over the kid's head and helping him tug oversized socks up his skinny little legs. It set him to thinking of all he'd missed, but somehow the remembering wasn't so painful as it had always been before.

His thoughts turned to the woman. She'd felt good in his arms, too. Quickly he tried to banish that thought, but it didn't let go easily. Looking into her eyes was like a summer day, sitting on the edge of a high mountain pool and seeing the snow-capped peaks and towering pines reflected in its calming depths. He wouldn't soon forget either, the picture seared into his mind of her rising to her feet, wearing that white coat and looking for all the world like some heavenly messenger materializing out of the mist of snow. The prospect of being marooned with Miss Kendra Emerson didn't feel like such a bad thing at all.

• • • • •

Kendra awoke to a soft snuffling sound. Her disorientation lasted only a moment, then she reached for the child who lay curled at her side, softly crying into his pillow. She sat up, pulling him into her lap.

"It will be all right, David," she whispered against his silky, blond curls.

"I want my mom," he sobbed.

"I'll take you back to her as soon as I can," Kendra promised and cuddled him closer, reveling in the feel of his small body pressed against hers. She stroked his hair and smelled the warm little boy scent of him, which brought a pang to her heart. She'd stopped thinking about a child of her own a long time ago. But now the old ache returned.

She'd cared for her sisters since they were younger than David so her mother could work, and later she'd had the responsibility of their sole care, but she'd never been their mother. Neither she, nor they, had forgotten she was their sister. After Katy and Cameron had both married and moved away, she'd felt light and free for a time. Then gradually this ache had stolen over her, and she'd longed for the feel of an infant, then a toddler in her arms, the noise and confusion of children's voices, and the serene moments when a child, fresh from the bathtub, lay sleeping in innocent abandon. She'd tried to console herself with the reminder that in raising her sisters, she'd had more mothering experience than many single women ever get to know.

"Am I lost?" the boy turned tear-drenched eyes toward her face. "Mom said I'd have to sit on a chair in the corner for a whole hour if I got lost."

"No, you're not lost," she hurried to reassure him. "We're at Mr. Kirkham's ranch. He knows the way back to the town where you live."

"Good! Can we go home now?" David's face brightened at the prospect.

"I wish we could, but it might take a little while. First we'd better see if we can find Mr. Kirkham and ask him how soon we can leave." She smiled as she tried to temper the news that they were stranded on this remote ranch.

"Okay!" David bounced to his feet and slid off the bed, completely unconcerned about his strange attire. Kendra hid a smile. Chase Kirkham had dressed the boy in one of his own tee-shirts, topped by a huge flannel shirt. The hem dragged on the floor and the sleeves fell over the child's thin wrists. One very large sock covered one foot and disappeared beneath the voluminous shirt. She suspected its mate could be found somewhere in the blankets she and the child had shared through the night.

David stopped abruptly before turning the door handle and turned with a woeful expression on his small face. "Did I miss Christmas?"

"No, there's still—let me see—two more days until Christmas." She smiled to reassure him, and he rewarded her with a broad grin before scampering out the door and disappearing down the hall.

She belted the robe around her waist and followed more slowly, entering the large room in time to hear David ask, "Where's your Christmas tree?"

Her eyes scanned the room, noticing again that the room was very masculine and comfortable, but there wasn't a hint of any kind of Christmas decorations. A bachelor sheep rancher probably never gave much thought to holiday decorating. In a way it was a shame. The large window on the east side of the room would be a natural for a large tree with old-fashioned bubble lights, and the lava-rock fireplace was just made for a row of bright red Christmas stockings.

"I don't have a Christmas tree," she heard their host reply in answer to David's question.

She turned toward his voice and felt a slight catch in her breath. Chase Kirkham stood at the kitchen end of the large room, stirring something that smelled heavenly in a large cast-iron frying pan. He wore faded denims, and his flannel shirt fit him a great deal better than its twin fit David. He was freshly shaved, and a few drops of water still glistened in his dark hair. She leaned against the doorjamb and blatantly eavesdropped.

"You got to have a Christmas tree." David approached Chase slowly and stared up at him with an earnest expression on his face. "Everybody gots to have a Christmas tree."

"Is that so?" The man glanced quickly toward the boy, then turned back to preparing breakfast. Kendra wondered if she should intervene. If the man didn't believe in Christmas, that was his business, and she certainly didn't want David to offend him. David's easy chatter and the simple prayer he'd offered had been enough to convince Kendra that David's family were members of the Church, but she didn't know about Chase. He'd been kind to them, and she was convinced he was a good man, but if he wasn't religious he might resent being told he should observe Christmas. They were guests in his home and should respect his views. They were in his debt. She shuddered to think what their fate would be if he hadn't been there to rescue them.

"Yes, sir." David nodded his head emphatically. "It won't get to be Christmas without a Christmas tree."

"And you think Christmas is pretty important, huh?" Chase scraped eggs and potatoes onto the three plates he'd already placed on the table. He glanced across the room and winked at her as though he sensed her dilemma and wished to assure her that he wasn't at all offended by David's earnest defense of the holiday. She felt a strange flutter in the pit of her stomach and suspected he'd been as aware of her presence when she paused in the doorway as she'd been aware of his. Unable to take her eyes from him, she continued to watch as he turned his attention back to David.

"'Course Christmas is 'portant," David informed him in no uncertain terms. "It's the baby's birthday."

A look of raw pain flickered across Chase's face, followed by a quick flash of sadness. Unconsciously she took a step toward him. Reaching for a plate of eggs, he turned his back for a few seconds, and when he faced David again, there was no sign of the emotion she thought she'd briefly glimpsed.

CHAPTER 8

When Chase set a platter of sausage on the table moments later the sadness was gone, making her wonder if she'd imagined that shadow reflected in his eyes. No, it had been real. Some silent bond linked her to this man and she knew he had suffered some terrible grief. As surely as she knew tendrils of pain still clung to him, she knew he wasn't ready to share that pain.

He motioned for them both to join him at the table, and she sat in the chair he indicated.

David folded his arms and bowed his head until his wild curls almost touched his plate. He screwed his eyes tightly shut and waited. After a moment he peeked sideways at Chase. Chase grinned and asked the little boy if he'd like to bless the food. Kendra scarcely had time to fold her own arms and bow her head before David finished praying and reached for a sausage. He stuffed the whole sausage in his mouth with one hand and clutched his fork in the other. Suddenly she realized she was famished, too, and dug into the food with almost as much enthusiasm as David was exhibiting. Either she was terribly hungry, or Chase was more than a passable cook.

Chase ate slowly, his attention on his two unexpected guests. Kendra ate with a healthy appetite, but the kid thoroughly amazed him. His own father had teased him as a boy about having a hollow leg he had to fill at each meal, but his own eating habits aside, he'd somehow gotten the impression little kids were picky. His sister claimed her kids only dirtied dishes and that they never actually consumed anything—other than french fries, anyway. Of course Lucy's kids had never been through an ordeal like this kid had, he acknowledged silently.

He'd caught the news on the radio this morning and put the story of a holdup in Darcy together with the story Kendra had told him. He knew law enforcement officials were searching for the thieves, along with Kendra and David, in five states, but that the search was being hampered by heavy snow at the higher altitudes and torrential rain at lower levels. The thieves, along with their hostages, had dropped completely out of sight. He decided not to tell Kendra about the bank guard who had been rushed to the hospital and who had not yet gained consciousness.

For some unexplained reason, he felt a touch of pride in Kendra's fierce protective stance toward a child who wasn't even hers. He hadn't spent much time around women for years, but he couldn't help thinking she was exceptional. She'd been a bystander, only in Darcy for a couple of hours while her tire was being repaired. She should be in California now, well on her way to a Christmas family reunion in the warmth and sunshine, instead of sitting at his table mothering a child who had accidently crossed her path. She wasn't excitable or dramatic like some women he knew, and she had a way of assuming responsibility without a lot of fuss. He liked that. She'd shown amazing strength through last night's ordeal and in keeping the child calm. He didn't doubt that her cool determination and die-hard inner strength had saved both her own life and that of the kid. *Carol's panic had rendered her incapable of even moving.* No, he wouldn't think about that. He wouldn't make comparisons. Besides it hadn't been Carol's fault; it had been his.

Unless he missed his guess, some of Kendra's inner strength came from a firm faith in God. It wasn't just the glimpses he'd caught last night of her praying or the interaction between her and the kid that gave them both away as members of the Church. Lots of people prayed when they faced danger, but there was something he couldn't explain about her, only sense, that conveyed an impression of real faith. For some undefinable reason, it was easy to picture her alongside those Book of Mormon mothers of Helaman's young warriors. He'd recently reread that story and it had stayed in his mind, causing him to speculate on what kind of women they must have been. In a way he'd envied those young warriors ever since he'd first heard their story as a troubled boy who longed to have his mother accompany him and his sister and their father to church each week.

He hadn't known many women with deep spiritual convictions of their own, but something told him Kendra was different. He'd always suspected his sister, Lucy, had married in the temple simply because she'd happened to fall in love with a returned missionary. His mother wasn't a member of the Church and had only occasionally gone to church with her family, and his wife had found church boring. Attending church alone had been difficult, and he'd gradually drifted into inactivity. Carol always claimed they could become active when they were old and gray and life wasn't filled with more exciting things to do. But Carol hadn't had a chance to become old and gray. Sharply he veered away from thoughts of Carol.

He didn't blame his mother or his wife for his own years of inactivity. He was the one who had let his faith slide. Still, he couldn't help wondering if the torturous climb back to faith in God had been prompted by the need for solace after his wife's death; otherwise, might he have drifted even further away? And would he have been a stronger, better person if he'd had memories of their faith to encourage him?

David's religious upbringing was apparent, too. Though Chase's church attendance wasn't as regular as it should be, he attended often enough to know most of the adults in the small Darcy ward. When the radio announcer mentioned Guy and Vicki Rolando, he remembered Guy taught the elders quorum class he occasionally attended; Chase had seen the young family sitting together during sacrament meetings. David obviously got his curly hair and compact build from his father, though the color of his hair came from his petite, blonde mother. Guy and his wife seemed like nice people, and Chase wished there was some way to let them know their son was safe.

Something about the boy touched him in a way he'd never experienced with any of his own nephews or nieces. He got along fine with them, but none of them ever made him think he was missing something in his own life. Of course, he hadn't spent a great deal of time with any of them. In a way he'd avoided close contact with his sister's children. He'd tried not to think about children at all after his baby died.

Maybe it was David's words when he stoutly defended Christmas that got him thinking about what might have been. Or maybe it was the way the boy had waited, in spite of his hunger, for a blessing on the food. Chase knew the little boy had meant the infant Christ child when he spoke of the baby's birthday; he had no way of knowing Christmas was his baby's birthday, too.

His eyes followed the rapid motion of David's hands as he stuffed sausages in his mouth with one hand and forked in eggs and potatoes with the other, only occasionally stopping to wash it all down with long, thirsty gulps of milk. Would his son have been anything like David? No, he was becoming maudlin. His son wouldn't be a little boy if he were alive today; he'd be a great, gangling teenager. They'd probably be fighting over a driver's license, grades, and chores, things like that. Funny, even that sounded good.

Having a child suddenly thrust into his life wasn't as painful as Chase thought it would be. It was true that David's presence turned his thoughts to his own child, but in some crazy way, it was almost comforting to imagine what his son might have been like today. And the boy wouldn't be here for long. He could handle it for a few days. The weather was bound to clear soon, and the child would be able to return to his own home.

"Are you going to take me home now?" Having finally stopped eating, David naturally wanted to go home.

"I would if I could," he tried to soften his answer and clarify the dilemma they faced. "My truck is broken down, so I'll have to take the tractor back to the river to see if the bridge washed out. If the bridge is safe, we can take the tractor to the next ranch. Ted Peters is my closest neighbor and he has a phone. But if the bridge is gone, we'll have to wait for someone to come looking for us."

Kendra hadn't understood how truly isolated they were. "When will that be?" she gasped.

"I know Brother Peters," David beamed as he spoke. "He comes home teaching to our house, so he knows where I live."

"Ted and Tracy Peters over on the Double T have a small plane," Chase explained. "She's the local veterinarian, and the plane makes it easier for her to reach outlying ranches quickly. Ted flies out to check his herd after most storms. He usually makes a pass over my place, and I fly a red flag on top of the barn if I need anything. There's a pasture south of the barn where he can land, if need be. As soon as this snow stops, I'll get the flag out."

Chase could tell Kendra wasn't thrilled by his explanation, but she didn't whine or complain either.

"May I watch TV now?" David asked. His chin trembled, and Chase suspected he was trying hard to be brave. He hated to disappoint him again.

"I don't have a TV. Reception isn't any good out here without a satellite dish, and since I don't watch much television anyway, buying one always seemed less important than putting my money into my herd or buying books." He doubted David understood any of his explanation, beyond the fact that there was no television.

"You got a Rudolph book?" David queried, and Chase's heart sank. What was a little boy like David supposed to do in his bachelor household? He didn't have any children's books, and no television, no toys, not even a blasted Christmas tree. Well, he could do something about the Christmas tree! There were those stunted little cedar trees down by the bridge. One of them would make a pretty good Christmas tree.

"David, how would you like to come with me to feed the sheep? When we get through, we could look around for a Christmas tree. I'll take my ax, and if we see one you like, I'll chop it down." He made an offer he figured the kid wouldn't refuse.

David's grin was like the sun coming out after a long winter and left Chase swallowing a lump in his throat. He was glad he'd thought of something to keep the boy entertained. It was a great idea. In the time since he'd taken over the ranch he'd never had a Christmas tree, but now he found himself anticipating the tang of cedar wafting through the house.

"Uh, Chase. He can't go out dressed like that." Kendra sounded hesitant, as if she hated to disappoint either of them. He looked at David and decided she was right. The kid couldn't go out without pants, and he'd likely trip and break his neck if he tried to walk outside with a shirt tail that dragged six inches on the ground. He should have tossed the kid's clothes in the washer, but he'd forgotten all about the wet, muddy clothes he'd dropped on the laundry room floor last night. David's face fell. Oddly, Chase felt almost as disappointed as the boy looked.

"If you have a washer and dryer, perhaps I could wash his things, and you could take him out later," Kendra said. Once more Chase spotted a quiver in the boy's bottom lip. He really hated to disappoint the kid.

He considered Kendra's suggestion, then turned to the little boy who was anxiously watching him. "I'm afraid she's right, partner. You'll have to be dressed real warm to go outside today. How about if I go start feeding the sheep, then when your clothes are dry, Kendra could take you out to the barn to help me finish up, then all three of us could go looking for that Christmas tree?"

David nodded his head and jumped down from his chair. "I'll help," he informed Kendra. She laughed as he ran from the table to the sink carrying his dishes, then dashed into a small room adjoining the kitchen. She hurried after him.

Chase rose from his chair and carried his plate to the sink, too, then reached for his coat, covered it with a plastic poncho, and headed for the door. Hesitating before stepping into rubber boots, he padded in stocking feet to the door of the laundry room where David stood on an overturned bucket pouring detergent into the washer.

"Kendra." She turned at the sound of his voice. Some silent message having nothing to do with their present situation seemed to spark between them, but then he cleared his throat and only said, "There are extra coats and boots in the closet by the back door. They'll be too large for you, but help yourself to whatever you can use." She smiled her thanks, and he found himself whistling as he made his way to the barn minutes later.

Snow was still falling, but the flakes seemed fat and lazy while the snow underfoot was mushy and soft. He wondered if the snow would soon stop altogether or turn back to rain. Even with all the problems the wet weather brought, he didn't look forward to the weather clearing up. Once the skies cleared, it wouldn't be long until Kendra and David would leave. That thought put an end to his cheerful whistling. Wasn't that what he wanted? Of course it was. He didn't want to get used to having them around. It was just that winter time tended to get a little lonely, and he was enjoying the novelty of having guests in his home. Even though he didn't wish their visit to end too soon, they both had families who were worried about them, and with whom they longed to be reunited. He chided himself for being selfish. Again he wished there was some way to let the Rolandos know David was safe.

CHAPTER 9

Vicki stirred the oatmeal listlessly. Morning had come, and there was still no word of David's whereabouts. She hoped he was somewhere warm and that the people who took him would give him some breakfast. For a moment she recalled how he'd looked when she'd placed his bowl of oatmeal in front of him the day before. He'd wrinkled his nose and looked disappointed, then looked up at her, a gleam of hope in his eyes, and asked, "Can I put brown sugar on it?"

She'd hated to tell him no, but there was very little brown sugar left, and she'd wanted to save it for a Christmas treat. Now she wished she'd put a heaping spoonful on his cereal, maybe two. She wouldn't touch that sugar until David was safely back home again she vowed. She turned at the sound of boots stomping on the front porch. In response to a loud banging on the door, she hurried to open it.

"Sheriff Hatcher!" She searched his face anxiously, hoping he brought good news.

"Sheriff!" Guy appeared behind her and reached for the sheriff's hand. "Have you found him?" Vicki held her breath, waiting for the sheriff's answer.

"No, folks. Nothing. There hasn't been a sign of them." The man was uncomfortable bearing bad news, but considered it his duty to speak to the Rolandos. He spun his hat between his fingers, looking for the words he needed.

"I thought you'd like to know the security guard is still in serious condition, but the doc thinks he'll pull through." He paused before going on. "Someone turned in a purse this morning that looks like it might belong to the woman who was taken along with David. Gus over at the garage said she was waiting for him to fix a flat tire before going on to California. We ran her I.D. through the computer. Seems to be an okay person."

"Her family must be as worried as we are," Vicki whispered through a tight throat.

"We haven't located her family yet, but there are pictures of two young families in her wallet. They're likely relatives. She works for a CPA firm in Salt Lake. I spoke with someone in their business office. Her name is Kendra Emerson, and he said she's not married and doesn't have any children." The sheriff summed up the scant information he'd learned about the woman who had been kidnapped along with their son.

When the sheriff left, Vicki, Becca, and Guy returned to the kitchen. The oatmeal had turned to a sticky, lumpy mess from sitting too long, but no one remarked on the unappetizing breakfast. Guy asked Vicki to bless the food, and she knew he was asking her to offer more than a simple blessing on the food.

For a moment Vicki's thoughts froze. Why was praying so difficult when now, more than at any other time, she needed God's help? She couldn't help feeling she was being tested and that if her faith wavered, she'd lose David. At the same time she'd never believed God was that harsh. A fleeting thought crossed her mind that perhaps her faith was so shallow, she didn't really believe God could help them. Or did she blame Him for taking David? No, Satan was taking advantage of her turmoil to cause her to doubt, to question her commitment to the gospel. Deep inside she knew that God would hear their prayers, and that He cared what happened to David. They couldn't help their son, only God could. She offered a blessing on the food, then without hesitating, asked God to protect David. An impression that David wasn't the only one needing her prayers stole into her heart and with deepest sincerity she asked God to keep Kendra Emerson safe, too.

• • • • •

The dogs came running to meet Chase the moment he opened the barn door. Rags was a young Sheltie and Roscoe an older version of the same breed of Shetland sheepdog. They had their own little door, so they could freely move between the barn, the lambing sheds, and the bulk of the herd that wintered in a large pasture behind the sheds. They were working dogs, not pets, but they always greeted him with eager excitement, and he stopped to pat them and refill their dishes before going on to the sheep. He enjoyed their company and took pride in the skillful way they handled their charges. They trailed behind him, occasionally uttering short yips as they darted about the edge of the herd, bringing any ewe who threatened to stray back in line.

He checked the ewes in the barns first. Lambing season wouldn't officially start until February, but there were always a few mamas who rushed the season, starting in January. Those due to lamb first were already in the lambing barns and didn't appear in any danger of giving birth right away, so he would feed them first and check the water lines before going on to the rest of the herd.

None of the water tanks were frozen, and he was glad he'd paid the exorbitant fee the power company had demanded to have an electric line run to the ranch, and that he'd installed heaters that kept the stock troughs from freezing over. If this storm continued much longer, the power might go out and he'd have to turn on the generators, but so far the line had proved pretty stable in all but the worst ice storms. Caring for the sheep didn't require a great deal of effort during this time of season, but when lambing began he'd work around the clock and get little sleep. Lambing was demanding work, but he'd always found a kind of satisfaction in helping new life into the world.

Using a small tractor to pull a low, flat trailer loaded with hay, he spread the feed in various places where the sheep could easily reach it. His herd was getting larger, and he needed to consider taking on help, especially during the lambing season. He'd started out with a small herd, using professional help to shear and transport the wool to market. Until the past couple of years, he hadn't envisioned moving beyond a one-man operation, but the last couple of lambing seasons had been tough to handle alone and the expanded hay fields he'd planted were going to be difficult to handle by himself. It wouldn't be easy finding someone willing to live this far out. Ted Peters had been trying for two years to find someone who would be willing to move to the Double T to take care of both his and his wife's books.

For a moment he wondered how it would be if he had a son working beside him. David's cherubic face came to mind. He pushed away that thought. If his son were alive, he'd be almost old enough to do a man's work. But if his son were still alive, then Carol would be too, and they'd still be living in Phoenix. He'd loved Carol, but she'd never shared his enthusiasm for the outdoors. She was a city girl, who had no interest in the kind of rural life he now led. She would have hated the ranch as much as he'd hated the stifling closeness of the city. Though he loved the ranch and the open freedom of his plateau home, he'd give it up in a minute to have Carol and the baby back, he mused. His desire to start a ranch had been the one area they had disagreed over. No, that wasn't quite true. He'd wanted to be more active in the Church, but she hadn't been interested. They'd planned to buy a few acres outside of town, when they could afford it—not a farm exactly, but a place where he could raise a few horses, keep a dog, and perhaps grow a garden. Shifting his eyes to gaze toward the cloud-shrouded hills, he knew what he'd never admitted to himself before—it wouldn't have been enough.

He'd bought the ranch after her death to escape his grief and to get away from the memories. He tried to imagine Carol and their son walking through six inches of snow, feeding bum lambs, or riding in his old pickup. The picture wouldn't come. It was Kendra and David who came to mind and caused him to frown. He wasn't forgetting Carol and Jesse, was he? No, he would never forget them, nor stop loving them. Just because he couldn't picture them in his present surroundings didn't mean he'd stopped caring.

He heard laughter and thought for a moment he was still imagining, but Roscoe lifted his head as though sniffing the wind, then streaked toward the barn with Rags at his heels. He whistled for them to stop, not wanting them to frighten either Kendra or David. The dogs halted and looked at him questioningly, and Rags began to bark and hop around in little circles. Roscoe planted his rump in the snow and cocked his head, obviously questioning his master's sanity to rein him in when strangers were encroaching on their territory. When Chase caught up to the dogs, he snapped his fingers and they fell in at his heels, prancing and eager to inspect the intruders. Chase was surprised by his own eagerness to see Kendra and David again. He had to remind himself it had only been an hour since he'd last seen them. Still, his heart gave a strange little jump when they came into sight.

David clapped his mittened hands together and began to run toward them when he saw the dogs. Roscoe stopped, his legs stiff, and his shaggy body assuming a territorial stance. Rags copied her older partner's position, but her thick, banner-like tail belied any serious intent.

"David, wait a minute," Kendra cautioned as she clasped his shoulder, impeding his momentum. "Let them get used to you slowly. Chase has to let them know you won't hurt the sheep before they'll be your friends."

"I won't hurt them! I wouldn't ever hurt a sheepie," David promised.

Chase smiled. No one had ever referred to his sheep in diminutive form before, but he didn't figure it would hurt any feelings if the boy called them anything he liked. He appreciated the way Kendra encouraged David to show caution around unfamiliar dogs, but didn't frighten him into fearing them. The dogs wouldn't hurt the boy. They only attacked predators who threatened the sheep, and even Roscoe was more bark than bite when it came to scaring off the occasional coyote who came looking for a free meal.

He knew the little boy wanted to tumble and play with the dogs, but taking his cue from Kendra, he asked him to stand still and let the dogs get used to his smell. Then he told him to take off a mitten and hold out his hand, palm down. David giggled when first Rags, then Roscoe, licked the back of his hand. By the time Chase let David pet the dogs they were fast friends. The sedate herd dogs appeared as anxious to play as did the small boy who had found unexpected playmates.

"Would you like to see some of the sheep up close?" he asked David, but it was Kendra he looked to for an answer.

"I would," she smiled. "I've seen, even touched, a few sheep at the fair in Salt Lake, but I've never seen as many as this at one time before," she told him with a look of awe on her face as she gazed out over the herd. Behind the splendor of her smile, he forgot the overcast sky and the light sprinkle of rain that continued to fall.

He led them inside the barn, with the dogs tumbling and showing off for David. They walked down a wide aisle between two long rows of pens, and Kendra stopped to pat the thick woolly head of one of his prize Columbias. David climbed the board fence and peered inquisitively at the stall filled with fresh, pale straw.

"Is this a stable?" David turned his face toward Kendra. He looked so serious and deeply concerned, Chase had to hide a smile. He had a hunch where the question was headed.

"Yes," Kendra answered simply. "A stable is another word for a barn or place for animals to sleep."

"Did Jesus get borned here?" This time his question was directed toward Chase. Chase stifled a chuckle, and bent forward so he could look directly into David's eyes. The kid's question had been sincere, and it deserved a straight answer.

"No, Jesus wasn't born here, but he was born in a place a lot like this. It was probably smaller, and there might have been other animals, not just sheep. It was probably warm and had clean straw for him to sleep on."

"You got any angels to sing to you at this stable?" David's gaze turned toward the shadowy upper regions of the barn as though searching for an angel.

"Afraid not," he answered seriously, and for just a moment he wondered if that were the truth. It seemed to him that maybe he did have a couple of angels visiting him right now.

"I like sheep." David reached across the fence to give a very large ewe a tentative pat. "Daddy read a story to me from his big Bible about sheep, and angels, and Baby Jesus. Three guys on camels like at the zoo came, too. They brought presents for the baby because it was his birthday. Mom said that's why we hafta get presents for everybody on Christmas, even Becca. On Becca's birthday she got all the presents, but when it's Christmas I get some, too."

David's parents had done a good job teaching the boy. Chase wondered if he would have done so well. Probably not. Back then his own faith had been pretty weak, and he'd had different priorities, but if he could go back, start all over again, he'd like a chance to raise a boy to look at life the way David's parents were teaching him. No, his mind shied away from that thought. Best not to think about might-have-beens.

"Becca must be your sister," he spoke to David. He already knew she was. He'd seen a little blond-haired girl a few years older than David with Guy one time.

"She's a girl," David explained, and Chase guessed that in a small boy's eyes that said it all. He regretted that his own son had never had a chance to have a sister. Funny how he'd never thought of Jesse before beyond the baby stage and he'd never considered that it wasn't only Jesse he'd lost. Seeing David with the sheep and the dogs, he couldn't help wondering what it might have been like if there had been other children and how different his life might be if they had been a part of it.

"Ready to go tree hunting?" He shut away the haunting pictures in his mind. Besides, he didn't want to keep David and Kendra out so long they got cold again. "There's a wagon and tractor parked behind the barn. Go jump on the wagon while I get my ax."

David scrambled down from the fence and took off running with both dogs at his heels. Kendra smiled at him with a hint of laughter in her eyes, and he nearly laughed out loud. He was enjoying himself. In fact, he felt downright happy. For the first time in fifteen years he could honestly say he felt good inside. That thought sobered him. Was it right to feel happy when Carol and Jesse couldn't share his happiness? What was there about Kendra and David that kept stirring old memories and inviting longings he'd thought he'd never experience again?

CHAPTER 10

Chase left a few bales of hay on the wagon to provide a small amount of shelter, and Kendra and David huddled against them. They peered over the edge of a tarp he'd grabbed at the last minute to help keep them dry. David had wanted the dogs to come with them, but Chase told him they had to stay behind to watch the sheep. The dogs looked comically forlorn as the tractor and wagon pulled away, leaving them behind.

The tractor moved as slowly as the truck had the night before, and David laughed each time they lurched across a bump or hole in the lane. Fence posts lined the lane and even with a coating of snow, Kendra could tell the large fields were hay fields, and she surmised that Chase grew his own feed for his sheep. In the distance, where sharp hills arose, she could see the darker shapes of trees. Clouds hovered low across the landscape, cutting off the tops of the hills and creating an illusion that they were on an island, separate from the rest of the world. She felt a moment's regret that she wouldn't be there in the spring to see those hills dotted with sheep.

The tractor slowed, then came to a halt, and David scrambled over the side. When she reached the edge, Chase's hand was there to assist her. A small thrill crept up her arm as she placed her hand in his, and in spite of the thick gloves they both wore, she registered a twinge of disappointment when he released her hand as soon as she was steady on her feet. Feeling heat rise in her cheeks, she hoped Chase hadn't noticed how his touch had flustered her.

He waved an arm toward a small gully and Kendra saw the trees. They were small and twisted, but one would make a satisfactory

Christmas tree. They were nothing like the long-needled ponderosa pines she had always admired. Still, they had a festive flair of their own, and already she could picture one of the thick bushy trees filling the alcove where the wide living room window jutted out at the front of the house.

She turned completely around, instinctively trying to get her bearings. Shock rippled through her when she realized she was staring at the river they had crossed the night before. Posts marked the place where the bridge had been, and thick cables trailed into the water and disappeared from sight. There was no trace of pilings that had supported the bridge from underneath. A small sound drew her attention to David and she looked down at his sober face. "The bridge is gone and we can't ever go home anymore." His words carried a terrible sadness.

"No, David, that's not true," Kendra tried to comfort the child.

Chase crouched beside him and held out his arms. With a sob David rushed into them and leaned his head against the big man's chest as Chase made their situation clear, "You can't go home today, but when this rain stops and it's safe for Ted Peters to fly his airplane, he'll know we're stranded and he'll come get you. You'll be just fine here with Kendra and me and the dogs to look after you until we can get you back home."

"Will the bad men find us?" David asked as he struggled to dash away his tears with the sleeve of his coat.

"I don't think we have to worry about those guys," Chase told him.

"I think they were in a hurry to get as far from here as they could," Kendra added. Smiling brightly she continued, "Let's go look for that Christmas tree."

"Yeah," David echoed and pulled himself free from Chase's embrace to look at the trees.

Feeling a lump in her throat, Kendra turned back toward the river as David started toward the trees. Dark, roiling water leaped and twisted, struggling to break free of the restraining channel. Her hands began to shake. There would have been no chance of survival if the bridge had broken while they were on it! Not only was the water swift and dangerous, but the sheer rock walls of the chasm would have made climbing out impossible.

"It's not usually like this." Chase touched her shoulder with a gesture he surely meant to be reassuring. His voice was soft and low, as though he too, was in awe of the spectacle before them. "I suspect we had a little help getting across last night." She'd felt that, too.

"Perhaps one of David's angels held the bridge together for us." She tried to lighten the moment, but the instant the words left her mouth, she knew they were more truth than joke.

"More like a whole legion of angels," Chase concurred, and she didn't think he was jesting either. His hand tightened on her shoulder briefly before dropping to his side. But it was enough to double her awareness of him and leave her feeling gauche and tongue-tied. She'd never known how to react to a man's casual touch.

"There's usually not more than a couple of inches running here, and by late summer it's often bone-dry. In fact, there's a spot about five miles downstream where a truck can ford the stream almost any time of the year." Though he no longer touched her, he hadn't moved away. His voice rumbled in her ear, and she felt a return of the prickly sensation she'd experienced when he'd touched her hand earlier.

From the corner of her eye she caught a movement and turned to see David plunging through the deepening snow toward the trees. The mushy, wet snow provided little traction and he slid and fell, soaking his pants as he worked his way to the trees.

"Wait, David," she called as he darted from one tree to the next as rapidly as the snow—which came to his knees—permitted, declaring each tree his favorite. She finally caught up to him beside a cedar that was only slightly shorter than herself, but as broad as it was tall. Its thick branches gave it the appearance of a large bush. When she brushed against it, the tangy scent of cedar filled the air. It was different, but she liked it.

"I want this one. It's the biggest," David called over his shoulder to Chase.

"A smaller one would be easier to carry," Kendra pointed out, realizing the tree would be much bulkier to carry than a conventional pine tree would have been.

"But this is the bestest one." David attempted to embrace the tree, but drew back when its rough branches brushed his face. He laughed and stretched forth a hand to shake the snow from a branch as though he were introducing himself. "Hello, tree," he giggled.

"This one it is," Chase grinned. "You guys clear away the snow around the trunk while I go back for the ax." David immediately dug in with enthusiasm. Laughing, Kendra stooped to assist him in brushing away the snow from the tree's base. Chase was back in a couple of minutes to help them. When they finished, he picked up the ax.

"Okay, short stuff, stand back!" Chase ordered David as he made a show of pushing back his sleeves and swinging the ax through a couple of fancy maneuvers before settling down to serious chopping. Kendra placed her arms around David and stood with him well back from the flying chips of wood. It had taken longer to clear the snow away from the base of the tree to provide access to the trunk than it did for Chase to chop the little tree down, but in those few minutes of watching him swing the ax, Kendra discovered she liked watching Chase work. He moved with a relaxed kind of grace that appeared almost lazy.

But he wasn't lazy. He was strong and kind, and suddenly she was afraid she was beginning to like him too much. Never in her life had she experienced this giddy reaction to a man before. What was the matter with her? She'd known Chase less than twenty-four hours! She glanced anxiously toward the sky, hoping it would clear and someone would come for David and her. The sky was no help, if anything it looked darker and closer to the ground than before. She mustn't care about Chase, she didn't want to miss him after she left this place. Intuitively she knew that if she let herself care about him, the loneliness would be that much harder to bear when she returned to her empty apartment.

• • • • •

After the supper dishes had been washed and put away, Chase looked around his living room and marveled at how changed it was. When they'd returned to the house with the tree, Kendra had taken charge of fixing lunch and drying both David's and her clothing once more. Amusement quirked the corners of his mouth when he saw she'd strung a cord across his fireplace and hung their wet socks on it, then spread cedar boughs along the top of his mantel. He'd found some boards he could turn into a tree stand, although he had found himself worrying what they would use for decorations. He needn't have worried. He'd only needed to provide paper and tinfoil. Kendra and David turned the paper into ornaments.

"Where'd you learn to do this?" he asked, fingering a fragile-winged paper bird.

Kendra laughed. "It really isn't hard. My sister, Cameron, learned about origami in school. She insisted on teaching Katy and me to do it, too. After a few weeks she lost interest, but I was hooked. I checked books out of the library and learned to make all kinds of paper figures and ornaments."

"It's neat!" David added his approval.

"Those stars are pretty neat, too," Chase applauded the little boy's dozens of shiny, lopsided creations and discovered he really meant it. Something about their unintended imperfections formed a harmonious whole.

"This one is for the top." David produced a cardboard cutout, obviously cut out by Kendra, which he had meticulously covered with tinfoil. Chase scooped him up in his arms and helped him attach the star to the top of the tree, then stepped back with the child to admire their handiwork. David's arm rested along the back of Chase's neck, just brushing his hair. He'd never given much thought to holding a child, but there was something terribly satisfying about the wiggly, warm little body in his arms. Kendra came over to stand beside them, and Chase discovered a lump in his throat and tears aching at the back of his eyes. Something stirred in his heart, and he wasn't certain whether it was pleasure or pain.

Since he'd moved into the house, Chase had never observed Christmas. He'd mailed a check to Lucy with instructions to buy stuff for her kids every December, but he'd never had a tree, and in a way, he'd resented even the gifts Lucy always sent him. He didn't send them back, but he opened the socks and shirts and stuffed them in his drawers as soon as he returned from town with her package each year. He made certain the fruitcake was all eaten before Christmas. He read a few verses from his scriptures almost every day, but he avoided Luke at Christmastime. To his way of thinking, the Savior had been born in the spring, late in the lambing season, so Luke was more appropriate then. For fifteen years he'd avoided Christmas—now the most beautiful Christmas tree he'd ever seen was right here in his front room. And there was a beautiful woman standing beside him and a trusting child in his arms, leaving him torn between a desire to protect himself by thrusting them as far away as possible, and the need to gather them close and savor every second of a Christmas he'd never expected to experience.

"Do you think Santa Claus knows I'm here?" David interrupted his thoughts, and Chase just looked at him helplessly. A tree was one thing, but there was no way he could conjure up Santa Claus. David was going to be one disappointed little boy Christmas morning—if he was still here. The way those storm clouds were hunkering down, there was a good possibility he would be. An ache spread across Chase's heart. It was all right for him to cut Christmas out of his life, but the boy shouldn't have to.

"David—" Kendra took the child from him and settled with him in a large easy chair. She looked awfully right there in that chair; so did the kid. Chase dismissed his sentimental thoughts, telling himself it was just all the years of loneliness speaking, but a determined burst of honesty reminded him he'd never noticed he was lonely before.

"Santa might not find you here," Kendra went on speaking to the boy. "But he'll still visit your house, and when you get home your presents will be waiting for you there."

"Will he bring the red train even if I'm not there?"

"I don't know what he'll bring you, but I'm sure it will be something nice. Your mom and dad will take care of your presents until you get home." She smiled and gave him a hug.

"Becca says Santa Claus won't come this year." He gazed solemnly at her, obviously hoping she'd refute his sister's dire prediction.

"Have you been bad?" Chase attempted to tease the child out of his suddenly woeful mood.

"Sometimes," David hung his head and admitted.

"I'll bet you weren't very bad." Kendra hugged the boy and attempted to reassure him.

"Becca says he won't come anyway, 'cause Daddy doesn't have any money to pay him."

"Listen, David." Kendra straightened him on her lap so he could see her face. "Some years Santa has a harder time than other years, and he can't always give all of the good kids the best presents every time. Sometimes mommies and daddies help him if they can, but sometimes they can't. Presents are nice. It's a lot of fun to give people you love presents, and getting presents is fun, too. But Christmas is more than presents. We can have a special Christmas Day right here without presents," she went on.

"But I like presents." The child's voice held a note of sadness along with an acceptance beyond his years.

"Christmas isn't really about presents, David. It's a feeling in your heart."

A sudden light replaced the forlorn look in David's eyes. "Like Whoville?"

Chase had no idea what the kid meant, but he could see Kendra was delighted with the boy's comparison.

"Yes, just like Whoville," she whispered. "Christmas really doesn't come in boxes and packages, lights, or roast turkey."

"It's in our hearts 'cause Jesus loves us," David added.

"Yes, he does love us," she repeated softly.

"Did he send Chase to keep us safe from the bad grinches?" he asked in all seriousness.

"I think he did." She hugged the boy closer and looked up at Chase with shining eyes. He cleared his throat and looked away. If he didn't watch it, he'd be blubbering like a baby first thing he knew. He remembered now the Dr. Seuss story about some mean character who stole everyone's Christmas. The thieves who stole Kendra and David right off the main street of Darcy and dumped them in the middle of nowhere to freeze to death certainly qualified as grinches as far as he was concerned.

Standing before the first Christmas tree to ever grace his house, he studied the scene before him and wondered if David was right. Had some heavenly power placed him where he could find Kendra and David when their strength was gone and they were numb with cold? Could that be the reason his truck stalled? It was sometimes hard to start, but that was the only time it had ever died right while he was driving it. He felt humbled when he considered the possibility. He'd heard others bear their testimonies and speak of coincidences they believed weren't accidents at all, but were really times when the Lord had stepped in to gently steer them in a particular direction. He wasn't sure how he felt about that kind of divine intervention. He wouldn't go so far as to say it couldn't happen, but he'd never given any thought to the notion God might use him in one of these near-miracles. Mostly he never gave much thought as to whether God was particularly aware of him at all.

He wasn't too sure what to think about the possibility that God might have a purpose for him or that He might have had something to do with his truck stalling out on the desert that night. But whether God was behind his rescue of Kendra and David or not, their presence had certainly given him something to think about. And it seemed that Christmas was one of those things he could no longer avoid thinking about. He'd forgotten a lot about Christmas, and he'd never known a whole lot about little boys, but he felt kind of responsible to see that this one didn't miss Christmas.

"Excuse me," he mumbled. "There's something I've got to do."

Kendra watched Chase leave the room and felt an ache in her heart. Perhaps she was being fanciful, but she had a strong feeling there was something about Christmas that caused him a great deal of pain. She would like to relieve the hurt she caught on his face at unexpected moments, but what could she do?

She didn't know how long she sat in the chair holding David. There was a warm fire in the fireplace, and flames reflected off the tinfoil stars on the tree, mimicking the little electric lights usually found on Christmas trees. Feeling drowsy and strangely at peace, she found herself drifting toward sleep until the buzz of some kind of saw pulled her back. She'd noticed a well-equipped shop behind the utility room earlier and she wondered what Chase was doing. Did he have work to do that their Christmas tree expedition had kept him from all day? She felt guilty for monopolizing so much of his time. She'd try to be more helpful tomorrow, though hard as she tried to regret the time they'd spent together, finding the tree and decorating it, she couldn't.

She glanced toward the window. The snow was coming faster now in hard frozen bits of ice that rattled as they struck the window. Wind added a keening wail to the storm and would perhaps move the storm front that had stalled for so long over northern Nevada, out of the area. If the snow stopped by morning, she might be on her way to California before the day was over. The thought didn't fill her heart with gladness.

Chase had turned on the radio earlier so she knew the bank robbers hadn't been caught, and that the police were still searching for them and their hostages. Her sisters must know by now why she was late and be frantic with worry. Her purse and car were all the police had needed to identify the stranger who had disappeared along with little David Rolando. It had sounded strange to hear her name spoken by the radio announcer, but it was nice to know the police had her purse and that she'd be able to claim it when she returned to Darcy. She'd been right about the bank security guard she had mistaken for a policeman. He had tried to stop the abduction and had been wounded as the van sped away. He hadn't returned fire out of fear he might hit one of the hostages. She was glad he was recovering, and that along with providing details of the crime, he'd become a local hero.

She didn't want her family to worry, and she ached with sympathy for David's parents. Still, a selfish part of her wanted to stay right here for Christmas. She'd never been happier than she was at this moment, in this house, listening to Chase work in his shop, and feeling David's gentle puffs of breath against her cheek. It was too tempting to imagine they were hers; the house, the child, and especially the man she'd first called a "cowboy."

CHAPTER 11

Guy swung the shovel with a vengeance. The snowfall had been slight. There was hardly more than a dusting on the walk and driveway, but it was an excuse to get out of the house. He felt like a caged animal, waiting inside for word of David. He needed the physical release that shoveling snow promised.

Where was David? Why hadn't anyone spotted the thieves and their hostages by now? Was David even still alive? A picture of his son lying, still and white, beneath a blanket of snow brought him to his knees. Despair filled his heart. *Why, God? Why is this happening? David is just a little boy, little more than a baby. He's much too young and innocent to be at the mercy of so much evil. I am his father. I would protect him with my life, but where do I look? What can I do? He needs his mother, and she needs him. She fears he is cold and hungry because she cannot emotionally admit he might not still be alive.*

His eyes closed and the haunting picture of his wife with tear-reddened eyes filled his mind. Vicki had been hesitant to leave Denver four years ago when he was offered a great job in oil exploration in the desert, but he'd wanted to go so badly she'd given in. He'd given up his job in the city, bought a trailer home, and followed the drilling rig for nearly a year and half. Unfortunately the company wasn't what he'd been led to expect and had fallen apart, leaving him stranded in Darcy, Nevada.

At first it hadn't been so bad; he'd gotten a job hauling feed for the mill, and he'd worked part-time at the feed yard. They'd developed a fondness for the little town. Vicki was happy in the ward and pleased with the small but excellent school the children attended.

Even though his salary wasn't large, they'd made plans to return to Denver to visit her father for Thanksgiving. Those plans hadn't materialized when the stockyard closed and the mill contracted with a larger company in Reno to do their hauling. He'd picked up a few odd jobs with ranchers, helping them finish haying and settling their herds for the winter.

It was winter now and there were no steady jobs available, and he didn't have the money to move on. Vicki didn't complain. She'd never once berated him for leaving a secure job in Denver, and even though she wasn't pushing him to return to the city, he could tell their financial situation frightened her.

If he could find a buyer for the trailer, he'd have enough money to move his family back to the city. Ironically, though Vicki worried constantly about her father back in Denver; she still expressed a reluctance to leave Darcy. None of them wanted to go. They'd fallen in love with this huge open land, but they had to eat, and pride wouldn't allow them to accept welfare. Guy had delayed searching further afield for a job, dreading the day when he'd have to wear a tie to work again each day, jockey for position on the freeway, and breathe stale city air. Now he feared he'd waited too long.

"Please, Father," he prayed aloud. "Bring David back to us. I'll go back to the city, I'll do whatever I have to, if only you'll bring him back to us."

He pulled himself up by leaning heavily on the snow shovel. The sky was bleak and nothing had changed. He'd brought his family to this place, and now they scarcely had enough to eat and David was gone. It was his fault. He'd foolishly chased dreams. He was a failure as a man, as a husband, and as a father. Why should God hear his prayers?

"Brother Rolando." A voice spoke his name and he looked up to see Bishop Samuelson. The bishop was a tall, thin man who had come to Darcy about the same time Guy had. The principal of the school, Bishop Samuelson had only come to the small town because a family emergency had delayed his availability to accept the renewal of his contract in Las Vegas. By the time the crisis was settled, he'd had to accept any school that was available. Just before contract time came around again, he'd been called as bishop of the Darcy ward and had agreed to stay.

Guy reached out to shake the bishop's hand. They stood silently for several minutes, both too choked to speak. Finally Guy asked, "Why?"

"I don't know," Bishop Samuelson responded. "There's so much we don't have answers for. Some theorize that problems come into our lives to humble us, and I've noticed that in some cases that may be true. Others see these same troubles as stepping stones in our preparation for greater responsibilities or blessings. I've seen the truth of that, too. I think people have always wondered why good people have to suffer and why the innocent often seem to pay for the wrong acts of the unrighteous. The men who stole David exercised their agency to make choices and they will ultimately pay for their evil choices, but that doesn't bring you much comfort now, I know."

"If only there was something I could do. I feel like the worst kind of father. I haven't supported my family as I should, and now my failure to watch my son closely enough has brought this tragedy on us." Guy admitted to the weight crushing him.

The bishop placed his hand on Guy's shoulder. "Perhaps you're taking too much blame on your shoulders. I've seen the way you've struggled to find work and your willingness to take on any job offered in order to provide for your family. And you're not the only father whose child has slipped away unnoticed for a few minutes. Jobs can fall through and economic problems can plague anyone. You're a good father, doing your best to care for your family and teach them the gospel. The Lord is not displeased with you."

"I wish I could be sure of that," Guy admitted. "The thought of David being hurt or forced to suffer is tearing both Vicki and me apart."

"You can't allow that to happen," Bishop Samuelson admonished. "The adversary lies in wait to attack our faith and lead us down the rocky road of depression and discouragement when we are the most vulnerable. What is needed now is to exercise every bit of faith you have, but you don't have to do it alone. Just as our ward family is willing to help you shoulder the responsibility for your family's material welfare for a time, so are we anxious to share our faith in your family's behalf. That's why we call each other 'brothers' and 'sisters,' because we share each other's sorrows and joys. I've had dozens of calls from ward members who want to organize a special fast, participate in the search, or provide Christmas for your family."

"Christmas. I'd almost forgotten," Guy mumbled. "David loves Christmas. I've never known anyone more excited about Christmas than David. If . . . if he isn't back by then, I don't think any of our family will be interested in celebrating."

"I understand." Bishop Samuelson tightened his grip on Guy's shoulder. "But let the sisters bring your family meals, and be assured that as many elders and high priests and as much of their equipment as the sheriff can use, will be assisting in the search."

"Thank you," was all Guy could manage.

"And Guy," the bishop went on, "I want you to think about Christmas. Remember our Heavenly Father saw His Son go into a world He knew was filled with cruelty and evil intentions. Unlike your son, His Son had a choice. Our Father knew the choice was His Son's and that ultimately the Son would triumph over His enemies. God could have intervened, but didn't—because it would have defeated the Son's mission. Still it must have been awful to witness all that was done to His Son and do nothing. You don't know why your son was torn from your family or if he will return in this life, but you can find peace in knowing God understands and that your faith can bring you understanding."

Guy was silent for several minutes, struggling to absorb the bishop's words. He did feel comforted to know that others, especially his Heavenly Father, shared his grief and worry, but it wasn't enough.

"Bishop—" asking for anything wasn't easy for Guy, "—would you give my wife and me a blessing?"

"It would be my privilege," the bishop responded. "I saw Ted Peters in town a little while ago. Since he's your quorum president, would you like me to get him to assist?"

Guy slowly nodded his head.

• • • • •

Vicki pressed her cheek against the glass and peered out at the night. The wind howled and sharp bits of ice made a tinny sound as they struck the window. The temperature had dropped and Sheriff

Hatcher had sent most of the men home until daylight. Several of the ranchers had been forced to drop out of the search early in the afternoon anyway in order to get feed to animals stranded on the unnatural islands formed by the persistent rain.

Where was David? Would she ever see her little boy again? She closed her eyes in an attempt to shut out the terrible thoughts that came relentlessly to her mind. She had to have faith; she had to believe he was warm and had been given food. She had to believe he was still alive.

"Mom, where should I put this?" She turned at the sound of Becca's voice. "Sister Anderson brought it, but there's no more room in the refrigerator. "

Becca stood with a large casserole dish in her hands. Vicki hadn't heard a knock on the door. There had been a steady stream of knocks on the door all day. Her visiting teachers had come, David's kindergarten teacher had stopped by, her closest neighbors, and several of the women she worked with in the Primary had dropped in to express their love and concern. Most had brought bread or cookies. The Elliot sisters had appeared with a big fruitcake. All had brought tears and an assurance that David was in their prayers. Now it seemed the Relief Society president had returned with dinner.

"Is Sister Anderson still here?" Vicki asked, knowing she should thank her. She'd have to thank all of the women who had beat a steady trail to their door all day with food and whispers of comfort. They had sympathized as only one mother can sympathize with another when her child is gone. She appreciated their concern and tried not to see the way they clutched their own children with guilty gratitude in their eyes. She didn't blame them for being glad it wasn't their children lost out there in the unknown with armed, dangerous captors who had already demonstrated how little they valued other peoples' lives.

"No, she said she didn't want to disturb you," Becca answered her mother's question. "She said we should eat this while it's still hot." The last was said on such a hopeful note, Vicki was instantly plunged into an awareness of her neglect. Becca had moved about the house all day like a ghostly shadow, while she'd been so consumed with worry about David, she'd scarcely given her other child a moment's thought. She didn't even know if Becca had eaten anything all day.

"Oh, I'm sorry, Becca. Set it on the table." She hadn't meant to keep her daughter standing with a heavy casserole dish in her hands. And she certainly didn't want her to be hungry. "I suppose we really should eat something." She looked at the dish without interest. Such a short time ago she was discouraged because there was so little to feed her family. Now the house was bursting with good food, and she thought she would choke if she attempted to swallow one bite.

Becca set the dish down and ran to the cupboard for plates and glasses. She set the table carefully as she had been taught. Vicki's heart ached to see Becca struggle to be an adult and to do everything so perfectly.

The back door opened, and she heard the sound of Guy stomping his boots against the rug to dry them a bit before proceeding into the house. Perhaps he had some news. She hurried to meet him.

"Guy?" His face was grim and there was a grayish tinge about his mouth. She knew without words that there was no news, at least not any good news.

He reached for her, and they held each other for long minutes. When he let her go, he moved toward a kitchen chair and lowered himself to it. Fleetingly it crossed her mind that he looked older than his thirty-four years. He was tired and scared. For so long he'd dreamed of escaping the regimented control of their city life for open spaces and the easy camaraderie of a rural lifestyle. Together they'd planned to leave behind urban crime and dirty air to embrace a simpler, more trusting way of life closer to nature. The past four years had been far harder physically and financially than either of them had expected, but they'd been happy. She'd watched her husband grow spiritually and felt a peace in him she wasn't sure he would have developed had he remained tied to a job and a city life that left him feeling caged. But now this! Seeing his pain was nearly as unbearable as feeling her own.

"Nothing. Not one sighting all day." Guy shook his head, and Becca slid a plate, overflowing with Sister Anderson's casserole in front of him. Mindlessly, he picked up a fork and began eating. She suspected he didn't even taste what he was swallowing. He would have eaten sawdust if it had been set before him.

"Sheriff Hatcher got a hold of some colonel down at the airbase, and he's sending choppers up as soon as the weather clears." Guy filled Vicki in on the little bit he'd learned from his trip to the sheriff's office. "There are so many bridges out, and gullies that should be dry are overflowing with rainwater, it's hampering the search. He said the highway patrol in several states have stopped a few vehicles that matched the description of the bank robbers' van, but nothing has panned out."

"They probably aren't even in Nevada anymore," Vicki spoke through tight lips. "They could be out of the country by now."

"David might be in another country? Where would they take him?" Becca looked up, alarm on her face.

"We don't know," Guy admitted. "They could be anyplace."

"Tommy Hunsaker came with his mom today. He said the robbers probably had another car, and they just went to where it was hidden, then drove it to their own house with David and that lady. He said the robbers would tie them up in the basement and no one would ever find them." Her eyes were round and scared, and she looked as though she were about to cry. "David won't like being tied up."

"The sheriff thinks those men had another car waiting, too," Guy agreed. "If not, then they must be holed up pretty close to here."

"No one likes being tied up." Vicki turned to her daughter, trying to offer her a measure of hope. "But we don't know David is tied up. They could be keeping him in a locked room where he can move around and even play or watch television."

"I hope he's not tied up," Becca spoke fervently. "Being tied up would make David really mad. He'd kick and yell and make those robbers angry. Tommy says if he makes them mad, they'll shoot him. I-I don't want them to shoot David." She started to cry.

"Oh, honey, don't cry." Vicki rushed to her daughter and took her in her arms. "None of us wants anything bad to happen to David."

"It's my fault." Becca buried her face in her mother's shoulder and sobbed out the words. "I told him to stay right by me while I looked at the Barbies, but I knew he wouldn't. He never minds me. I looked at the Barbies anyway, even when I knew he'd gone off to look at something else."

"Oh, Becca." Guy reached down and picked her up in his arms.

"It's not your fault. If anyone is to blame, it's me. It wasn't your responsibility to watch David; it was mine. I'm the one who started watching a football game and forgot about both of you."

Vicki heard her husband's and daughter's words with a kind of shock. She hadn't seen that they had both been blaming themselves for David's disappearance, because she had been wallowing in guilt herself! After all, it had been her idea to go to Decker's in spite of the rain to look at washing machines.

"Listen, both of you," she said, then paused. She had to say this right. Her father had once told her that guilt was a wasted emotion, useful only as far as it got a person to start changing what he wasn't doing right. All by itself, it just made someone feel bad and accomplished nothing. "I've been blaming myself, too," she told them. "We could have waited until another day to look at washers, but I wanted to go right then, even though it was raining. We could blame David. He knows he isn't supposed to wander off by himself, and he certainly shouldn't have gone outside on his own. The truth is, it wasn't any of our fault. Those men, who chose to steal what wasn't theirs and broke Decker's window, then used a woman and child to hide behind, are the ones responsible. We can be more careful in the future, but we can't blame ourselves for other people's wrongs."

"You're right," Guy sighed. "Perhaps none of us are completely blameless, but wishing we'd done something different won't change a thing. David is still gone. Bishop Samuelson was here earlier and he said pretty much the same thing."

"Tommy says that lady was a stranger and she probably helped the robbers kidnap David," Becca went on. Vicki turned startled eyes to her husband. She hadn't given much thought to the woman. If the woman was part of the gang, could it be possible they'd taken David because she wanted a child? If so, surely she'd take care of him. She wouldn't let them kill him.

"No, that's not true," Guy assured his daughter. "Tommy's imagination is running wild." He turned to Vicki as though he could read her thoughts. "Sheriff Hatcher checked on her. Kendra Emerson is an accountant with a reputable firm in Salt Lake. She has two sisters who live with their families in California. She was on her way to spend Christmas with them. She's in her mid-thirties and unmarried. She's active in her ward in Salt Lake. The sheriff spoke with her bishop, who assured him Ms. Emerson is a fine person, quiet, but completely dependable. He's very worried about her."

"I guess it's a good thing we prayed for her, too," Becca mumbled.

"Yes, and we'll keep on praying for her," Vicki promised.

"I've been thinking about what Bishop Samuelson said this morning and about how we've all been blaming ourselves for what happened. It seems to me that our preoccupation with guilt is interfering with our faith. It's saying we believe all of us, including David, are being punished by God for our mistakes. That's not right." Guy paused before going on as though he were thinking out loud. "We're suffering because two men who had nothing to do with us chose to do evil. I've been angry because I feel helpless. I want to do something. I want to be the one to go get David and bring him back. But it's David's and that Miss Emerson's welfare that matters right now. We need to stop feeling guilty, stop focusing on how terrible we feel, and remember that the only weapon we have against evil is faith in God's goodness. We need to exercise that faith by praying not only for David's protection, but we should ask God to soften the hearts of those who took him, and to be with and strengthen all those who are searching for him."

"In Primary, Sister Thompson said God protected Daniel from the lions and those other three guys from being burned up in a furnace because they had strong testimonies," Becca added. "Could we pray for David to have a strong testimony?"

"Yes," Vicki hugged her daughter, "we can ask Heavenly Father to help David remember all he's been taught of the gospel and to be unafraid."

CHAPTER 12

Morning brought a halt to the falling snow and Chase hurried to the barn to hoist his red flag. The sky was still overcast and wind stirred across the barnyard, which was covered with six inches of snow. He let David accompany him to the barn because the little boy wanted to help feed the sheep and play with the dogs again. Besides Kendra had let him know she'd appreciate a little time alone in the kitchen without either of them under foot.

He smiled. He'd been doing that a lot lately, smiling. There was just something about making his way to the barn with a little boy beside him and a pretty woman back in the kitchen, whom he suspected had every intention of baking some kind of surprise, probably cookies. It had been a long time since he'd had homemade cookies. And he'd never before straightened his shoulders in the self-conscious way he was doing now while sort of hoping a woman was watching him from the kitchen window.

David watched with avid curiosity when he pulled the square of red cloth from the box in the small room off the main part of the barn.

"What's that?" the boy asked, fingering the bright piece of fabric.

"It's a flag," Chase grinned down at the boy.

"There aren't any stars." David looked skeptical.

"It's not that kind of flag," Chase chuckled. "This flag is a signal flag. We'll put it on the flag pole over there in front of the barn so it can be seen by someone flying above us in an airplane. It's to let my neighbor, Mr. Peters, know there's some kind of trouble here, and that I need some help."

"I'll help you, Chase," David volunteered. "I can help feed your sheepies."

"Yes, I know, but that's not the kind of help I meant. When Ted Peters sees the flag, he'll let the sheriff know, then the sheriff will come see what I need. That way he'll know you and Kendra are here and find a way to get you back to your mom and dad."

"Will I be home for Christmas?" David asked.

"I don't know, but if Peters flies over before it starts raining again, there's a good chance," Chase answered. "Tomorrow is Christmas and he might not be able to get here that quickly," he added, not wanting to get the boy's hopes up too high.

He carried the flag outside and David watched as he attached it to the pulley that would hoist it into the air. David beamed when Chase let him pull on the rope that carried the flag to the top of the pole where it whipped in the wind above the barn.

David happily carried armfuls of feed to the ewes inside the barn, then Chase encouraged him to play in one of the stalls with a stack of empty baling twine spools while he hauled feed to the sheep in the sheds and pens outside the main barn. He ordered Rags to stay with the boy. Roscoe would be enough help with the sheep this time.

Hearing a deep cracking sound far in the distance, he paused, wondering if the obstruction holding back the river was beginning to break up. He hoped so; he didn't want to have to blast it. Earlier he'd considered finding the obstruction and setting a charge to break it up this morning, but waiting another day wouldn't hurt anything. His house and stock were all high enough that they were in no danger if the river overflowed the gully, and there was nothing but BLM land for more than a hundred miles downriver, so no one was in any danger of being flooded out when the obstruction did break free.

Besides, he didn't want to leave the project he'd set himself. It was Christmas Eve, and for the first time in fifteen years he had something to look forward to on Christmas Day.

As he drove the tractor back toward the barn after delivering the last load of hay, he saw David standing in the wide doorway, a happy smile on his face. One small hand was buried in Rags' thick fur, the other was raised to wave to him. Chase waved back. He started to smile, then a picture rose in his mind. He could see himself in all the years to come, driving up the incline toward the barn, watching for a small boy happily anticipating his return. He'd lift his arm to wave at a shadow forever.

What was the matter with him? He'd accepted the loss of his family a long time ago and had never gone looking for substitutes. His sheep, his dogs, and the wide open sky had always been enough for him, so why was he suddenly picturing his future as something bleak and lonely?

Shaking off the melancholy picture, he motioned for David to move back, then chuckled as Rags immediately understood his signal and began herding the child safely clear of the approaching tractor. When he parked just inside the barn and shut off the engine, David ran to meet him. It was the most natural thing in the world to swing the child onto his shoulders for the trek back to the house. He told himself he should be disappointed that a light dusting of snow had begun to fall again, but in truth, the snow felt more like some kind of reprieve.

Stepping inside the house, he set David down and they both removed their muddy boots and hung up their coats. Chance eyed his coat hanging next to Kendra's with David's little coat completing the threesome and felt a certain rightness in the grouping.

Good smells were drifting from the kitchen and he wondered what Kendra was cooking. She'd asked if she could use his kitchen and cooking supplies before he and David had gone outside. He'd assured her his kitchen and pantry were well stocked, and it would be okay to use anything she liked. If what she'd baked tasted anywhere near as good as it smelled, it was more than okay.

His kitchen looked different; maybe it only felt different. To him, his kitchen was just a room full of appliances, a place where meals were prepared and dishes washed. Today it seemed like more. Without consciously being aware of what he was doing, his eyes began searching for Kendra. He found her standing beside the stove, stirring a dark brown mixture in one of his heavy-bottomed saucepans. On the table lay a pile of chopped nuts. Warmth crept through him, filling him with a sense of homecoming as he watched the way she chewed on her bottom lip as she worked and a lock of hair almost the color of the mixture in the pan fell across her eyes. He smiled at the picture she made as she swept it away with the back of one wrist.

He'd noticed from the start that she was slender and tall for a woman. Now he observed the gentle sway of her body and the way she'd tied a dishtowel around an incredibly small waist to serve as an apron. She only came up to about his chin, he speculated, and was struck by the picture she presented of being younger than her years, yet competent and strong. The direction his thoughts were taking him brought him up short. Since when had he started noticing the way a woman looked?

• • • • •

"Hi, Kendra!" David greeted her. "Me and Rags took care of the sheepies that are going to have babies!"

"I'll bet they were happy you took them their breakfast." Her eyes sparkled as she talked with David about his adventures in the sheep barn.

Chase wandered closer to the stove where he sniffed the mixture in the pan. It was either frosting for the cake he could smell, or fudge. His mouth watered. His mother had made fudge for Christmas when he'd been a boy. The aroma brought back memories of a time when Christmas was much anticipated and deeply enjoyed. He had a hunch David would find fudge in his sock come morning. A remnant of the little boy he had once been hoped Kendra would save a piece or two for him.

She reached for the pan and he watched as she poured the mixture into a buttered baking dish. When she finished she asked David if he wanted to "lick the pan."

He giggled. "Daddy says only puppies and cats lick pans, I have to use a spoon." Kendra laughed with him and handed him a spoon. Chase's mouth watered at the sight of the rich fudge clinging to the sides of the pan and for just a moment he wished he were a little boy again.

"Want some?" David held out the spoon toward him.

"That's all right. You eat it," he told the boy.

"It's really good." David continued to urge him to share a spoonful of the fudge.

"All right." He yielded at last and his lips closed over the spoon David held. "Mm-m," he murmured. "That is good!" And deep inside he knew the feeling encompassed far more than just the sweet candy he savored in his mouth.

After lunch David asked if he could go back outside to play in the snow. Chase considered his request then said, "Okay, we'll all go, but I think you should dress warmer. Jeans aren't a lot of protection from the cold, and they didn't do much to keep you dry yesterday."

"I don't have any more pants." The boy spoke mournfully as he sat down on the arm of Chase's chair wearing a flannel shirt that trailed on the floor with every step he took. His jeans were in the dryer where Kendra had placed them as soon as David returned from helping Chase do his chores that morning.

Chase felt David's disappointment as keenly as though it were his own. He'd loved playing in the snow when he was a kid, and there was something about the first real snowfall of the season. He couldn't remember the last time he'd experienced the exhilaration of a rowdy game of fox and geese or built a snow fort. A fierce yearning to play the games he'd once played came over him. Adult or not, he was going to play in the snow with David—and Kendra, too.

"We'll think of something," Chase promised. He stalked off to his bedroom and returned minutes later with the bottom halves of two pairs of winter thermal underwear and an armful of socks, which he handed to Kendra. "These are the smallest I've got." He indicated the thickly woven pants that looked like old-fashioned long johns. "I wear them to do chores when the temperature dips really low and during lambing season to keep me warm. I forgot and washed these in hot water and they shrank a bit. Do you think you might wear one pair, and perhaps you could cut down the other for David?"

Kendra picked up the clothing he'd handed her and eyed it critically. He became aware David was watching her with bated breath. That was okay; he was practically holding his own breath in hopeful anticipation, too.

"That might work, and I could turn some of those socks into leg warmers," Kendra agreed slowly. "Do you have scissors?"

"Yippee!" David whooped, and it was all Chase could do to refrain from echoing the child's enthusiasm.

He produced the scissors, and David stood on a chair watching as she spread the items out on the table, trimmed the legs of the pants, and cut the toes off a pair of tube socks. "I hate to cut up perfectly good socks," she commented as she held up the leg warmers the socks had become.

"Don't worry about it," Chase drawled. "My sister, Lucy, is convinced I'm going to freeze to death out here, so she keeps sending me flannel shirts and thick wool socks. I've got enough to last me through about a hundred blizzards." The little lines at the corners of her eyes deepened, and he was glad he was able to amuse her for just a moment. She seemed to be a practical woman who was able to take a lot in stride, but the shadows under her eyes told him her abduction had taken its toll and her sense of responsibility for David was never far from her thoughts.

When she finished cutting makeshift winter garments for David, Chase persuaded her to retire to the bedroom to dress herself warmly while he dressed David. After he had helped the little boy place one foot then the other inside the thermal pants, Chase rolled the waistband over four times. The seat of the pants still bagged, but that would just give the kid a bit more padding on his skinny little rump, Chase decided. He reached for David's jeans, which Kendra had removed from the dryer before disappearing into the bedroom. Getting them on over the thick thermals took some tugging, and when Chase added the legwarmers over the top of the denim pants, he wondered if the boy would be able to bend his knees. At least he'd be warm, and hopefully dry.

David attempted to run across the room to the door and found himself waddling like a fat goose instead. He burst into giggles and finding the sound infectious, Chase's laughter joined that of the boy. It sounded rusty to his ears and reminded him he hadn't laughed much for a long time.

Kendra struggled to pull her jeans over the thick thermal pants Chase had loaned her. Fastening them proved more of a challenge, and she vowed to stick to a diet when she got back home. Catching a glimpse of herself in a mirror, she groaned. She looked like she'd gained twenty pounds. Self-consciously she smoothed her hair back and wished for a tube of lipstick. There wasn't much she could do to improve the image staring back at her from the mirror, so she might as well join her men. The unconscious thought burst to the forefront of her mind. They weren't *her* men, and she'd be better off if she didn't let herself start thinking of them that way.

Rejoining the males, she hid a smile at the sight of David, who looked like he'd suddenly gained weight, too. Chase's grin as he surveyed her attire made her suddenly self-conscious and much too aware of how tight her pants were. Her thoughts brought the warmth of a blush to her cheeks. Wordlessly he handed her a knitted cap. His hand brushed hers, adding fuel to the fire that burned inside her each time he came near. A small whoosh of air as he caught his breath told her he wasn't unaffected by the brief contact either.

"Lucy knits, too," he said by way of recovery as he reached for a scarf to wrap around his neck which almost covered his ears, then perched his Stetson atop his head. Once outside he whistled for the dogs, and they came running to chase and play in the snow around the humans who were laughing and playing as well.

The dogs paid particular attention to David as he struggled to form a ball he could roll about and enlarge for a snowman. Each time he tripped over one of the dogs, he would squeal with laughter as he rolled in the snow. Thinking it part of the game, the dogs rolled and barked along with him.

The wet snow proved ideal for building snowmen. The first ball was so large they had trouble placing the second and third atop it. The second snowman was smaller, and David insisted it was a snowlady and that they had to build a little snowman to be their little boy. When she stood back to study their work, it touched Kendra in a strange way and she turned away to hide a sudden rush of emotion. The snow figures mirrored too closely the dangerous mind game she could feel herself falling into.

A snowball glanced off her shoulder, and she gasped before reaching for a handful of the white stuff to launch back at David. He quickly made another snowball and threw it toward Chase this time. Reaching down with both hands, Chase scooped up a pile of snow. David shrieked as he ran toward her, and she caught the brunt of the double handful of snow Chase launched toward the boy.

Laughing, she reached for more snow and quickly formed it into a ball. Raising her arm to throw it toward Chase, she noticed he was ready to launch a counter attack. Instead of throwing her snowball, she began running, only to slip on the treacherous wet snow and fall to her knees. She heard Chase yell before somersaulting over her, pressing her, face first, into the snow as he frantically tried to prevent himself from landing on top of her as he too lost his footing.

"Are you all right?" His arm came around her, and he helped her to sit up. "I didn't mean to knock you down. When you slipped, I found I couldn't stop."

She continued to sit, looking up at him, and discovered his face was only inches from hers. The falling snow, David's whoops of laughter, the excited barking of the dogs, even the cold, wet air, all faded far into the distance. There was only Chase and an aching, breathless spot in her chest. He leaned closer. She stared at his mouth, and for one crazy minute, she thought he was going to kiss her. His head moved nearer hers, and she lifted her lips toward his.

CHAPTER 13

Snow, wet slushy mush, slid down the back of her neck and she jerked her shoulders backward. Only Chase's quick reaction saved her from tumbling over once more.

"David," he chided. "No fair hitting a lady while she's down."

"I'm sorry." David threw his arms around her and pressed his cold cheek to hers.

"It's all right." She touched her nose to his. "But I think it's time to end this game. Your nose feels like an icicle."

"Don't want to stop playing," he protested half-heartedly. But she didn't miss the way he glanced around apprehensively, making it clear he didn't wish to remain outside alone. She sensed the child, even as well-adjusted and resilient as David seemed to be, still harbored a small amount of lingering fear from their recent ordeal.

"It's raining again. Our snowmen are getting littler." His voice held a touch of sadness, and she was surprised to discover he was right. The snow had turned to rain, and the little snow family was slowly melting away.

"All right, we'd better head back inside," Chase spoke as he rose to his feet and reached a hand down to assist her. "Rags! Roscoe! Back to the sheep." The dogs headed back to the barn with only an occasional sorrowful peek back at David.

Once back in the house and all attired once more in warm, dry, oddly mismatched clothing, Chase retired to his shop, where from time to time he caught enticing aromas coming from the kitchen. He heard David's high-pitched voice and Kendra's melodic laughter, and an undefinable longing filled him. It was the loneliness, that's all.

He'd been alone so long he was making too much of his holiday visitors. Choosing not to examine the fact he'd never thought of himself as lonely before, he ran a strip of sandpaper across the block of wood in his hands and forced himself to concentrate on planning for the coming lambing season.

He'd almost finished the task he'd set himself when Kendra tapped on the door, calling him to dinner. He dropped the block of wood back on his workbench and hurried toward the kitchen, telling himself it was only polite not to make her call him twice.

Dinner was a festive affair with a sprig of cedar and a paper rose for a centerpiece. Kendra had roasted a chicken with stuffing and mashed potatoes, and had made wonderfully light dinner rolls. There was carrot pudding with caramel sauce for his and Kendra's dessert and iced sugar cookies for David. Judging by the imaginative decorating, David had helped with the icing project. A man could quickly grow accustomed to dinners like this, he mocked himself as he reached for a second helping of pudding.

After dinner Kendra coaxed him into joining David and her in singing a few Christmas carols. The rain on the roof provided a steady accompaniment. David only knew the words to the "Jingle Bells" chorus and the first verse of "Away in a Manger," but that was more than Chase remembered. Kendra tried to teach them the words to "Joy to the World," and he finally caught on to the melody and hummed along as she sang. Slowly, carols once familiar, became familiar once more.

"Do you know the rumpa-pum-pum song?" David asked Kendra.

"Yes, I do, but you and Chase will have to do the drum part." There was a mischievous sparkle in her eyes as she glanced his way. Accepting the challenge, he showed David how to slap the table in an imitation drum beat. Getting the beat right involved a lot of giggling, and when they finally made it all the way through, David showed Chase how to do a high five.

"I think it's bed time," Kendra told David when she caught him rubbing his eyes.

"You didn't read the story yet." David turned to Chase in an attempt to put off going to bed.

"No, I didn't." He knew which story David meant. In a way he'd known since David had asked about his missing Christmas tree that this moment would come, and he hadn't known how he would handle it. Surprising himself, he walked to the bookcase and pulled out an old well-worn Bible. It took only a moment's searching before he settled back on the rug beside Kendra and David. For just a moment he closed his eyes and the memory of sitting beside Carol, reading these words aloud as they anticipated the birth of their own son, flooded his mind and he wondered if he could do it. Opening his eyes, he saw the look of anticipation on David's face and began. Slowly at first, he read and found himself marveling at the simple beauty of the story of the first Christmas. The words didn't bring the pain he expected. Instead a quiet peace filled the room, and it was as though he were experiencing his child's first Christmas. Understanding began to fill his soul. He'd been wrong to cut off memories of Jesse and of Christmas. Instead of letting the love and promise of Christmas provide solace to his heart, he'd branded the holiday as the source of his pain and denied himself the comfort of believing his son still lived.

When he finished, he saw David had fallen asleep. His eyes followed Kendra as she picked up the sleeping child and carried him to the bedroom. She hummed softly, and he recognized the lullaby strains of "Silent Night." He'd always loved that simple carol, but for fifteen years its tender message had laid bare his soul. Carol had hummed that song as she painted the nursery, folded soft, little clothes, and moved about their home in happy anticipation of their Christmas baby. Tonight it didn't hurt in the old way. It wasn't so much a painful reminder of the past, as it was a tender promise of what might be.

Hearing David cry out, he quickly stood, but then Kendra's soft consoling voice reached him again, and he settled back in his chair. Was David's small cry the result of remembered fear or did it spring from the pain of missing his family? He didn't know, but it saddened him and filled him with a vague longing of his own. Though Kendra sang softly to the child, he felt a soothing sense that she was comforting him, too.

He wasn't sure whether Kendra would return to the front room or go to bed, too, and it pleased him when she not only returned, but stopped in the kitchen for two glasses of milk and a plate of cookies. He figured the milk was probably almost gone. In three days they'd consumed more than he usually used up in a week, but he didn't care. He'd cheerfully buy more when he made it to town again. He had plenty of the powdered variety he could mix up once the real thing was gone. It wasn't as good, but it wasn't too bad either, if it was really chilled or served hot with a couple of scoops of chocolate mix added to it.

They sat in front of the fire drinking their milk and eating cookies. The peace he'd felt earlier while reading from Luke seemed to linger in the room and he felt content. When they finished their snack, they carried their dishes back to the kitchen where Kendra retrieved several small packets of the fudge she'd made earlier and a handful of cookies. He watched her drop them into each of their now dry stockings hanging before the fire. Chase added a handful of nuts.

"I wish I'd bought oranges in town," he whispered.

"Did Santa put an orange in your sock when you were a kid?" Kendra asked, a twinkle in her eye.

"Always," he answered solemnly. "Except one year I got a big red apple."

"Me, too," she laughed and the sound brought a touch of delight to his soul. "Did you mind?"

"Mind? No, of course not. I always liked apples better than oranges." He found himself grinning as he relived a long ago Christmas. "Did you?"

"I barely held back the tears. I didn't get many oranges, and I'd been counting on one." A whisper of sadness crossed her face and without considering his action, he reached out to touch her cheek with his open palm. The touch of her soft skin sent ripples of warmth sliding up his arm, filling him with a longing to pull her close and touch the softness of her mouth with his own. Feeling suddenly awkward and unsure, he only let his hand move down her face in a gentle caress before stepping back. He couldn't be sure, but he thought he saw a flash of disappointment in her eyes. Already he regretted the hesitancy that had cost him a kiss he suspected he would have savored for the rest of his life.

"There was always a chocolate Santa in my sock, too," he continued as though there had been no break in their conversation.

"That's probably where I developed a weakness for sweets."

"You don't look like you indulge in many sweets," Kendra responded impulsively, then blushed. Seeing her embarrassment filled him with tenderness, and he didn't respond with the teasing comment that rose unexpectedly to his tongue. Instead he marveled not only at the long-dormant desire to laugh and tease that had been reborn in him, but at the gentle joy this woman awoke in his heart.

Before sitting back down, Chase turned the radio on and fiddled with the dials. Reception was never good, but sometimes an all-night station out of Salt Lake could be picked up in the evening. Soon the faint sound of Christmas carols filled the room. He leaned against the back of the sofa and patted the spot beside him, inviting Kendra to join him. She hesitated a moment, then took the spot he'd indicated. They sat without speaking or touching, enjoying the fire and the music. It had been a long time, maybe not ever, since he'd felt so comfortable and at peace.

His mind drifted back to a night several months ago at the end of summer. He'd heard the dogs fussing and had gone out to see if a coyote might be harassing the sheep. Not finding any cause for the disturbance, he'd sat down in a grassy spot, and watched the sky. He'd leaned back until he was lying flat, picking out various constellations he knew. He'd begun thinking about his own insignificance in the vastness of the universe and his thoughts had turned to God and the scriptures he'd read about His knowing even when a sparrow fell. The question popped into his mind, did God just know, or did He care? That question was quickly followed by another. He'd been attending church more often the past year, and his bishop had lent him several books by Church leaders. Scripture study had become an integral part of his life, but there were still questions. Did he have the courage to do as the fourteen-year-old boy-prophet had done—to ask God?

He considered getting to his knees and praying, but he hadn't. He'd fashioned a prayer in his mind, but some prompting urged him to speak aloud. He'd tried praying aloud a couple of times, but those attempts had left him feeling self-conscious and a little foolish. The feeling persisted though, and he began speaking his thoughts out loud while staring up into the velvety blackness of a canopy sprinkled with billions of tiny points of light. The comforting sense of a caring ear hearing the words that came straight from his heart had filled him with peace, something like the peace he felt now sitting beside Kendra in the aftermath of an evening spent with David and her, observing the simplest of Christmas traditions.

"Thank you, Chase." Kendra broke the silence.

"For what?" Her words puzzled him. If anything he should be thanking her for the best dinner he'd ever eaten and for bringing joy and laughter back into his life along with these few hours of peace.

"You saved our lives and not only provided us with food and shelter, but turned a bleak experience into one of peace and comfort. I should apologize for disrupting your plans. I don't think you really wanted to celebrate Christmas, but Christmas means so much to David," she tried to explain.

"And to you," he added softly, pleased to hear that she had felt the peace, too.

"Yes, to me, too. I've always loved Christmas, but I wasn't looking forward to spending Christmas with my sisters' families. Don't misunderstand," she hastened to explain. "They love me and truly welcome me into their homes, but sometimes it's hard not having a home and family of my own. For an experience that started out so badly, I believe this has become the Christmas I'll always remember with the greatest fondness." Afraid she'd revealed too much of herself, she lapsed into silence again.

"Why don't you have a home and family of your own?" he asked after a few minutes. "Perhaps it's none of my business. Just tell me if I'm butting in where I've no business to be, but it seems to me you have all the qualities necessary to be a good wife and mother. You're easy to be around. You're pretty and smart; you're good with children, and you certainly can cook. I think you have spiritual depths as well that would go far in binding a family together."

His words touched her greatly, but she shook her head. "I'm really quite ordinary. Even so, I might have married if I'd had time to cultivate friendships with young men when I was younger, but I always felt so awkward, and I had responsibilities. My father died when my sisters were very small. Mother needed my help after that, then she passed away when I was only eighteen. Working two jobs to keep what was left of our family together left no time for much of a social life."

"Your sisters are both married now with families, aren't they?" he probed, encouraging her to tell him more.

"Yes, but it's too late for me." Her laugh sounded forced.

"Why is it too late?"

"I'm thirty-five years old." She sounded defensive and he feared he'd hurt her.

"You're a beautiful woman," he sought to assure her, but she looked dubious and turned the conversation.

"Was it so difficult to disrupt your life to let David celebrate Christmas?" she asked.

"No," he admitted reluctantly. "I thought I couldn't do it, but I discovered I wanted to for David. I'd do more if I could. I'd like for him to have a sled and the red train. I'm glad you made cookies and fudge for him. I made a little something for him, too, so he'll have one present under the tree in the morning."

She reached across the space separating them and touched his hand. "You would make a wonderful father. You're so very good with David." Before he could hide it, she saw the flicker of pain in his eyes. "Please tell me about it," she invited.

He closed his eyes, bowed his head, and covered the lower half of his face with one hand. With the other hand, he took the hand she'd placed on his in a gesture of comfort. He sat hunched forward, tightly gripping her fingers as though they were a life-line. She waited, not certain he would confide in her. At last the words emerged as though being ripped from his soul. "Carol and I had been married two years when she became pregnant. We were both excited about our 'Christmas' baby. We decorated the nursery, and Carol bought fuzzy red pajamas in the tiniest size imaginable. She made a quilt from red and white striped flannel and tied it with green pieces of yarn. I bought a miniature Christmas tree for the nursery with those little blinking lights, and we waited. He was due almost a week before Christmas, but when we went to bed Christmas Eve, he still hadn't arrived. Carol said she didn't mind; she was sure he'd be born on Christmas Day. Early Christmas morning she woke me up saying she couldn't breathe. I thought she meant the baby was coming.

"I jumped out of bed and started dressing. I asked if her bag was packed and if she'd started timing the contractions. I found her robe and slippers and insisted she put them on. I guess the excitement of imminent fatherhood slowed my wits because it was several minutes before I realized the room was smoky. I opened our bedroom door to find the hall and stairway full of smoke. Carol screamed, and I called to her to follow me, but she was too frightened to move. I ran back to the bedroom, wrapped Carol in a blanket, and tried to carry her to the front door. I didn't make it. I'd wasted too much time. A couple of firefighters found us just five feet short of the door. They rushed us to the hospital, but Carol died shortly after giving birth to our baby. He died ten minutes later. I recovered, but I never could face Christmas after that."

"You were burned trying to rescue your wife and child?" It was more statement than question and he could hear the horror behind her words.

"It was a far smaller price than they paid," he muttered.

"I'm so sorry," she murmured and without quite knowing how it happened, wrapped her arms around him and held him until his trembling stopped. With an aching heart, she realized he blamed himself for his wife and son's deaths.

"You weren't responsible for what happened," she told him.

"When I learned the fire was caused by an electrical short, I blamed the Christmas decorations until the fire investigator assured me the fire started in the garage. The house was old, and he said mice had eaten the insulation off the electrical wires, resulting in bare wires touching the wooden framing. After that, I could only accept my own responsibility. If I'd acted quicker, they might have both lived."

"You don't know that," she attempted to wipe away his guilt. "I do a lot of work for several insurance companies, and I know something about wiring fires in old houses. It was probably too late by the time Carol awakened you. The miracle is that you survived."

"I never felt like it was a miracle. It always seemed wrong to me that I should live when both of them died," Chase admitted to Kendra what he'd never voiced even to himself before. "They were buried together, with Jesse in Carol's arms. Neither one was burned and they looked as though they'd simply gone to sleep. Seeing them like that, I think I lost my mind for a little while. It filled me with anger to think they'd gone on to peace and happiness and left me with hideous scars and all the grief. I didn't stay angry long and soon found myself thinking of all they would miss because I'd let them down." With the admission came an uncomfortable illumination of his life since the death of his family. Could it be true that his guilt had driven him to bury himself away from other people because he felt unworthy to go on living? Had he, in fact, not been living, but merely surviving?

"It was a miracle," Kendra insisted. "As difficult as losing your family must have been, God must still have work here for you to do."

"I guess I want to believe that. I told myself that getting past the pain of their loss was impossible in Phoenix, and the horrified gasps I heard each time someone new saw my face encouraged me to cut my ties with the city. I quit my job and bought this ranch. The earth and sky, along with the animals, have helped the healing process. I've come to depend on God a lot more than I used to, but I still feel a failure in some way because I had lived when they had died." She pressed her cheek against his scarred one, thinking that his scars might well be a badge of honor.

"I read somewhere that survivors of terrible disasters often experience those same feelings," she told him. "And I suspect your physical scars appear far worse in your mind than they actually are. At first they must have been red and startling. Now they can still be seen, but they've faded to little more than roughened skin only slightly different in color from the surrounding skin."

He appeared skeptical and she continued on, "In some ways my experience has been just the opposite of yours. Instead of feeling guilty for living when my parents died or considering all they've missed, there have been times when I resented them for dying and leaving me with so much work and responsibility. My head always told me the resentment was childish—they didn't choose to abandon me—but the feelings were there anyway."

Chase chuckled wryly. "Someone once called death the great cheater. I guess we can both attest to that."

"In a way," Kendra agreed half-heartedly. "It has also been called the liberator, too. Who knows what mistakes I might have made if I hadn't been weighed down with responsibility. I'm truly sorry for the pain losing your wife and baby cost you; still a selfish part of me can't help acknowledging that if those terrible things hadn't happened, you wouldn't have been here when David and I needed you."

There were no words to respond. In a way her words offered a healing balm, a kind of absolution. Two lives had been lost; two had been saved—but something deep in his soul told him there was more to it than that. He would have died for his family. In a way, he had. He'd ceased living fifteen years ago. That same quiet voice told him he'd been wrong. God hadn't asked for his life; He'd asked him to live.

They sat wrapped in each other's arms until the fire died down and they both yielded to sleep. It might have been a few minutes, or it might have been hours later, that Chase awoke. He wasn't certain what had awakened him, but he was glad something had. His neck felt kinked, and he knew Kendra would be stiff the next day if he didn't send her to bed. Besides he had a present for David that needed placing under the tree.

Carefully he extricated himself from the woman snuggled beside him. She didn't wake up, so he lifted her in his arms and carried her to the bed where David slept. Reluctance to let her go held him motionless for several minutes before he settled her on the bed and carefully tucked her beneath the quilts. He stood for long minutes watching her sleep and wished he could tell her how much her being here for Christmas meant to him. Instinctively he'd associated Christmas with spring; now he knew why. It had little to do with the actual season. Christmas was a harbinger of birth and hope, needed more sorely during the depths of winter than in the spring, when everywhere a person looked there could be seen the verification of life.

Softly he tiptoed out of the room and went to his shop. There he gathered up the gift he'd made for David and walked back to the living room to arrange it under the tree. He ran a finger tenderly across a piece of shaped wood and hoped the little boy wouldn't be too disappointed. After one last look around the room, he closed the fireplace doors, turned off the radio, and shut out the lights.

Minutes later he climbed into his own cold, lonely bed. That's when he knew what had awakened him. The storm had stopped. All was silent. Through his bedroom window he could see a sprinkling of stars shining against a smooth black sky.

CHAPTER 14

"I know, Daddy," Vicki struggled to keep the tears at bay while she spoke with her father on the telephone. "You always told me it was easier to think I'm strong when things are going well, but the real test of faith comes when I have the least reason to trust in God. I haven't lost faith. I truly believe He's looking after David, but it's just so hard not knowing . . ." She gripped the receiver tighter and listened. A few minutes later, she hung up the phone and turned to face her family.

"Daddy said to give you his love and tell you he's praying for David, too. He wishes there was some way he could be here with us."

"I wish that, too." Guy reached for her hand, and she saw the sincerity in his eyes. "He shouldn't be alone now. When we left Denver, your mother was still alive and your brother appeared settled in his job there. But now with your mother gone and Daniel living in Florida, we should be there with your father. Before I got laid off, we talked about getting him to come for a long visit. Now I'm thinking that as soon as we can find a way to return to Denver, we'd better look for an apartment large enough for him to come live with us."

"I don't want to move back to Denver," Becca protested. "David won't ever find us there."

"Oh, Becca," Vicki put her arm around her daughter. "We won't leave David. Your father was talking about after David comes back."

"David won't like it," Becca continued to resist the plan. "He wants to be a cowboy, and he can't be a cowboy in the city."

"I don't think any of us wants to go back to the city," Guy sighed. "But you're a big girl. You understand we can't keep living here if I can't find a job."

"I know, Daddy, but I won't ever get a horse or see Tommy again if we move away."

"You'll be closer to Grandpa, though." Vicki tried to give her daughter a coaxing smile, but her own heart was breaking. She'd known returning to the city was inevitable; Guy had been unhappy there before, and he would be again. This time the children would be unhappy, too. She couldn't even imagine subjecting David to apartment life again after four years of practically running wild.

"Couldn't Grandpa come live with us here?" Becca pleaded. "I wish he was here right now."

"He wishes he were here, too," Vicki hugged Becca again. "It's hard for him being so far away when he thinks we need him here. He told me he's going to get his Bible and read the Christmas story tonight. An old friend came by earlier today to leave him a box of chocolates, and he told me he plans to eat a couple of those before he goes to bed. He says we should go ahead with Christmas, too, just the same as we would if David were here."

"I don't feel much like Christmas," Becca expressed her reluctance.

"I don't either," Vicki concurred.

"No, I think your father is right," Guy spoke slowly, as though he were still thinking it through. "Christmas means a lot to David. He wouldn't want us to pretend tonight was just like any other night. I'll read the Christmas story, then we'll sing a few carols. Becca can hang up her sock . . ."

"And David's, too?"

"Yes, you can hang up David's sock, too."

• • • • •

Light streamed across the bed from an unshaded window when Kendra awoke. It was Christmas morning and the sun was shining. Turning quickly, she saw David was stirring and would soon be awake. She slipped out of bed, hoping for a few minutes alone in the bathroom before he was completely awake. She was startled to discover she was already fully dressed except for her boots. Memories of the previous night flooded through her mind, and she realized she'd fallen asleep and Chase had put her to bed. The warmth she felt wasn't all due to embarrassment. Some was an appreciation of his gentle, considerate ways.

In the bathroom she bathed quickly and traded her wrinkled shirt for one of Chase's flannel shirts. She shoved the too-long sleeves back to her elbows, then faced herself in the mirror and wished for a blower and styling brush. Fortunately her hairstyle was simple and wouldn't look too bad, but she certainly wished she'd stuck a tube of lipstick in her pocket when she grabbed her purse and left her car at the garage three days ago. She reminded herself she should be thankful Chase had a couple of spare toothbrushes on hand when she and David suddenly arrived without luggage.

What was she primping for anyway? She'd only known Chase a few days and had no business weaving romantic fantasies around him. He'd been kind to her, but he didn't mean anything special by his actions. He would be kind to anyone he rescued under similar circumstances. He was lonely and she was lonely. They had each been facing their own bleak Christmas, and now were doing the best they could to keep David's Christmas from being miserable. She shouldn't read more into their accidental friendship than truly existed. Nevertheless, she vigorously scrubbed her cheeks to bring out a bit more color, and her heart stubbornly refused to listen to the careful reasoning of her head.

Back in the bedroom she found David kneeling on the bed with his nose pressed against the window. His small hunched figure filled her with sadness.

"It's not snowing," he spoke almost listlessly.

"Isn't that what you wanted?" she asked. "Chase said when the storm passed, his neighbor would be able to fly his airplane over the barn, and that he would see the red flag. After that it won't be long until you will be home with your mom and dad."

"I want to go home," David spoke fervently and he appeared worried. "But the snow is all gone, and there's just mud. Do you think there was snow at my house last night so Santa Claus could come?"

"He probably came whether there was snow or not," Kendra attempted to reassure him. "Santa doesn't need snow. He goes to places that never have snow, just like he visits places where the snow is as high as the houses."

"Really?" The skepticism was evident in his voice.

"Oh, yes. I have two nieces and a nephew a little younger than you who live in Los Angeles, California. They've never even seen snow, but Santa comes to their house every year."

"But Santa Claus has a big red sleigh, and sleighs won't go if there's no snow," David argued from his personal knowledge of sleighs.

"Santa's sleigh isn't like any other sleigh," she whispered as she pulled the oversize shirt over his head and helped him into his own shirt and pants. "Santa's sleigh doesn't need snow. All it needs is the magic of love."

He still looked dubious. "If Santa came, will Becca get to open my presents?"

"Probably not," Kendra attempted to reassure him. "Your mom and dad may just leave them under the tree until you get there." At least she hoped that's what they would do.

"If Santa Claus brought me the red train, it's okay if Becca plays with it until I get home," David announced in a suspiciously martyr-like voice. Kendra smiled at his simple generosity, then she sobered. From reading between the lines of David's conversation the past few days, she was pretty certain there wouldn't be a red train under his tree, or much of anything else. She suspected David's parents were going through a financially difficult time and his father was out of work.

"Look, here comes Chase!" David shouted as he turned back to the window. She followed his gaze in time to see Chase wading through the ankle deep mud that spread between the house and the barns. He saw them at the window and stopped to wave before continuing on to the house. She felt a flutter in her chest when he grinned their direction, and she hoped his smile wasn't just for David, who was grinning back at him. The light in David's eyes faded as Chase disappeared from sight.

"Do you think my mama misses me?" David said, a wistful expression on his face.

"Yes, I do. I think she misses you very much," Kendra hastened to assure him. "I think your daddy misses you, too."

"And Becca?"

"Yes, I'm sure your sister misses you, just like you miss her." She gave David a hug, knowing what he was really saying was that he missed his family. Christmas morning had brought a serious case of homesickness.

"Becca likes sheepies, too. And dogs. She 'specially likes horses. How come Chase doesn't got any horses? He has a saddle. I saw it in the room where he keeps the dog food."

"I don't know," Kendra laughed. "Maybe you could ask him."

"Okay!" He slid off the bed and charged toward the door shouting, "Chase, why doesn't your stable got any horses?"

Chase was standing in the kitchen in his stocking feet when they walked in the room. In two long strides he reached them and scooped David up on his shoulder. "What brought this on?" he laughed. "Aren't the dogs and sheep enough?" he teased.

"Becca likes horses," David explained, though it really wasn't an explanation at all. Chase looked at Kendra with a question in his eyes.

"He's a little homesick this morning and thinking about his sister," Kendra explained.

"Ah, that's it." He smiled, and an almost indiscernible dimple appeared in his chin. Kendra found she couldn't stop watching him. A strange sense of distraction kept her absorbed in watching his movements as though she were memorizing each one. Almost from a distance she heard him say, "I do own a horse."

"Where is it? Can I ride your horse? I didn't see a horse." David's eyes were round with excitement.

"You didn't see her, because she isn't here right now. She's going to be a mama pretty soon, and Sister Peters over at the Double T is taking care of her. She's a veterinarian—that's an animal doctor," Chase explained. "She's keeping Bluebelle for me until after her baby is born."

"Wow! Can I see her baby when it's born?" David asked.

"I'll try to arrange it," Chase promised. He whirled David around, then stood him on the counter top where the boy's eyes were almost level with his own. Bracing one hand on each of David's shoulders, he asked, "Now, do you know what day this is?" He met the child's eyes with a sparkle of mischief in his own.

"It's Christmas," David answered solemnly, his sadness back.

"Don't tell Kendra," he dropped his voice to a conspiratorial stage whisper. "I peeked, and it looks to me like she has a wing-dinger of a Christmas breakfast planned for us."

"Do you?" David turned to her.

"I sure do, but I think before we have breakfast you need to finish dressing. Go get your socks on."

"What's a wing-dinger? Do I like them?" David continued to question her.

"Chase is just being silly," she told him. "He means I have something really special planned for breakfast, and yes, I'm sure you'll like it."

"Okay," he leaned forward expecting Chase to set him down. Instead, Chase carried him to the fireplace and encouraged him to peek inside his sock.

"Candy!" David squealed.

"Not until after breakfast," Kendra reminded him, and pretended she didn't see when he pinched off a smidgen of the chocolate and popped it into his mouth. She turned her head and saw what Chase had placed under the tree for the boy, and her heart swelled with emotion.

"David, tell Chase to put you down by the tree. There's something there you need to see," she whispered with a catch in her voice.

Chase let him slide slowly to the floor where the boy hunkered down on his knees and stared in rapt astonishment. "Are they really for me?" he asked. Chase nodded his head and David let out a whoop. "Look, Kendra. There's sheep and Roscoe and Rags. They got a stable and an angel. And this is a manger!" He picked up a small wooden box filled with bits of straw. Resting on the straw was a baby. Reverently he stroked the tiny wooden infant. "I got my very own baby Jesus." He went on to exclaim over Mary and Joseph and a shaggy gray donkey.

Kendra picked up the small, blue-robed mother and felt a strange kinship to the woman who so long ago ended what must have been a difficult trip with the joy of holding her child in her arms. An inkling of the love Mary must have felt for the man who had stood beside her, helping her over the rough spots, and protecting her from the rabble who filled the city filled her heart.

"A donkey is almost a horse, isn't it?" he asked Chase.

"Don't let Bluebelle hear you say that," Chase grinned back. "She thinks she's pretty special. But yeah, they're quite a bit alike."

"Chase, it's wonderful." She squeezed his hand and felt tears slipping down her cheeks. "They're works of art. How did you make them so quickly?"

"I made the sheep and the dogs last winter. It didn't take long to do the other stuff." He ducked his head and looked embarrassed by her praise.

"Hey! There's king guys and camels!" David's small hands picked up the figures that had been half hidden beneath a cedar branch. Again she was impressed by the color and detail Chase had put into the figures when he'd had so little time to prepare them.

Kendra left David happily arranging and rearranging his nativity set while she started breakfast. As she slid the Swedish braid she'd made the day before into the oven to heat, Chase joined her. He took over preparing a Southwestern omelet, while she mixed frozen orange juice and heated milk for chocolate. Working together felt so natural and comfortable, it was easy to imagine they were a family and had prepared breakfast together many times. She wished it were so. Guilt swarmed in right behind the wish. Chase was simply trying to make an unfortunate set of circumstances a little less frightening for them all. He still mourned Carol, and David had a loving family of his own. She had no right to wish for what was only hers temporarily because of someone else's loss and grief.

David brought his wooden dogs to the table, then fetched a couple of sheep partway through the meal. He spent more time helping his dogs guard the sheep than eating. His usually voracious appetite took a back seat to the unexpected gift he'd received. Not so with Chase. He savored every mouthful and delighted Kendra when he asked for a third slice of the fruit-filled braid.

Following breakfast, David settled on the rug in front of the fireplace to play while she cleaned up the kitchen. It was a comfortable kitchen, and she felt right at home in it. The only changes she'd recommend, she mused, would be bright gingham curtains at the window, and perhaps, a matching rug in front of the sink. She'd put the plastic glasses on the lower cupboard shelf, saving the higher shelf where they now sat for a nicer set of glass goblets.

"Need some help?" Chase came up behind her and placed his hands on her shoulders. She struggled to resist an urge to lean back against those sturdy hands and revel in the sense of coming home and of belonging she felt in his presence and in his house. She'd never felt a stronger sense of peace and good will on Christmas morning than she did this morning. The temptation was too great, and she allowed herself to relax against the warm pressure of his hands for just a moment.

"I thought you still had chores." To her dismay, her voice sounded slightly breathless.

"I do, but the sheep can wait." His eyes met hers and it was hard not to imagine his words meant more than a simple offer of assistance with tidying the kitchen.

"No, it may be Christmas, but not even animals should have to wait for their breakfast." She could feel herself blushing even as she urged him to finish feeding the sheep.

"All right," he agreed. "The sooner I finish chores, the sooner I can join you and David back here in the house." The look he gave her made her heart lurch, and she wondered if she was reading more into his words than he meant, or if his eyes were truly saying all those things she'd waited all her life to hear.

Humming a Christmas carol, she filled the sink with hot soapy water. She paused when a strange sound caught her ear. She listened intently. It sounded like an engine, but it was far away. Her heart sank. The sound had to be Chase's neighbor flying over to check his stock. He'd see the red flag. Before the day was over, David would be back with his family, and she'd be on her way to Los Angeles. The prospect of being rescued shouldn't sadden her. She was being selfish to wish they wouldn't be found. And of course, she was anxious to relieve Katy's and Cameron's concern.

It was strange how the most disastrous experience of her life had turned out to be something else entirely, she couldn't help thinking. At the least, this had certainly been the most unexpected Christmas of her life. Her mind returned to that moment in the snow when Chase had almost kissed her. She wished he had. Falling asleep in his arms last night was surely the greatest Christmas gift she'd ever received. Their Christmas had been simple, but in her heart she would always treasure this Christmas as an interlude out of time.

• • • • •

Becca opened a present listlessly. She turned each small gift over several times, then began to remove the tape bit by bit, stretching out the time it took to open each one. David would have ripped each package open with a burst of enthusiasm, shredding the paper as he went. Guy could tell Becca was trying to act excited for his and Vicki's sake, but her heart wasn't in it. Neither was his, and Vicki looked as though it was taking every bit of control she could muster to keep from bursting into tears. It wasn't just that the gifts they had purchased for their daughter were inexpensive trinkets, with the Barbie that Becca had wanted significantly absent. Becca kept looking over at the pathetic little pile of packages that should be David's, and it was obvious that she was acutely aware there was no David to open them. If he were here they would all be telling him to calm down, to stop jumping around, to be quieter. Strange how his absence was more noticeable than his noisy presence would have been.

There was no special surprise under the tree for Vicki this year. It was the first Christmas he hadn't managed to buy his wife some small gift. They'd agreed not to spend any of their small cash reserve for gifts for each other. It had seemed more important to spend the little they had for the children. If he had been able to buy Vicki a gift, he suspected she wouldn't have noticed it anyway. All she saw was her missing child.

"Here, Daddy," Becca walked over to place a small box in his hands. She handed an identical one to her mother. "We made these at school. Mrs. Brown had all the classes from kindergarten to third grade make them together."

He watched Vicki pick at the red wrapping paper until Becca reminded him he was supposed to open his at the same time. From the many layers of paper, a small plaster oval emerged. He stared at it for several minutes, then felt a tear slide down his cheek. He reached to touch the outline of David's hand. Vicki did the same to the matching mold of Becca's hand, then reached across to touch David's handprint, too. The small, chubby handprint preserved in plaster of Paris hurt unbearably, yet Guy treasured it beyond words. Would this and memories soon be all he had left of David?

"Thank you, Becca." He had to clear his throat before the words would come out.

"We'll keep them always," Vicki added in a choked voice.

"They're supposed to be from both of us," Becca hung her head.

"I know, honey." He hugged her, then cleared his throat again. "Okay, let's go have breakfast. I don't think any of us are in the mood for any more Christmas presents. We'll open the rest when David comes home."

"Look, Daddy," Becca paused when she reached the kitchen door. Hope gleamed in her eyes as she pointed at sunshine spilling through the curtains, creating a bright puddle all around the table. "The sun is shining. Will the helicopters come today to look for David?"

"I don't know. It's Christmas, but I certainly hope so," he answered fervently and Vicki seconded his wish.

He had the strangest sensation the sunshine was a sign, something like the star that led the wise men to Bethlehem two thousand years ago.

"If they find him today, we could still have a merry Christmas." Becca's eyes shone with anticipation.

"Indeed we will," Vicki added with a fervency that sounded almost like a prayer. "When David comes home, it will truly be Christmas."

CHAPTER 15

The space between the house and the barns was a sea of mud. Chase was glad David hadn't insisted on accompanying him this morning. He'd already checked the ewes in the barn, but he still needed to feed the sheep who huddled in the protection of the sheds outside. It wouldn't take long.

He worked quickly, loading bales onto his wagon, from the huge haystacks he'd built last summer, then dispersing the feed to his hungry stock. The sheep came running, bleating a chorus of Christmas cheer, as they saw the wagon approach. There was enough straw beaten by small sharp hooves into the mud of the feeding area to prevent his getting stuck, and he finished in record time. Shutting off the engine, he started to step down, but a distant sound caught his attention. He glanced at the sky, but there was no sign of Ted's plane or any other aircraft.

Hackles rose at the back of his neck. He could plainly hear an engine revving and straining as though it were stuck in the mud not too far away. Sound carried long distances on the high plateau, but he doubted it was possible to hear a vehicle on the interstate nearly sixty miles away, no matter how perfect the conditions. He'd have to investigate. It was probably Sheriff Hatcher's deputies still checking the back roads—which in most cases weren't even really roads—for any sign of the robbers and their hostages. Some dark premonition warned him to be careful.

Before starting out, he stepped into the small tack room in the main barn, unlocked a cabinet, and reached inside for his rifle. He could shoot and had gotten quite good at target practice. A couple of times he'd chased off a coyote, but he wasn't interested in hunting, and had never killed anything with the gun. He'd thought more than once of purchasing some good field glasses, but he'd never gotten around to it. The rifle would have to do. It had a scope and might save him miles of walking. He wished his mare were here, but she was too close to foaling for him to ride anyway.

Out of years of habit, he checked the safety on the rifle, then pointed the barrel toward the ground as he struck out toward the river. Mud sucked at his boots, and he sought rocks or any bits of vegetation sticking through the muck he could find to walk on. Belatedly, he recalled, he should have told Kendra he'd be gone a while. He wasn't accustomed to accounting to anyone for his time, but it would have been the polite thing to do and might have saved her some worry. Of course she might not worry at all, might even be glad of a little time to herself, but some instinct insisted she would worry. And in a way he found the notion she might worry about him kind of nice.

At the river's edge, he paused to search the opposite bank for a vehicle that might have made it that far. The old dirt road was empty as far as he could see. Its washboard surface, riddled with potholes, gave no indication someone had passed that way recently. He looked down at the muddy water and noted that whatever had obstructed the river had finally broken free. The swirling water was down fifteen or sixteen feet from the top of the gorge, which meant it was still more than ten feet deep. He tried to estimate how long it would take to rebuild the bridge and wondered how he'd get back and forth to town to pick up his mail and groceries until he got it done. He hoped he could get it rebuilt before lambing season started. He didn't like the idea of being cut off from the Double T if he should need the assistance of a vet. Ted's wife, Tracy, was the best vet around, besides being the only one for miles. She would do almost anything to save an animal, but even she couldn't swim the river.

He walked a mile further downstream, occasionally pausing to listen. A couple of times he heard the engine sound, but it seemed to be growing weaker. Then he heard it no more. He suspected someone had run a battery down.

At last he topped a bluff and gazed out toward the BLM land. Thousands of acres of brush and dried grass fell away before him.

From his lofty advantage point, he could see the river wending its meandering way toward the desert floor where it usually dwindled to a small stream, sometimes disappearing altogether before it joined its puny waters with a slightly larger stream miles away. Now he could see that from the point where the rock walls of the gully ceased, the river had spread out to form a vast lake. Near the edge of the lake, around the area of the old ford, he could see what looked like a vehicle.

Raising the scope to his eye, he watched the tableau below. A dark colored sports utility sat in mud and water with its nose tipped deeper in the muck. It was stuck where someone had tried to drive it across the lake the river had become. Three figures stood behind the vehicle, their jerky movements indicating a great deal of agitation.

Who were they and how had they gotten on his side of the river? Had they somehow crossed the bridge before he had a few nights ago? Surely, he would have seen tracks if someone had crossed ahead of him. No one had passed him on the road where he'd been stranded for several hours, so he doubted the vehicle had been ahead of him. No road stretched on this side of the river from the bridge to the ford. For years he'd intended to build a road along this side of the river, but he'd never gotten it done. There was a roundabout way to drive from the house, up into the foothills, then around to the ford, but he would have known if anyone had driven past the house to take that route. The dogs wouldn't have let anyone open the gate leading to that road. Roscoe would have defended that gate to the death.

The only way that vehicle could have gotten on his side of the river was for it to have been driven across the ford before the obstruction in the river broke, sending a flood to spread across the desert floor. Now the first sunny day had them trying to make their way back the way they'd come, but the rush of water from the gorge made the ford impassable.

Answers began to form in his mind, but he didn't much like what they were telling him. Those men had to be the bank robbers who abducted Kendra and David. They'd left their hostages and taken off in a sports utility, Kendra had told him, headed into the desert. They'd probably expected to follow one of the BLM trails back to civilization, but in the storm they'd either met with a downed bridge or taken a wrong turn and arrived at the ford. With the water blocked somewhere in the gorge, the ford had been shallow and they'd easily driven across. Later when the blockage cleared, the angry accumulation of weeks of rainfall had spread across the land, eliminating the ford and forming a broad lake.

On a small bluff above the ford stood the old rock house that had been built by the previous owner of the Krazy K when he had homesteaded the land nearly a century ago. The house was a simple four rooms and an attic. It boasted few amenities, but Chase kept it in good repair for those occasions when the Basque shearers needed a place to stay, or he himself needed a roof over his head on a stormy summer night when the herd was pastured down that way. He figured the robbers had found the house and waited out the storm there. This morning with the sun shining, they'd tried to leave and become stuck.

It didn't take much deductive power to figure out that when the desperate men realized they couldn't get their vehicle free, they'd start looking for another escape route. Because of the storm, the men hadn't heard the soft putt of his tractor or noticed smoke from his chimney until this morning. The bright, still morning had changed everything. Just as he'd heard their engine, they had probably heard his. A glance over his shoulder revealed just what he expected; a thin plume of smoke rose from his fireplace chimney. They'd come looking. Fear filled his heart, then turned to determination. Somehow he had to make certain they didn't find Kendra and David.

The radio announcer had mentioned several times that the police were looking for two men. Only Kendra and David knew about the third man, a man Kendra could identify, because unlike the two who had abducted her, he hadn't worn a ski mask. If Chase were some kind of movie hero, perhaps he could hold off the intruders with his rifle. Reality told him the attempt would be foolish. He was only one man with limited skills. There were three of them, and undoubtedly they were armed better than he and were probably better shots. At any rate, he didn't want any shots aimed toward Kendra and David or his sheep.

The men still seemed intent on getting their truck out of the lake, but he doubted that would be possible. He considered returning for his tractor and attempting to pull the stuck vehicle free. If they never saw Kendra and David; they wouldn't know they were here. He could pretend he knew nothing about the men's wanted status. He'd just be doing a good turn.

It wouldn't work. Even if he managed to pull the vehicle back to more solid ground, the men would still be on his side of the river, stranded in the large, but limited crescent of land circled by mountains on three sides and the river on the fourth. Even if they could drive through the relatively shallow water of the newly formed lake, when they reached the river channel their truck would be completely submerged. Freeing the vehicle wouldn't accomplish anything worthwhile.

But he couldn't do nothing. Men who were willing to abandon a woman and small child in the remote high desert during a freezing winter rain wouldn't hesitate to make certain no witnesses remained alive a second time.

He looked skyward praying for a glimpse of Ted Peters' plane, but the sky held no answers. Tucking his rifle under his arm, he began retracing his steps, moving rapidly through the rocks and brush. Urgency consumed him. He had to make it back to Kendra and David as quickly as humanly possible. Gut instinct told him it wouldn't be long before the robbers would follow.

CHAPTER 16

Chase had been gone far longer than Kendra had expected. She found herself repeatedly watching through the kitchen window for his return and pacing about the great room. Chase kept a considerable supply of magazines and his bookcases overflowed with a wide spectrum of reading material, but she couldn't seem to settle to anything. She prepared a salad and placed it in the refrigerator and checked the roast she'd placed in the oven earlier for their Christmas dinner.

She fussed over setting the table, wishing she had her pretty china with its narrow ivy border—instead of Chase's heavy stoneware—to give the table a festive look. Her mother's rich, creamy linen tablecloth would be nice, too. It was much too easy to imagine her own household items scattered among Chase's. Too soon, she finished the table preparations and looked around for something else to do. She'd already prepared rolls and pies the day before, so there weren't enough preparations left to keep her busy.

She forced herself to sit in one of the easy chairs and thumb through a magazine. Over the top of the pages she watched David play. Over and over Joseph and Mary, riding on the little donkey, approached the stable. Then the baby would appear, to be placed lovingly in the manger. Next the sheep and dogs were spread across the rug, and he would hold the angel in the air above them. He paused each time at this point to sing a few lines from "Away in a Manger" before setting the angel down and turning his attention to his wise men. She smiled when David's wise men treated the baby and his family to rides on their camels. Her heart filled with tenderness for the little boy, and she knew it would be difficult telling him good-bye when the time came.

Restlessly she rose to her feet and paced to the window again. The sunlight wasn't as dazzling as it had been earlier. There was still no sign of Chase, but his dogs stood in front of the barn with their noses pointed toward the river. There was an alertness to their stance, and they seemed to be listening. Chase must have gone to check the river's flooding. Thinking of Chase anywhere near that churning nightmare of a river channel sent chills down her spine. Surely he wouldn't get too close. She didn't think she could bear it if anything happened to Chase.

She was letting her over-active imagination get carried away. Chase wasn't a child and he wasn't the kind of man who took needless chances. Something else was at the root of her worry. No matter how many times she'd cautioned herself against letting herself care too much for him, she'd gone right ahead and fallen in love with the man, her "cowboy." She'd thought herself a mature, sensible woman. But loving him would make leaving him so much harder when she returned to Salt Lake, and her life would feel dark and lonely because she had foolishly fallen in love with a man who couldn't possibly care for her as she'd come to care for him. Still, she couldn't really regret loving Chase; just knowing him had somehow made her life richer and fuller.

"Look, Kendra!" She turned to see David had propped a large book against a stack of smaller books. He held the little manger at the top of the slope he'd created and let it zoom down carrying the wooden baby. The manger, transformed into a sled, carried each of his figures one after another, down the hill to dump them unceremoniously on the rug. She remembered seeing a table leaf in a closet and helped David turn it into a longer, not-quite-so-steep hill. He grinned his enjoyment of the new game, and she hoped David's parents wouldn't find something sacrilegious in their son's game of providing sleigh rides for the holy infant and all his entourage. Perhaps she was being irreverent when she imagined the Christmas Child, like David, would probably have loved sleigh rides if snow had been part of his childhood.

Once again she wandered to the window. There was still no sign of Chase, and the dogs were no longer in sight. She wondered if she should go look for him. The mud was slippery and he might have fallen. She wouldn't think about the river.

"The snowmans are all gone." David stood beside her, looking regretfully at the small spot of white that was all that was left of the largest snowball. It was almost as though he, too, was beginning to wonder if the magical day they'd spent together, playing in the snow, had been some fantastic figment of their imagination.

"I know." Kendra placed a hand on his shoulder. "We had a good time making them, and it's sad to see them melt, but they won't ever go completely away as long as we remember them in our hearts. I'll bet if you close your eyes really tight and think about us rolling the snow into big balls and finding rocks and sticks to make their faces, you'll still be able to see them in your mind."

David squeezed his eyes tightly shut and did as she suggested. "I see them! I see them!" he shouted. "And I see you running away and Chase tripping over you." He laughed and opened his eyes. "You were funny."

She laughed with him and turned her eyes back to the window. Something wasn't right. An uneasy premonition had haunted her ever since Chase had gone outside. And there was something about the engine sound she'd heard earlier that continued to bother her.

"Let's go help Chase," David's voice intruded on her thoughts. "I want to show Rags and Roscoe my Christmas present."

"Okay," she smiled down at him. That might be the best way to relieve her own anxiety. "It's not snowing or raining, but it's still cold outside, so I think we'd better put on the heavy clothing we wore yesterday. They're sitting on top of the dryer if you'd like to go get them."

"Long johns!" David giggled and dashed from the room. He'd latched onto the words when he'd heard Chase use the term, and for some reason, he found it as amusing as the long insulated pants. Kendra helped him dress, before retiring to the bedroom to dress herself in warm layers.

When she returned to the living room, David was trying to stuff the stable and all the little wooden figures into a big plastic bag.

"David, they won't fit. Just put the ones you think Roscoe and Rags will like best into your coat pockets and leave the rest here," she advised him.

He looked disappointed, but did as she asked. He set the plastic bag on the table and returned the bulky stable to its spot on the floor beneath the tree along with the camels and wise men. Most of the sheep had to stay, too, and Joseph and Mary. Kendra turned off the stove, and pulled the roasting pan from the oven and set it on top of the stove before stepping into the galoshes Chase had loaned her to wear over her shoes. When they were both dressed to Kendra's satisfaction, she took David's hand.

Stepping out the back door, Kendra stared in amazement. Chase had told her his house was close to the mountains, and she'd seen the dark shapes through the storm, but this was incredible. Huge rock slabs pointed to the sky less than a mile from Chase's back door and ended in a jumble of cliffs and towering peaks covered with snow. Towering clouds behind the western peaks warned that the dazzling sunlight wouldn't last. Slowly she turned around and was amazed by how far she could see. Before her stretched a vast vista of brush-covered hills. An occasional solitary cedar dotted the land and she caught occasional glimpses of the river which defined the lower border of Chase's land. In the far distance a gleam of silver hinted at a small lake. It had never occurred to her that the ranch was actually a high plateau caught somewhere between desert and mountain. It was beautiful, and she understood why Chase chose to stay in his remote aerie.

As they walked toward the main barn, the dogs ran to meet them. Kendra insisted they wait until they were inside the barn before David could pull his treasures out of his pocket to show the dogs. The heavy door moved easily on well-oiled rollers, and she blinked several times as her eyes adjusted to the darker interior of the building. The large ewe Chase called Old Glory bleated a welcome. She looked around but didn't see Chase.

"See, this is Jesus. Today is his birthday," she heard David tell the dogs. "And this is you, Roscoe, and this one is Rags. I just brought one sheep, but I got lots. This one is a donkey. It's sort of like a horse, but littler. The baby's mommy rode on a donkey the night Jesus got borned in a stable just like this one."

With great care he pulled the little angel from his pocket and set it on a small ledge next to Glory's pen. "Chase made an angel for me, too. Angels watch over things so's they're safe. You can keep the angel today 'cause it's Christmas." The dogs tilted their heads to one side and did their best to look as though they understood. Their interest increased greatly when David pulled a small plastic bag from his pocket and broke off a chunk of chocolate for each of the dogs.

"I'm not sure dogs should eat fudge," Kendra warned David. "Candy might give them a tummy ache."

"I'll ask Chase." David returned the treat to his pocket and broke a cookie he'd stashed in his pocket into little pieces for the dogs. Kendra smiled. Chase was obviously some kind of hero to the little boy, and David trusted him to have all the answers to his questions. He reached for her hand again, and they walked down the wide aisle of the barn, occasionally stopping to pat a woolly head. Roscoe trailed behind, pausing now and then to cock his head and look back toward the barn door. Rags stuck close to David and frequently sniffed at his pocket. David gave her another cookie crumb.

At the far end of the barn they walked through another set of doors into the feed area with its sheep and sheds. The tractor and feed wagon were parked in the shelter of one of the sheds, but there was no sign of Chase. Something wasn't right.

"Chase!" she called his name. There was no answer, and David added his shout to hers. Rags gave several short yips. Each time there was no response, her uneasiness escalated another notch. Many times in her life she'd felt the warmth in her chest that confirmed the rightness of a choice she'd made, and some instinct told her that the growing sense that something was terribly wrong came from the same source.

"Maybe he went to look at the river," David offered a possible solution and Kendra shuddered. She'd never been overly fond of water, and that river terrified her.

"He might have," Kendra conceded reluctantly, hoping he hadn't.

"We could go see," David began tugging her back inside the barn.

"I don't think we should," she responded hesitantly. "It's a really long walk. I think we should go back to the house and finish getting dinner ready." She wasn't sure why she felt reluctant to go back to the river, but something prompted her not to go that way. She recognized that prompting; she'd felt the Spirit many times in her life and had learned to obey, even when her own reasoning suggested a different solution. This prompting didn't bring her comfort. It only increased her fear. If she and David shouldn't go near the river, then there was all the more reason to fear Chase being there.

David hugged the dogs and mimicked Chase as he told them to watch the sheep. The dogs watched him hopefully for several seconds, then loped off to do his bidding. Their obedience to his command brought a proud grin to his face. Leaving the dogs and sheep behind, David and Kendra picked their way across the muddy yard to the house.

"Wipe your feet before going inside," she cautioned David and turned to drag the soles of her boots across the boot scraper beside the back door. A prickling sensation at the back of her neck brought her head up. Straightening, she let her gaze wander across the slope, which fell away to the desert below. Her eyes lit on a tall figure traveling up the lane in long, ground-eating strides. He seemed to radiate some kind of urgency.

"Chase!" Her instinct was to hurry toward him.

"Stay there!" he called, and she placed a hand on David's shoulder to restrain him from rushing forward. The dogs recognized his voice and came bounding out of the barn to tear up the lane to meet their master. He ignored them and hurried on. She became aware of the rifle he carried, and that added weight to her fear.

Chase didn't slow down as he came closer, and by the time she could see his face, she knew her earlier premonition had been right. Something was wrong. He didn't seem to be injured, she noted with relief, but he was greatly agitated. Perhaps his injury was hidden by his heavy clothing.

"What is it?" She reached out as though to touch him as he rushed up the step. "Are you hurt? Has something happened to one of the sheep?"

"I'm fine," he said as he gasped for breath, and she knew he'd been running for some distance. "But we've got to get out of here," he panted. "We have to hurry."

"Chase, what's wrong?"

"In the house." He ushered them ahead of him.

"I got mud . . ." David started to protest entering the house without scraping his boots.

"Don't worry about it." Chase picked him up and swung him

through the door. Once inside, Chase set the boy down and ran toward his shop, returning almost immediately with a sturdy back pack and a tightly rolled sleeping bag. He began stuffing items in the pack, and when he grabbed the plastic bag David had left on the table and tossed her roast inside it, Kendra let out a frustrated wail.

"Chase Kirkham, tell me what is going on this minute," she demanded.

"It's them." He glanced apprehensively toward David. "The men who abducted you are here on the Krazy K. They've been here all along, but the storm kept them from knowing we were here, just as it hid their presence from us."

"You saw them?" He nodded, and she felt her legs buckle. A wave of dizziness sent her reaching for a chair back for support. The dizziness lasted only a second or two, then she was back on her feet, demanding to know more. "Do they know we're here?"

"I don't think they do yet, but they soon will. Their SUV is stuck in the mud and they won't be able to get it out. I think they crossed the river onto my land that first night by driving through a ford that has since become part of a wide lake. Even if they could get their vehicle out of the mud, they can't get off my land the way they got onto it. It's just a matter of time before they come this way, looking for another way across the river. We have to be gone before they get here."

"Lock the doors so they can't get in!" David shouted. His face was pale, and Kendra knew he understood more than she would have guessed. He rushed to the door to follow his own suggestion. Her heart ached to see the panic in the child's eyes.

Her eyes went to the rifle Chase had leaned against the cupboard. His gaze followed hers, and he spoke softly, "It's not enough. I'm not a marksman, and I don't believe I could hold off three armed men. There's no question I would want to return fire if we were cornered and it became the only hope of saving you and David, but I don't know if I could actually pull the trigger against another human being. I don't want to risk your lives to find out."

She understood the futility of trying to fight off the robbers when they came. There was little choice but to leave, but where would they go? She must have spoken her thoughts out loud because Chase answered her.

"There's not another road out of here, but there is a narrow suspended bridge a couple of miles up the gorge the river passes through on its way out of the mountains. It was built before Ted turned the Double T into a cattle ranch. His father ran sheep, and in summer when the grass was in danger of being over-grazed on his side of the river, he'd bring them up here to pasture on the side of the mountain. He had to have a way to get the sheep across the river, so he and his hired hands built a swinging bridge out of steel cables and split logs."

A suspended, swinging bridge didn't sound highly promising to Kendra. "What if it has washed away?" she asked.

"It's too high. It spans the chasm at its narrowest point, and I'm certain the water didn't reach that high." He passed over the hot kettles of mashed potatoes and vegetable on the stove and reached for the pan of rolls she'd baked the day before and had ready to pop back in the oven to reheat. He dumped them in another plastic bag, and the rolls followed the roast into his back pack. Opening the refrigerator, he hesitated a moment, then passed over the salads she'd prepared to the plastic food saver of fudge. It disappeared into the pack also along with all of the cartons of juice he could find. He glanced longingly toward the pies, then shook his head. "Too fragile," he muttered, and she had a depressing picture of the sticky mess the pies would become if he'd dropped them into plastic bags. She shook off the feeling; there was no time to mourn the ruin of the dinner on which she'd lavished so much care.

"Find some warm shirts and extra socks for us." It was practically an order, but she hurried to do his bidding while he continued to load his pack with matches, ponchos, and other items he deemed essential.

When she returned to the room, he added the clothing items to his cache of supplies. "All right. Let's go." He swung the pack onto his back, added the rolled sleeping bag to the top of his load, and adjusted the straps.

"I should carry something," Kendra protested as she looked around the warm kitchen for the last time, her eyes searching for some item they might need. She couldn't bear to leave this way. It was silly, she knew, but she'd formed an attachment to the small bright kitchen. It felt like home in a way her apartment never had.

"You'll probably have to carry David part of the way," Chase warned. "You'll need your hands free in order to help him."

"I can walk!" David protested, as he took Kendra's hand. "Only babies have to be carried."

As Chase reached for the door, David's voice brought him to a halt. "We didn't say a prayer. Daddy says we should always pray before we go on a journey."

"Your daddy is right." Chase swept his hat off his head and muttered a prayer, almost as short as David's first blessing on their food. It was short, but covered the essentials and seemed to make David happy. To be perfectly honest, it made him feel better, too. One thing was for sure; they'd need all the help God could give them. He stepped out the door and closed it firmly behind them before moving quickly toward a row of bushes and trees he'd planted years ago for a windbreak. The trees would provide some cover should the trio of desperate men be closer than he expected.

The dogs came bounding toward them. "Can Roscoe and Rags come with us?" David asked as Rags sniffed his pocket then swiped his tongue across the boy's face. David dropped to his knees to wrap an arm around Rags.

"They better stay here and watch the sheep. With us gone, the sheep won't have anyone but the dogs to keep them safe," Chase tried to soften the disappointment for the boy. Kendra heard the worry in his voice and knew it was difficult for the man to leave the dogs behind, but understood the risk that the dogs might bark, giving away their escape route. Living alone the way he did, she suspected the dogs were almost family to him. He'd told her they were working dogs, not pets, but she knew a deep affection existed between them anyway. She didn't know whether his only fear was that they would bark and give away their position, or whether he really thought the dogs could somehow keep his sheep safe.

Surely the robbers would have no reason to hurt the dogs. But the dogs were trained to protect the sheep, and if they saw any threat to their charges they would attack, and the thieves might retaliate. Without the dogs, the sheep might break through the fence and wander away or coyotes could wreak havoc on the flock.

David's lip quivered when Chase sent the dogs to the barn. She felt a similar urge to cry when she glanced back toward Chase's house. She didn't want to leave any of it behind, not the house, not the barns or the sheep, not those two dear dogs, and certainly not the cozy Christmas the three of them had started to share.

CHAPTER 17

Chase moved quickly at first, but as the rocky trail grew steeper, he slowed his pace to accommodate the woman and child. He felt a little easier once they were out of sight of the house and into a grove of cedars. The thick trees provided some shelter from the wind that had sprung up, preceding the storm that was swiftly moving their way. He stopped to let Kendra and David catch their breaths for a couple of minutes, then led out again. They didn't speak, and even David seemed to understand the urgency of their silent flight.

No real trail existed from the house to the sheep bridge. He'd climbed up this way on occasion, but only in summer. Even in summertime he generally drove his truck or rode Bluebelle along the road if he had reason to search out this remote corner of his ranch. The more circuitous route would be easier. Unfortunately, it would also be riskier. He didn't deem it safe to follow the route beyond his hay fields and along the curve of the mountain to the meadow where his sheep fed during the summer and on up to the higher pasture on the upper side of the bridge. That route was too visible to anyone approaching the house. Besides it covered a good ten miles, while straight up was less than two.

There had been no threat as long as he'd watched the men work at freeing their vehicle, but still the threat was there. They would come. Some prompting deep in his soul told him his window of opportunity for securing Kendra's and David's safety was extremely slim. He meant to obey that prompting. He'd failed to act quickly enough to save one woman and child he'd loved; he wouldn't fail again.

Brush scraped against their clothing, impeding their progress, and rocks turned into boulders as they scrambled to climb over them. Sometimes the mud was slippery and held them back. Sometimes the soft goo threatened to suck them into its depths. The wind picked up and clouds blotted out the sun. Always they moved upward, and their lungs felt tight and strained. The two miles were beginning to feel like ten, long before they reached the rocky ridge where the bridge's cables were anchored into solid rock.

He led Kendra and David as they climbed over the ridge and down into a cup-like depression where the bridge began. Here there was some shelter from the wind, which was beginning to carry tiny shards of ice that stung their faces as they pushed against it. Grateful for the reprieve, they huddled against the rocks. There were still patches of snow at this elevation and the temperature felt colder. Kendra sank down on a flat boulder and stared grimly at the bridge, which spanned a chasm more than a hundred feet wide.

Little puffs of white punctuated each breath they took. Chase watched Kendra and instinctively knew she didn't want to set one foot on the bridge, but that she would. He might have only known her a few days, but he knew about that deep well of faith and courage she drew on when the going got tough. She'd do whatever she had to do to save David. And if the only way to save David was to cross that bridge, she'd swallow her fear and cross it.

"Kendra." He sat down beside her. Perhaps if he explained the bridge's construction she'd be less afraid. "It's perfectly safe. These two heavy cables over our heads are firmly planted in solid rock on both this side and the other side of the gorge. Four similar cables stretch across that gap a little lower and are attached to these at ten-foot intervals. They support the planks we'll walk on. See, there's a railing on either side and mesh wire running from the cables under the planks to the wooden rails."

"What's the wire for?" Chase looked at David and was surprised to see rebellion on the little boy's face. David was tough and adventurous. Chase hadn't expected him to mutiny at the prospect of crossing the bridge.

"Sheep get kind of playing around when they cross the bridge or sometimes they get spooked, so we have to have a fence to keep them from falling or pushing each other off," he explained.

"Do I have to go across that bridge?" Chase heard a note of challenge in the boy's voice that clearly said, "Just try to make me cross it."

"You know we have to go across it," Chase spoke sternly. "There are some bad men following us who will hurt us if they catch us. It's the only way we can get across the river to get away from them."

"It looks scary." David looked mutinous and Chase could tell Kendra agreed with the boy's estimation. A gust of wind swept across their lofty perch and the bridge creaked. Far below, the water crashed against boulders and sent spray flying high against the rocky walls. It didn't touch them, but Kendra shuddered.

"Chase, won't they follow us across the bridge and catch us anyway?" Kendra asked. Wind whipped her hair across her face, and he watched a fat, lazy snowflake flutter to the rock beside her, invading their sheltered space. It reminded him that the sun had disappeared behind the clouds some time ago, and that a storm was rapidly taking shape around them. They'd better be on their way if they hoped to reach some kind of shelter before nightfall. He didn't want to be caught in the open when the temperature dipped into single digits.

"No, they won't follow us. I'll make sure of that. Once you and David are across, I'll remove enough planks to discourage them from following us," Chase tried to reassure her.

"Remove planks? But how?" Her voice held a hint of alarm. He could tell she figured that if the planks were easy to remove, there was a chance they'd fall off on their own.

"Two years ago Ted and I replaced some of the planks. We discovered the old wood is soft, and the nails pull free quite easily. I brought a claw hammer." He patted his back pack that now rested beside him, then stood. He held out a hand to her, and just as he knew she would, she stood beside him. David put his hands behind his back and shook his head.

"I not go," he pronounced stubbornly, reverting to childish language as if to protect himself from the danger an adult world had thrust upon him. Chase could easily pick the boy up and carry him across even if he kicked and screamed every step of the way, but he'd prefer not to frighten the child or for him to start yelling.

Chase hunkered down beside the boy and spoke quietly. "When my friend Ted was a little boy, he had a bum lamb. That's a baby sheep who doesn't have a mama. Ted fed that lamb from a pop bottle with a rubber nipple on it just like a great big baby bottle. As that lamb got bigger, it followed Ted wherever he went. He trusted Ted more than anybody or anything in this whole world, so when Ted's daddy and his dogs brought their sheep up here, and the sheep decided this old bridge was just too scary, he sent for Ted and his lamb. Ted walked right out on the bridge, and his little lamb followed him. Then all of the other sheep followed the lamb, and they all got safely across.

"Son, you've had some bad experiences the past few days, but Kendra has taken care of you and done her best to keep you safe. Don't you think you might trust her the way Ted's lamb trusted him?"

Pulling the little wooden lamb Chase had carved out of his pocket, David looked at it for a minute then up at Kendra.

"David," Kendra spoke softly. "That little sheep is like the ones that belonged to the shepherds who heard an angel tell them the Christ child had been born. Those sheep were like the little lamb Chase told you about, too. Sheep aren't terribly strong; they get scared, and they can't protect themselves very well. That's why they love the shepherd so much who takes care of them and keeps them safe. Sometimes Jesus was called the Good Shepherd, and those who followed him were called his sheep because he loved them and took care of them. Do you think you could think of yourself as one of Jesus' lambs and trust Him to lead us across that bridge?"

David looked at the bridge and squinted his eyes as though struggling with a weighty question. He then looked at Chase, then back at the bridge.

"Chase is a shepherd." David spoke as though he were deep in thought. "Sometimes I get scared, and I'm not big."

"You're getting bigger," Kendra assured him. "Will you come?" She held out her hand.

"You took care of me when the robbers broke Decker's big window," he continued. "Are you a shepherd, too?"

"I don't have any sheep," Kendra smiled encouragingly at the small boy.

"Just one small borrowed lamb," Chase spoke softly, but Kendra and David both heard.

"Me?" David sounded a little confused.

"Yes, will you trust Chase and me to get you across the bridge?" Again she held out her hand.

Tentatively David reached out to clasp her fingers. Suddenly his grin flashed across his face. "I can do it," he announced. "I got lots of shepherds. You and Chase and Jesus."

CHAPTER 18

"Guy!" Vicki sat straight up in bed and screamed her husband's name. The bedroom door exploded open, and Guy was beside her in two steps.

"What is it?" he asked as he lifted her into his arms. She was shaking so uncontrollably he could scarcely hold onto her. "What's wrong?"

"It's David! He's in danger," she gasped. "I saw him! There are men with guns chasing him, and he's about to fall into a terrible black hole."

"Honey, it was a dream," Guy attempted to soothe his wife. "You came in here to be alone, and you fell asleep." He'd checked on her more than an hour ago and found her restlessly moaning in her sleep. Her ravaged face and fearful cries had torn at his heart.

Christmas Day had passed like the two days before in dreary sameness. They'd gotten their hopes up when Christmas Day had dawned clear and bright, enabling an aerial search to begin, but the good weather hadn't lasted long and the search planes had been grounded by noon. There had been no news, and they'd felt the passing of time like a clock ticking off the minutes of their son's life. They both knew that the more time that lapsed between their son's abduction and his recovery, the greater the risk was that he wouldn't be found alive, if he were found at all.

Guy looked down at Vicki, knowing how desperately she needed sleep. He hadn't wanted to awaken her, so he'd drawn a quilt over her and sat beside her until she'd drifted into more peaceful slumber. Then he'd tiptoed from the room to call Sheriff Hatcher one more time.

"It was more than a dream," Vicki insisted. "I know David is in some kind of danger."

Guy felt a chill, almost as though Vicki's nightmare was reaching out to touch him, too. He picked up the blanket and pulled it around them both.

"We have to do something." Vicki turned desperate eyes toward him. "We have to help him."

"You know I'd do anything to help him, but what can I do?" Guy voiced his own frustration. "I would go anywhere, do anything for him, but I don't know where to go or what to do." He wasn't discounting her dream. He'd felt his own restless uneasiness growing all afternoon. More than once he'd felt this senseless nightmare was building toward some frightening climax.

"God is the only one who can help him, isn't he?" Vicki's voice revealed how desperately she clung to her faith even though she shook with fear. When Guy agreed that their son was in God's hands, Vicki's face took on renewed determination. "He's in terrible danger. I think we need to pray as we've never prayed before."

Mutely Guy bowed his head in agreement. They slid off the bed onto their knees, and Guy straightened the blanket around their shoulders. Tucking Vicki's hands in his, Guy began to pray. Unitedly they pleaded with God to protect their son. Urgency filled his heart. He had prayed countless times since David had been taken, but he hadn't felt this urgent desperation since that first night. He'd never given the words 'to intercede' much thought before, but now his mind opened, and he caught a glimpse of the Savior's role as he interceded with the Father for all mankind. Born of the love he held for his son and his desperate desire to save him came an awareness of divine love, humbling him further, as he continued to pray.

• • • • •

The snowflakes now coming in full force, Kendra clutched at Chase's hand and whispered a plea to God under her breath for their safe crossing. She was nearly as frightened as David, but as long as Chase held her hand, she'd be all right, she attempted to reassure herself. He led the way, holding to the cable rail with one hand and to her hand with the other. When she hesitated before stepping onto the bridge, he tightened his grip on her hand and slowly she followed with David practically glued to her side. David gasped as the bridge wobbled beneath his feet, but gamely continued on, clinging tightly to her hand, and together they followed a step behind Chase.

The wind tugged at their clothes, and though the bridge didn't move much, it swayed enough to leave them clutching each other's hands. Hard crystals of ice assaulted their faces, and she imagined the boards beneath their feet throwing back a hollow, empty echo with each step she took. She tried not to look down at the water churning beneath them, knowing her courage would fail if she actually looked at it. The roar of the water blended with the wail of the wind, and she fought the urge to clap her hands over her ears. David made a small whimpering sound, and she set aside her own fear enough to draw him closer to her.

Carefully placing one foot in front of the other, they progressed toward the center of the bridge. The planks grew slipperier and the snow nearly blinded her. Here there was no protection from the wind and the sway of the bridge became more noticeable, or perhaps her imagination only made it seem so. Swirling white obliterated the end of the bridge, lending an illusion of being trapped forever in an endless nightmare without beginning or end. From her heart came a plea for God to protect them and carry them safely across this abyss.

David's hand loosened from hers, and she felt him lurch away. He'd slipped on an icy plank and was sliding, screaming, toward the wire mesh. Jerking her hand free from Chase's, she lunged toward David, and her fingers closed around his coat sleeve. As she attempted to pull him toward her, she felt him frantically clutch at her leg. But instead of breaking his slide, she lost her footing, and was pulled after him on the slick planks. Fear that their momentum would carry them over the top of the mesh sides had her frantically grappling to find a handhold in the wire.

A sharp jerk on her shoulder broke their skid, and the rough fabric of Chase's parka brushed against her face and mouth. Gripping her shoulder tightly, Chase halted their slide and steadied them on their feet. David buried his head against her leg, and she felt his small body quiver as he struggled to hold back tears of fright. It was over in seconds, but the experience left her trembling. It didn't take long until she realized they'd been in no serious danger; her fear had been unrealistic. The mesh sides of the bridge would have stopped them even if Chase hadn't grabbed them. In moments his gentle comfort and solid presence gave her the courage to go on. Chase seemed to know without her saying a word when she was ready to move ahead.

"We have to keep moving." Chase's mouth was practically against her ear, but still he had to shout. She drew herself upright and tugged on David's arm, urging him to keep walking. He didn't move, and one look at his terrified face told her he couldn't move. Reaching down, she pulled him into her arms, then slowly straightened. His arms locked around her neck, and he buried his face just under her chin. Her fear receded as an overwhelming need to protect David became greater than her own terror.

Keeping her balance would be harder while carrying the child, but he was far too frightened to take another step on his own. The only way to get David safely off of this bridge would be to carry him. For a moment she wondered if she would be able to take a step, but then Chase's arm settled around her shoulders, and she followed where he led. When her strength was tested to the limit, she felt his pouring into her. A strange, comforting calm settled over her as she lengthened her stride to match Chase's. Together, they could conquer the bridge.

Chase's arm suddenly tightened across her shoulders, bringing her to an abrupt stop. Cautiously she looked around, then glanced down straight into a gaping hole. She forced herself to look at the spot her next step would have taken her. A plank was missing, leaving at least a ten-inch gap. She began to tremble. A scream rose to her lips, and fearfully she swallowed it back. One more step and her foot would have gone between the planks. It wasn't wide enough for her entire body to slide through, but she had trouble convincing herself she wasn't in any real danger of falling through to crash onto the rocks and sink into the foaming water beneath.

"We can make it," Chase encouraged. "It's just one board."

"Just one board!" her mind screamed. "If one board is missing, others could be, too." She looked ahead fearfully. Chase took her hand and urged her silently on.

Nervously she let him help her across the open space, but her trust in the bridge was shattered. From that point on she kept her eyes riveted to the shaky path, testing each plank carefully before trusting her weight to it. Her diligence was rewarded by finding gaps where four more planks were missing, two of which were right together, creating a formidable gap.

David's arms gripped her neck in a stranglehold, and she wondered if she might suffocate rather than fall through the holes in the bridge. At least David didn't have to see the holes. His eyes were so tightly closed, he couldn't see anything. Nonetheless, she held him to her with all her strength and whispered soothing words she had no doubt the wind blew away the moment they left her lips. Over and over she thanked God for Chase's strong arm around her shoulders and for allowing him to see the holes in the bridge in time to prevent them from falling through.

At last the bridge ceased to rock, and she knew they were once more over solid ground. It was all she could do to keep from weeping when she stepped off the last plank and felt solid rock beneath her boots. She'd heard of people falling to the ground and kissing it upon safely arriving at some destination, and knew exactly how they felt.

Chase hurried them off the bridge and into the shelter of a deep indentation in the rock. She slid to the ground with her back against the cold, hard rock, welcoming its solidity, then drew David onto her lap and pulled him close. Only half aware, she watched Chase fling his pack and the rifle down beside them and pull out his hammer. He was returning to the bridge! Unable to bear the thought of him returning to that bridge, she held out her hand as he walked away, in a silent appeal to stay with her.

Whether he failed to see her gesture or ignored it, she didn't know, but he left her there with David huddled in her arms while he went back to the bridge. He disappeared quickly from her sight behind a curtain of falling snow. Never had she felt so lost and alone in her whole life. She hadn't felt so abandoned since her mother had died.

David made a soft snuffling sound, reminding her she wasn't alone. David was with her, and he was counting on her to comfort him and keep him safe. Suddenly she was filled with purpose. She raided the pack for ponchos to shelter David and herself from the cold ground and the driving sleet. As she arranged the ponchos, she talked to David, assuring him he was safe now. He sat up and looked around timidly as though he couldn't quite believe the bridge was behind him.

Tearing off a chunk of the now cold meat, she fitted it inside a roll which she encouraged the boy to eat. Then needing to keep busy, she prepared sandwiches for Chase and herself as well. David took a couple of bites of his sandwich then reached into his pocket for a piece of his hoarded fudge. He probably needed something more filling than candy, but she didn't have the heart to argue with him. It was still Christmas, and with all the child had gone through this day, if he wanted fudge for his dinner, then fudge he would have!

She peered into the falling snow, hoping to see Chase emerge from the thick curtain, as she ate her sandwich. It wasn't the Christmas dinner she had planned, but she was glad Chase had thought to bring the meat and rolls with them. When her vigilance wasn't rewarded by a glimpse of Chase, she leaned back against the rock again and lifted David back onto her lap. He was sleepy and rubbing his eyes, so she cradled him in her arms. Softly she began to sing a Christmas lullaby.

CHAPTER 19

Chase leaned back, pulling and tugging at a rusty nail that resisted leaving the spot where it had rested for more years than Chase had even known of the bridge's existence. It didn't come free as easily as the others had, but finally it yielded to the pressure he exerted. He'd removed six planks so far. A couple more should do it. It would take someone with a lot more courage than he suspected the bank robbers possessed to attempt to cross that gap on nothing more than slippery cables, especially in this storm with night coming on. He wished it were possible to break the cables and send the bridge tumbling into the chasm below, but he had no tools capable of snapping steel cables.

He stood to knock apart the railing beside the hole he'd created, and paused to listen. The storm muffled sound, but he thought he'd heard something, possibly a rifle shot. His heart froze and he paused to listen. Visions of the robbers scattering his flock or shooting his dogs brought a lump of fear to his throat. He stood still, straining to hear over the high-pitched, keening wail of the wind.

Hearing nothing but the rush of air, he resumed the task he'd set himself. When he finished removing the protective wire mesh, he broke apart the wooden rail. Moving as fast as he dared, he tried not to think of the narrow rocky gorge beneath him that harbored a frenzied torrent of seething, angry water. If he fell, death would be swift—but he had no intention of leaving Kendra and David alone to fend for themselves. He'd been only half alive for fifteen years, not really caring much whether he lived or not, but now he wanted to live. He'd been wrong to turn his back on life. The past few days had stirred a remembrance of the joy he'd once taken in being alive, reminding him that life was to be treasured.

On his hands and knees, he retreated to the end of the bridge. With mere feet to go, he heard Rags' unmistakable yip and turned to see a small dark shape leap onto the bridge and bound toward him.

"No, Rags! Go back," he screamed into the swirling curtain of white. But the dog continued on at breakneck speed, coming closer to the yawning hole Chase had created. Enough light remained to see the dog bunch his muscles and leap forward when he reached the gap. Chase closed his eyes in horror. Nausea rose in his throat, choking him with its bitter gall. The distance was too far; surely the little dog wouldn't make it. If she didn't die from the fall, the icy, churning water would soon crush her against the boulders and steep cliff sides below.

Above the wind, he thought he detected the scrabble of claws on wooden planks. Dare he hope? He opened his eyes in time to see Rags cross the remaining space between them, the yawning gap behind her. The little dog's tail was between her legs and drops of red stained the planks with each wobbling step. He dropped to his knees and the dog sprang into his waiting arms. Laughing and crying, he hugged the dog to him.

"That was an incredible leap, little girl." He buried his face in the dog's thick ruff and stroked her sides. He didn't want to even think about why the dog had disobeyed and come after him, or how she'd managed to jump a more than six-foot gap.

His hands were bare. He'd removed his gloves while working on the bridge, and now he felt something sticky. Carefully he traced a welt across the dog's rump. She'd been shot! He had heard a shot! A shot aimed at Rags! Anger swelled in his chest. He checked the wound more closely and saw the crease wasn't deep. The bleeding had nearly stopped. A couple of her back toe claws were broken and one was still bleeding a little bit. That had probably happened during her frightened leap across the gap in the bridge.

Anger turned to sadness and he wondered what kind of events had molded a person's life, making him capable of firing a shot at the hard-working little dog. Memories of the wiggly puppy she had been blended into pictures of her eagerness to learn from old Roscoe, and ended with a picture of the dogs rolling in the snow with David. Gone was any pretense that the dogs were only stock dogs, merely a necessary convenience in working his sheep. They were loyal friends and companions and had come the closest to being family he'd known since his tragic loss fifteen years ago.

Chase stood with Rags still in his arms and looked back the way she had come. Worry creased his forehead as he wondered about Roscoe and his sheep. Through the slashing snow, he could just make out the shape of a man at the far end of the bridge. One of the robbers had followed Rags! Chase felt his heart pounding in his chest and thought he might be sick. Slowly he let Rags slide to the ground. "Go find David," he ordered sharply, and the dog turned to streak toward the rocks that hid Kendra and David.

Chase could barely make out the rifle held to the man's shoulder. The snow swirled and parted, revealing the rifle clearly pointed toward him. His own rifle was with Kendra and David. Time stood frozen as he stared across the chasm at a man who might put a bullet through him any second. Kendra's face swam before him, and he knew he didn't want to die. Even more he didn't want any harm to come to her. *Please, God,* he found himself praying over and over like a stuck record. A sense that he didn't pray alone filled his soul. As if echoing down a tunnel in his mind, he seemed to hear the voices of David's parents, Bishop Samuelson, Lucy, and other less familiar voices join with his in prayer.

The man lowered his rifle and turned away, as though defeated by a greater force. In seconds he was lost in the swirling snow.

Chase continued to stand, reeling under a sense of bewilderment. What had happened? Why hadn't the man fired? Was it possible the man hadn't seen him through the falling snow? Was he the one thief Kendra said had expressed a reluctance to kill David or her? Gradually he became aware of a comforting sound. Music reached his ears, and he remembered David's talk of angels. He'd had a definite sense of not being alone as he stood facing the gunman. Was it possible he hadn't been alone, that an unseen being had stood beside him, adding his prayers to those Chase uttered in that moment of terror?

Turning his head, he listened. The sound came again. He knew this angel's voice. Kendra's clear, sweet tones drifted on the air. *Silent night, holy night,* she sang and a shiver slid down Chase's spine. In his heart he knew he'd just witnessed a Christmas miracle.

• • • • •

Kendra thought she heard Chase shout once, but it was likely the wind. At times it sounded almost like human screams. She huddled under the plastic poncho and continued to sing to the sleeping child until a bundle of fur catapulted into her lap, and began eagerly licking David's face.

"Rags! Where did you come from?" She struggled to keep her balance and hang onto David. David opened his eyes and threw his arms around the dog.

"Rags! You came!" He hugged the dog and laughed as the dog attempted to lick his face once more. "We crossed a scary bridge. I just about falled off. Did you cross the bridge, too?" he asked as though he expected the dog to answer.

"She sure did!" Kendra looked up to see Chase standing above her. He crouched down to run his fingers through the dog's thick coat. A lump rose in her throat, and she decided she'd never been happier to see anyone before in her life. "She's been hurt, but she's okay," Chase went on. "There's a little blood on her coat, so be careful you don't get it all over you," he cautioned David.

"Did the bad men hurt her?" David demanded to know as he hugged the dog.

"I think so," Chase answered honestly. "But she got away."

"What about Roscoe?" Kendra asked. The dog's appearance seemed a little strange to her. She couldn't imagine either dog disobeying Chase to come after them unless they'd been threatened in some way.

"I don't know," Chase admitted soberly.

"Do you think my angel will keep Roscoe and the sheepies safe from those bad men?" David asked with a tremor in his voice.

"Your angel?" Chase clearly didn't understand and the question startled him.

"When you were gone so long, David and I went to the barn," Kendra explained. "He left the angel you carved for him on a ledge over one of the stalls for the dogs, so they would have a little Christmas, too."

"I wouldn't be at all surprised if your angel keeps an eye on Roscoe, David," Chase answered the boy with convincing sincerity. His glance at her told her there were things he didn't wish to speak about in front of the child. "I hate to move on in this storm, but I think we need to get away from the bridge and onto lower ground. It's almost dark, and I'd like to try to reach a place where we can settle down for the night before the temperature dips much lower."

Chase helped Kendra slip one of the ponchos over her coat and he wrapped David in another one. The last one he donned himself. Kendra handed him the sandwich she'd made, and he wolfed it down ravenously before thrusting his arms through the pack's straps and shrugging it into position on his back. Kendra picked up David. Chase offered to carry the boy, but she insisted his pack was a heavy enough load for him to carry. Ducking their heads against the onslaught of blowing snow, they left the limited shelter the rock had provided.

Wind immediately flung sharp specks of ice in their faces, and they had to bend almost double to escape its stinging force. Chase helped her down a sharp incline where she stumbled and bumped against rocks and brush for what seemed an endless period of time, then the ground leveled out to a more gentle incline. Each time she slid on an ice-covered rock, Chase was there to steady her.

Kendra walked until her arms ached and she feared she would drop David. Still she moved forward, occasionally glancing nervously behind them. Each time Rags, too, would look back, then satisfied they weren't being followed, would trot on. Her arms turned numb and she wondered if David would slip out of her grasp and she wouldn't even be able to tell. At last she asked him if he could walk again.

"Me and Rags can walk." With the bridge far behind them, his usual bravado returned. He let her lower him to the ground, where he hugged the dog before marching off behind Chase with Rags prancing at his side. Once more he was the bouncing exuberant little boy she'd grown to love. She shook her arms to encourage circulation to resume its normal flow and stumbled along after them.

The wind seemed less fierce as they moved away from the river gorge, and the snow changed from icy shards to softly falling flakes. She'd feared they would lose their way in the storm, but a sense of peace enveloped her as the half-light turned to night and the snow petered away. When the snow stopped falling, the air turned noticeably colder. The cloud cover moved aside, revealing glimpses of a silvery blue moon, and an occasional star peeped through trailing wisps of white. David's steps began to lag and Kendra's movements became slower. It became harder and harder to ignore the cold seeping through her clothes or to place one foot ahead of the other. She couldn't remember ever being so tired or cold before in her life except for the night she and David had been abandoned by the robbers.

"It's not far now," Chase encouraged them. "There are a couple of large haystacks right ahead and parked behind them is an old sheep camp trailer. It belonged to Ted's father, and now the Double T boys use it in the summer time when they're haying out this way. In the winter it comes in handy as a place where the men can take a break from the cold."

"Will we be able to get inside?" she wondered aloud, hoping there would be a way to get warm once they reached the trailer. Her feet were so cold they were beginning to feel numb, and she was worried about David making this long trek in the snow and cold. He'd been through so much, and she hoped he wouldn't end up having to fight pneumonia or some such illness as well.

"Ted never locks it. There's nothing valuable inside, and the only people who would think of using it are folks like us looking for emergency shelter."

Two large, dark shapes soon loomed ahead and Chase picked up David who was now stumbling with every step. He lengthened his stride, and Kendra struggled to keep up. She wondered how he could move so fast, encumbered by both the heavy pack and David. They passed the haystacks, and Chase urged her ahead of him to the small wood and tin house set on wheels. It looked something like a covered wagon, but she was glad its walls weren't made of canvas. He pushed open the door and she stumbled inside.

Chase must have carried a flashlight in his coat pocket because he flicked it on before he set David down on what looked like a bed. Kendra looked around the small space and decided it held everything important. One end of the box-like room was taken up by a wide bunk and right beside her stood a small stove with a box of dry wood beside it. That was all she wanted—heat and a place to sleep.

Chase lost no time lighting a fire and as warmth seeped through the little stove's metal sides, she and David drew closer to it. They removed their gloves and stretched their fingers toward the faint warmth. The heat felt heavenly, and in a short time she removed David's boots and coat along with her own. The heat brought a tingling pain to their toes, and Kendra and David both winced as their feet began to warm.

They made sandwiches of the roast and rolls, and washed them down with juice while standing beside the stove, with the flickering flames from the open firebox their only light. It wasn't the Christmas dinner she had planned, but she relished each bite. And there was something satisfying about being together with Chase and David in the crude shelter, warmed as much by their sense of shared camaraderie as by the flames.

Before long she could see David's eyes beginning to droop. He looked as though a whisper might send him toppling over.

"Get him ready for bed," Chase spoke in hushed tones. "While I get a place ready for him to sleep."

Kneeling before Chase's backpack, she began pulling out the items Chase had so hurriedly stuffed inside it. Finding one of Chase's thick flannel shirts, she wrapped David in it while Chase pulled a thick, square package from his pack. He unfolded the package to reveal a tarp, which he spread across the lumpy, dirty mattress on the bunk. His sleeping bag was next.

"Here let me take him. He's already asleep, poor little tyke." Chase lifted the sleeping child from her arms when she had finished buttoning him into the shirt. Carefully he tucked David between the tarp and the sleeping bag, which he had unzipped and spread flat across the bunk forming a heavy blanket.

David mumbled a few words, and Kendra sat down beside him. As she soothed her hand across the boy's forehead, Rags jumped up on the bed and snuggled next to him. She hesitated, thinking she should make the dog get down, then decided it was all right this one time. Her mother would have had a fit over permitting a dog to come inside a dwelling, and she certainly wouldn't have allowed one to sleep with her or her sisters. But Kendra didn't care. Rags would help keep David warm, and they would comfort each other. David stirred, whimpering slightly in his sleep. Softly she began to sing the lullaby she'd sung earlier back at the bridge.

Chase picked up David's coat, thinking that if he rolled it up it would serve as a pillow. His hands stilled when he encountered several hard lumps. Gingerly he reached into the little pockets and drew out the carved baby, two little dogs, the donkey, and a sheep. He held them in one hand and thought about today being Christmas Day. Long ago another man had struggled to find shelter for a woman and a child. Had Joseph felt the same strong protective emotions that assailed him now? Had he known an inexplicable peace in his heart as well, when he'd looked into the faces of the woman and child when that shelter was found?

Chase slipped the make-shift pillow under David's head. Then he remained on one side of the sleeping child and examined the nativity figures that he'd cut, sanded, and polished for the boy as though he'd never seen them before. They seemed to be telling him something he had to strain to hear.

"They made him very happy." Kendra stopped singing to whisper. "I want you to know that even with all that's happened, perhaps because of all that has happened, this has been the most spiritual Christmas of my life."

He turned the carved dogs over in his hands several times and swallowed deeply. He wasn't accustomed to sharing his feelings. "It's been that way for me too," he finally said, his voice gruff.

She looked down at the figures in his hand. "Do you think Roscoe is really all right?" she asked softly.

"I hope so. Someone took a shot at Rags. That's why she came after us. Roscoe wouldn't leave the sheep no matter what, but he's also a lot more wiley than Rags. I hope he's found a way to stay out of sight." Chase admitted his concern for the dog left behind.

"Do you think those men are following us? Will they find us here?" she worried aloud.

"I think we're safe. I pretty well tore the bridge apart." He was quiet for several minutes, then he reached for his pack and pulled out the fudge. He wanted to tell her about what had happened on the bridge, but it was hard to find the words. He munched on the candy for several minutes, then looked over at her. She was almost asleep.

"Kendra," he called her name softly, and she gave a little start. "One of those men followed Rags. I saw him at the bridge with a rifle. I don't know if somehow he missed seeing me, or if a speck of Christmas spirit touched his heart, but I saw him turn away. Something I can't explain happened out there on that bridge. It was almost like a whole army of angels stood behind me when I faced that man. In my head I could hear other voices praying for that man to spare us. I'd already disabled the bridge, so I can't explain how Rags got across, I just know no man will be able to cross it. You can sleep tonight without worrying about being followed."

She murmured something unintelligible, and he went on, his voice hesitant, "This is the only bed, and we both need sleep. Do you think it would be all right if you crawled under the sleeping bag on that side of David, and I sort of scooted under on this side next to the dog?"

She didn't answer. She was already asleep. He pulled the sleeping bag over her shoulders and watched her snuggle closer to David. An odd sort of jealousy touched him. It wasn't really jealousy, just a strange longing for someone to snuggle close to him. Well, not just anyone—so maybe it was jealousy—but he couldn't help thinking how nice it would be to feel her cuddle close to him.

He arose from the bed and fed the fire a couple of heavy chunks of wood. Raising his arms, he pulled the last thick flannel shirt from his pack over his head, kicked off his boots, and returned to the bed.

He was exhausted, but still he lay awake thinking. Something he couldn't explain had happened out there on that bridge. He supposed some folks would say it wasn't a miracle, but in his soul he knew it was.

From a few feet away he could hear Kendra breathing. She was no ordinary woman. Saying she was attractive and well-educated barely scratched the surface in describing her. She'd done more to turn his lonely house into a home in the few days she'd been there than he could quite comprehend. He liked her gentle way of caring for David and her acceptance of his animals. Admiration for her courage in the face of adversity swelled his heart. A kind of rightness swept over him as he lay still, listening.

Today was Christmas Day, but down deep inside he figured it had been Christmas ever since he first saw Kendra struggling through the rain and snow with the boy in her arms. He wondered why the Lord would bless him with such a special Christmas when he'd spent fifteen years trying to forget the day. Even so, during his years alone on the ranch, he'd felt a gradual pull toward things spiritual, and his faith had grown as he studied the scriptures and learned to talk to God. Today was the day the world celebrated His Son's birth; was it possible God had chosen this day to let him know it was time for a rebirth in his own life?

CHAPTER 20

Kendra awoke to a light patter of rain on the metal roof of the camp wagon. Curling deeper in the warm cocoon her body had formed beneath the sleeping bag, she lay still listening and enjoying the warmth. All was quiet. She sat up and looked around. Gray light filtered through a small, dirty window telling her morning had come. David was still asleep curled tightly in a nest of shirts beneath the sleeping bag. He looked peaceful and trusting, as though all the fears of the day before were forgotten. There was no sign of Chase or Rags. A fire burned in the stove, and though the wagon wasn't exactly warm, it wasn't terribly cold either.

Feelings of gratitude filled her heart and she felt blessed. Such a short time ago she'd told herself she should be grateful her sisters wanted her to spend Christmas with them and she should be grateful for rain instead of snow when she'd had to change a tire. She'd spent a lot of time telling herself she should be grateful for this or that, but this morning there was no sense that she should force herself to be grateful. She truly was grateful for life, for warmth, for shelter, for David, and for Chase.

She climbed off the bed, making certain David was still covered, and donned her coat. It had dried overnight hanging on a nail behind the stove. One side was a little longer than the other, a button was missing, and it sported a number of stains. It looked nothing like the fashionable garment she'd purchased a week ago, and she didn't particularly care. She didn't feel much like the woman who had purchased the coat a week ago, either. Cameron and Katy would fuss and insist she buy a new coat. They'd offer to buy it for her, but right now, this morning a glamorous coat didn't matter at all.

Easing the door open, she climbed down a couple of wide steps to find a light drizzle instead of snow still falling. Puddles dotted the saturated land. To the west a few wide slashes of blue contrasted with trailing white clouds, hinting at a break in the stormy weather. The air smelled clean and new with a hint of hay and sage. She breathed in the aroma and felt almost giddy with the clean, new scent of survival.

"Good morning," Chase spoke from where he leaned against the side of the wagon. "Did you sleep well?"

"Actually, I did, though I hadn't expected to," she answered with a smile. Her heart lifted at the sight of him, seeing beyond the dark stubble on his face, his battered hat, and his torn and muddy clothes. It was still raining, but somehow she didn't mind. She'd come a long way from the woman who had complained of a flat tire in the rain such a short time ago.

"You were tired." An understanding smile accompanied his understated words before he went on to tell her, "I did a little checking around, and found Ted has a herd of cattle wintering pretty close to here. From the looks of these stacks, I'd say he's hauling feed for them from here. If we sit tight, someone should be along pretty soon. But if you'd rather keep moving, I suspect we're no more than six miles or so from the ranch house."

It was hard to believe they were that close to other people. The news was oddly disappointing. She should be shouting with joy to know they were so close to safety. Instead, she felt a strange stirring of disappointment. For four days her world had narrowed to just three people. Those few days had become her life. She'd experienced the greatest terror she'd ever known, been truly needed, laughed and played as she'd never done as a child, caught a glimpse of all her dreams, and known the most sacred Christmas of her life. It was almost as though she'd never truly lived until Chase had plucked her from certain death and carried her to his home. That other life, the one without Chase, seemed so far away and unreal.

Her heart did a crazy little tap dance as she looked at him, seeing past his heavy, sheep-lined coat and stained Stetson, to a man like no other she'd ever known. How could she explain her desire to be reunited with her sisters and assure them she was safe, to end David's family's suffering, and to know the bank thieves were safely locked in jail, while another part of her didn't want this adventure to end, because when it ended, she'd no long have an excuse to be with Chase. A word kept creeping into her mind, but it couldn't be. She was too practical and sensible. She'd known him less than a week; she couldn't have fallen in love with him. Could she?

Who was she kidding? She'd known for several days what she felt for him. Only she didn't believe love could happen that fast. There was a logical explanation for her feelings, her *imagined* feelings. She knew from all her reading that men and women who share an intense crisis together develop a heightened awareness of each other. She'd just have to be sensible about this, though sensible didn't have much appeal at the moment.

"If you'd like a few minutes privacy, you won't be disturbed over there between the haystacks," Chase informed her. "I'll just go inside and see if there's enough food left for breakfast."

He started to walk past her, then stopped when she placed her hand on his arm. "There's no way to express my gratitude for all you've done." The words sounded too stiff and formal. She wished there was a way to really tell him how much his rescuing her that first night, his generous sharing of his home, and the Christmas they'd spent together meant to her.

His eyes met hers, and she had the strange feeling that he understood exactly what she couldn't find the words to express. Something changed in the back of his eyes, and she felt an answering response deep inside herself. Slowly he leaned closer, and she felt a flutter of panic. Carefully, allowing her plenty of time to protest if she wished, he placed a hand on either side of her face. His thumbs lightly stroked her cheeks and her breath caught in her throat. Lowering his head, his lips briefly touched the corner of her mouth. She sighed and reached to place her hands on his shoulders and his mouth settled firmly against hers. No, she didn't feel the least bit like being sensible.

The kiss might have lasted two seconds or stretched out for minutes, she lost all concept of time. Rags whined, and Chase gently stepped back with a soft smile that lifted one corner of his mouth. "Go tend to business," he told her as he gently touched her chin with one long finger as though reluctant to sever contact. "I'll check on

David and see what we've got for breakfast." Her legs felt weak as she stepped away.

She had little time to dwell on Chase's kiss. David's voice reached her as she walked back to the camp wagon, and she saw Chase and David hurrying toward her. Chase winked at her as he passed her with the boy and pointed toward the west. As the two disappeared behind the haystack, she looked where he had indicated. There coming toward them was a flatbed truck.

She stood still, watching it bounce across the field, sending mud flying on either side as it moved closer. In minutes Chase and David joined her again. David was jumping up and down with excitement. The harrowing crossing of the night before seemed forgotten. Rags, too, seemed to have forgotten the previous night's ordeal. She leaped exuberantly against David, nearly knocking him down, before Chase ordered her to stay down.

"If we hurry, I think we'll just have time for the last of the rolls before they get here." Chase urged them toward the trailer. Was she mistaken or had she seen a hint of regret to match her own in his eyes before he turned away to climb the camp wagon steps?

In the sheep camp wagon, they quickly consumed the last of the juice and rolls. Chase and David finished off their breakfast with the few remaining pieces of fudge, and David held out the last small chunk of the roast to Rags. Over the occasional soft splat of rain on the roof, they could hear the truck coming closer.

It took less than a minute for Chase to roll up the sleeping bag and return the few items they'd used to the backpack. Kendra scanned the small space to see if they'd forgotten anything, then taking a deep breath, followed Chase and David out the door. Watching Chase test the knob to be certain the door closed tightly behind them, she felt as though a door was closing on more than the camp wagon.

The truck slid to a stop a few feet from where they stood waiting. They could clearly see the curious expressions on the faces of the three men in the cab.

"Chase, what are you doing here?" Ted Peters called, surprise in his voice, as he climbed out of his truck, quickly followed by two lanky cowboys. He stopped to eye Kendra and David. His eyes widened and his attention slowly shifted back to Chase, but before

Chase could answer the first question, Ted asked, “Who are your friends?”

“I’m David William Rolando,” the boy giggled. “You know me, Brother Peters.”

Ted’s eyes snapped to David and his jaw fell slack. “David Rolando? Guy and Vicki’s kid!” He reached for the child and swung him up in his arms. Moisture glinted in the stockman’s eyes, and it was several minutes before he could control his voice. “Can I assume you’re Ms. Emerson?” he asked at last, turning to Kendra.

“She is,” Chase answered for her. “As you can see they’re both safe, tired, and anxious to get home, but standing on their own two feet. The problem is, there are some boys back at my place that I’d like the sheriff to clear out, so I can get back there and feed my sheep.”

“Won’t take but a minute to get the sheriff on the horn.” Ted announced, grinning as though he might never stop. He set David back on his feet and stepped back to his truck. He returned with a cell phone and was already punching in the numbers before he rejoined them. He demanded to speak to the sheriff personally and when the law officer came on the line, he smiled broadly and started right in. “Sheriff, you’re not going to believe this . . .”

The two cowboys stood with their hands in their hip pockets, looking bemused and a little punch-drunk, as they listened to their boss talk to the sheriff. When he hung up the phone he turned to them, “Why don’t you boys see how fast you can load some hay and get the herd fed? There’ll be a couple of choppers here in about half an hour. One will pick up these folks and the other one will head on up to the Kirkham place. I’d like to be ready to help out, if it looks like they could use a little help.”

The men scrambled to do his bidding, and the rancher turned back to Chase, “Perhaps David and the lady might like to wait inside the truck where it’s warm. If you’d care to help me and my boys with the hay, we’ll be done before the sheriff gets here. Then we can drive almost to the sheep bridge and get there in time to back up the sheriff and get your stock fed. While we’re at it, you might fill in a few details, like how you happened to end up with Ms. Emerson and Guy’s boy.”

"Sure," Chase answered. "But we won't be crossing the sheep bridge. Just give me a minute and I'll explain." He took Kendra's arm and began walking toward the truck. The air felt thick and heavy. Speech was impossible.

CHAPTER 21

"Isn't it ever going to stop raining?" Becca pressed her nose against the glass. She sounded petulant and tired. Vicki didn't bother to answer. She felt as though gloomy skies and rain had become her whole life.

"The forecast is for clearing by midmorning," Guy told them as he joined them at the window. With one hand on each of their shoulders, he, too, peered through the glass, seeing little but rivulets of water streaming down the smooth surface.

"David isn't ever coming home, is he?" Becca sighed.

"Don't say that!" Vicki's voice was sharper than she intended. Becca burst into tears, and Vicki wrapped her arms around her. She didn't mean to take out her worry and frustration on Becca. It was only that she was so tired and scared. It had been five days now, and there hadn't been one hint of their son's whereabouts.

"Sh-h," she crooned as her own tears joined those of her daughter. "We can't give up. We have to keep believing and hoping."

"But what good does it do?" Becca pulled away from her mother to look back at her with despair clearly written on her face. "He's gone, and he's not ever coming back!"

"Come here." Guy put an arm around each of them and led them to the sofa. "Let's talk about this."

"Talking won't change anything," Becca stubbornly insisted.

"No, talking won't change anything, but it might help us put what has happened in perspective. First, we know Sheriff Hatcher is doing everything he can to locate David. And second, we know a lot of people are praying for his safe return."

"I don't think God is listening to all those people," Becca muttered under her breath, but Vicki heard her, and she knew Guy did, too. The possibility that they might never see David again in this life was more than she could bear, but neither could she stand it if this horrible experience cost Becca her trust in God.

"God always hears prayers," Vicki reminded Becca. "It's at times like this, when it appears He couldn't possibly be listening, that our faith is tried." When Becca merely looked puzzled, she went on. "It's easy to say our prayers and believe God is watching over us, when everything is going well. When we don't get the answer we want or when it takes a long time to get an answer, then we get angry and say He isn't listening or He doesn't care. But He *is* listening, and He does care. Sometimes we can't understand why an answer takes so long to come or why we get the answer we do. That's where faith comes in. God has His reasons for answering when He does and in the way He does. We have to remember, too, God didn't take David from us; two evil men did that." Just saying the words, she discovered, was a test of her own faith. It was becoming harder and harder to believe this nightmare would end, and that she would hold her son in her arms again.

"Do you think God is telling us no, that we can't have David back?" Becca looked miserable as she asked the question.

"It's too soon to know that," Guy spoke carefully. "The sheriff thinks the men who took him might still be close by. They might be stranded somewhere, just like so many cattle are, because of the flooding. He thinks if that is the case, they'll keep David alive because they might still need a hostage. If the robbers are stranded by flood water, David is probably cold and hungry, but otherwise safe."

"I don't want him to be cold or hungry," Becca wailed. "David gets really cross when he's hungry. If they don't have any food, he might kick and scream and those bad men will hurt him to make him be quiet. And what if nobody finds them?"

"I think they will," he spoke softly. "Last night after both of you had gone to bed, I sat up for a while reading the scriptures, trying to find some comfort there. Here it was Christmas and our home had never felt *less* like Christmas. I was reading in the Doctrine and Covenants of a time when the Prophet Joseph was in jail and about all of the terrible persecution he had to suffer. One verse seemed to speak directly to me. It said if the heavens should blacken and the elements combine to hedge up the way and it seemed that the jaws of hell gaped open to swallow Joseph, he should remember that those things were to give him experience and would be for his good. I thought of how it has rained so long here, and of how David's disappearance could be compared to having the gaping jaws of hell open after us. Right now it's hard to imagine that this experience might bring about some good. Then I read the next verse that reminded me that our Savior, whose birthday we celebrate at Christmas, suffered far more than even Joseph Smith did."

"They both died, Daddy," Becca reminded him, obviously feeling far from comforted.

"I know, Becca. I thought the same thing when I first read that scripture, but a voice inside me reminded me that they neither one died before their missions were completed. I felt impressed that David's mission in this life is not yet finished. Then I went on to read the last verse in section 122. Here, let me read it to you." He reached for the book lying face down on a table beside the sofa. His finger scanned the page until he found the place he wanted.

"When I read this, I felt the Lord was talking to me about David, not just to Joseph Smith. "*Therefore, hold on thy way, and the priesthood shall remain with thee; for their bounds are set, they cannot pass. Thy days are known, and thy years shall not be numbered less; therefore, fear not what man can do, for God shall be with you forever and ever.*" Guy closed the book and looked at his wife and daughter.

"With those words I felt the first peace I've felt since this began. I believe he's alive and we'll get him back," he told them.

"What does it mean about the priesthood?" Becca scrunched up her face in puzzlement. "David's too little to have the priesthood."

"He is," Guy agreed. "But I'm an elder and David is my son. The bishop, the elders quorum—in fact, the whole ward—has been praying for him. I think that entitles him to the power of the priesthood watching over him."

"Oh, Daddy," Becca leaned against his chest. "I've prayed and prayed and I really do believe Heavenly Father and Jesus are taking care of him, but I'm still scared."

"We all are," Vicki breathed against her daughter's hair. "We wouldn't be human if we didn't fear for him. I think that's more a symbol of our love for him than our lack of faith in God."

The strident ring of the telephone froze them in place. Recovering first, Guy dived for the wall phone hanging just inside the kitchen. Vicki and Becca grasped each other more tightly. Some sixth sense told them this wasn't a neighbor calling to check on them or to learn if they'd heard anything yet. They held their breaths, watching as Guy held the phone to his ear listening. His back was to them, and they couldn't see his face.

"Sheriff," he acknowledged the caller with a single word. He listened intently and Vicki saw his shoulders tighten as though bracing himself for what was to come.

"You're sure?" His voice sounded harsh, then he was quiet, listening.

"Yes, yes we can make it," they heard him say in response to some unheard question. Something in his voice caused their pulses to quicken. "Thank you." He set the phone back in its cradle, then continued to stand with his back to them, unmoving. Vicki saw his shoulders begin to shake and a sound reached her ears. Guy was crying! He never cried!

"David!" she screamed and ran toward him. He whirled about and caught her in a fierce embrace.

"They found him! He's alive!" Joy mingled with shock as he spoke the words in a hoarse shout. Tears streamed down his face. "The sheriff will pick us up in ten minutes to go get him."

"Alive? He's all right? He isn't hurt?" She sank against her husband's shoulder and felt her own tears begin to flow.

"David's coming home?" Becca sounded awestruck and began to weep when Guy nodded, his face raw with emotion.

Small arms slipped around Vicki's waist and she turned just enough to pull Becca into their embrace. All three faces, damp with tears, glowed as they held each other. Slowly they slipped to their knees and tears continued to fall as Guy whispered a quiet prayer of thanksgiving.

• • • • •

Chase helped Kendra and David climb inside the truck. He threw his pack in beside them, then stood awkwardly, not knowing what to say. Finally he mumbled, "When the truck is loaded, Ted or one of his men will drive it to where his cattle are waiting to be fed. I'll be in the back." He jerked a thumb toward the flatbed where the cowboys were already stacking bales.

"I want to help," David protested.

"Not this time, sport." Chase picked him up and set him in the middle of the truck bench seat. He reached for the seat belt and buckled it around the small form. "You stay inside with Kendra, out of the wind."

All while he tossed the heavy bales from the stack to the truck, Chase spoke in short bursts to Ted about Kendra's and David's harrowing experience, ending with the trio's flight across the sheep bridge. He didn't mention their Christmas celebration or the newly awakened emotions that had surfaced in the last few days. Those things touched him too deeply to speak of so soon.

The cattle were fed and they were almost back to the stacks when he caught a glimpse of not two, but three helicopters moving steadily toward them. The heavy throb of turning rotors filled the air and something akin to dread lodged in his heart. In a few minutes Kendra would leave; David, too. David, he would see again. If he didn't leave church the minute sacrament meeting ended anymore, he could talk to David and be sure the little guy was doing all right, but would he ever see Kendra again? Endless days of open skies and mile after mile of grass and brush stretched before him, no longer as the escape he'd once yearned for, but as a lifetime of bleak loneliness. He longed to turn back time and once more savor those moments when the three of them had been warm and happy, sitting around his kitchen table or pausing to pet Old Glory while the dogs leaped around them in the barn. He wanted to roll in the snow amidst laughter and barking dogs, and he wanted to learn how to make paper birds. He wanted to sit before a fire with a sleeping woman in his arms and the scent of cedar and pumpkin pie teasing his senses.

Chase straightened his back. It wasn't like him to get emotional. He had things to do. His stock needed to be fed, he'd have to talk to the sheriff and see if he could get a lift back to his place, and he'd have to make sure Tracy got a chance to look at Rags' wound.

Kendra choked back tears when the first people off the first helicopter were a thin, wiry young man followed by a tiny woman with long blond hair, blowing across her shoulders. She looked about hesitantly and raised her hand as though shading her eyes.

"Mommy! Mommy!" David shouted as he catapulted toward the couple. The man reached him first and swept him up. The woman's arms came around them both, then David leaned forward to throw his arms around his mother's neck. The three of them hugged each other, laughing and crying, and Kendra ached with jealousy. No, it wasn't really jealousy. Over the past days she'd come to love David as her own, but she'd never forgotten he wasn't her child. She could take joy in his joy. Feeling ashamed of herself for her momentary pettiness, she plastered on a bright smile and turned toward the man with a star pinned to his coat who loped across the ground toward her.

"Ms. Emerson?" He held out a huge rough hand and she grasped it.

"Yes, but please call me Kendra." She smiled up into his broad homely face, immediately warming to the man.

"Are you all right? Did those men hurt you in any way?" His concern was genuine and she caught a glimpse of the kind of man who enforced the law in a land as vast as several large cities, but who saw the scant human inhabitants as a small and close family—his family.

"I'm fine," she assured him. "Chase Kirkham has taken splendid care of the both of us."

"I'd like to ask you a few questions if you don't mind before we head back to town. There's bound to be reporters hanging around by the time we get back to Darcy." His tone was almost apologetic.

"No problem," she smiled back, and he led her to the haystack where a couple of bales formed a kind of bench. He indicated she should sit.

She answered the sheriff's questions as quickly and thoroughly as she could, then was hurried toward one of the choppers. She turned her head toward the other helicopters which bore military logos and had evidently been borrowed from the nearest air base. Her eyes searched for Chase among the men gathered around them. She found him standing with his back toward her and his head bent toward his dog. He straightened and turned, as though she'd called his name. Their eyes met and she hoped he'd come to her, but someone touched his arm and he turned back toward the group of men. As good-byes go, it wasn't much. A kind of melancholy settled in her heart.

The pilot took her arm and urged her to board. David and his parents were already buckling themselves in seats and David was talking a mile a minute. She stepped up, then paused when she heard Chase speak her name. Her heart accelerated. He had come to say good-bye, after all. With a jolt she realized that deep inside she was hoping he'd come to ask her to stay.

"Kendra," he hesitated, and she felt frustration grow inside her. He shifted nervously, clearly unable to put into words whatever he was thinking. It wasn't the first time she sensed he wished to say more than he could put into words. "I wish . . . If you . . ." Someone called his name, and he turned back to the man who had called.

"What about Rags? Can she go with you?" she asked, attempting to draw his attention back to her.

"I'll shut her in the sheepherder's wagon for now," he explained. "Ted called his wife, and she's on her way out here to pick her up. I'll feel better knowing Tracy is looking after her and seeing to her wound. She'll be okay until I can get the bridges fixed and take her home again."

"Isn't Rags coming with us?" David jumped from his seat and ran to kneel beside the open door. His parents both reached for him and he struggled to escape, intent on reaching the dog.

Chase put out his hand to stop the boy from leaping to the ground. "Rags will be all right," he promised. "She'll be home in a day or two, and if it's all right with your mom and dad, I'll bring her to town once in a while so you can see her."

David turned to his mother and she nodded. A bright grin spread across David's face as he looked down at the dog sitting at Chase's feet. "'Bye, Rags," he called softly. "Come see me soon and bring Roscoe."

David scrambled to his feet, but before his mother could urge him back to his seat, he threw himself at Chase. Tears sparkled in his eyes. "I lefted my stable and the king guys and everybody at your house." Tears rolled down his cheeks, and he clutched Chase in a fierce grip. "I love 'em. Will you take care of them for me? Roscoe can keep my angel in his stable place if he wants."

"Yes, David, I'll look after them for you. And one day soon I'll take them to town for you," Chase assured the child, and Kendra could see the silvery gleam of moisture in his eyes. She'd seen the bond develop between Chase and David and knew it was as difficult for Chase to tell the boy good-bye as it would be for her to do so when her turn came. But at least he would occasionally see the child and would be able to watch him grow up, she thought sadly. She would probably never see either of them again.

"What if the grinches smashed them?" David's question drew her attention back to the conversation between him and Chase. Recognizing his concern for the nativity pieces he'd left behind when they'd had to abruptly flee Chase's house, she thought about the little figures that had brightened Christmas morning for the three of them. The memory brought a lump to her throat, and she hoped with all her heart that the evil men who had forced them out into the cold on Christmas Day hadn't wreaked their vengeance on the lovingly carved symbols of peace and good will.

"They're pretty strong, so I'm sure they're okay." Chase really wasn't certain he would find the pieces intact when he returned home, but he'd carve new ones if those rotten skunks had harmed them. He patted the boy's back awkwardly. "You just remember what Kendra told you about that Whoville place."

The little boy swiped at his tears with the back of his mittened hand, and his smile returned. "Thank you, Chase. My heart had the bestest Christmas." He gave Chase a fierce hug.

"Mine did, too." Chase spoke to David, but his eyes met Kendra's over the top of the boy's head. "The very bestest," he murmured softly for her ears only, and she wished their good-bye weren't quite so public.

"Chase!" a voice called impatiently.

"Good-bye, Chase," Kendra managed to whisper. With two rough, calloused fingers he lightly brushed her cheek. Then he was gone.

CHAPTER 22

Instead of flying them directly to Darcy, the helicopter—which she realized belatedly was actually a medical life flight transport—took them to the regional hospital twenty miles beyond Darcy. Enviously she watched Guy and Vicki Rolando point out landmarks to their son as he excitedly bounced in his window seat, reveling in the unexpected treat of a helicopter flight. She felt an almost maternal pride in the boy when he asked if they could stop to get Becca so she could ride in the chopper, too.

Vicki explained that Becca was staying at the Sheriff's office with the dispatcher because no one had been certain there would be enough seats for everyone on the helicopter. Also the sheriff hadn't wanted to take any chance of exposing Becca to danger if the men who held up the bank were in the vicinity. That reminded David of the ride in the bank robber's van, and he rushed to tell his mother how there hadn't been enough seats, and he and Kendra had to lie on the floor, and how they bounced against the sides because they didn't have seat belts.

"I told them you said I always had to have my seat belt on," he explained earnestly to his mother. "But there weren't enough, so Kendra held me tight so I wouldn't get bumped." Vicki wiped her eyes and hugged him once more. Over his head her eyes, filled with gratitude, met Kendra's and Kendra had the strangest feeling she and David's mother were meant to be friends.

"How come we have to go to the hospital?" David asked as his dad pointed out the facility as they began their descent.

"Sheriff's orders!" the pilot laughed. "He said you were both to be taken to the hospital for checkups before David could go home and Ms. Emerson can be on her way."

"Nobody shooted us!" David protested. "Just Rags." Kendra saw the way both of David's parents winced at the mention of someone shooting the dog. Eagerly David told them all about the brave little dog and the mean men who hurt her. Watching, she saw the expressions on the Rolandos' faces change from anger, to sympathy, then to laughter. Behind the changing emotions she caught glimpses of their pride in their son and their joy at his return. The love binding the little family was unmistakable and brought an ache of envy to Kendra's heart.

The checkup didn't take long. A nurse put antiseptic on a couple of scrapes Kendra had received during their trek to safety, and put a bandage on a small blister on one toe. Almost everyone in the emergency room of the small hospital found a moment to stop by and ask about her ordeal. Feeling self-conscious over her sudden celebrity status, she didn't tell them that she'd never think of those five days as an ordeal.

When she finally got a chance to call Katy to let her know she was safe, they both ended up crying. As Kendra wiped away the tears, she chided herself for becoming a crybaby. It wasn't like her to be so weepy.

"I think I'll turn around and go back home now," she told her sister. "Christmas is over, and . . ." Kendra tried to justify returning to Salt Lake rather than continuing on to California for the remainder of the holidays. She hadn't wanted to spend Christmas with her sisters this year, and now she felt even less desire to travel to California. She simply wanted some quiet time to think and reflect about all that had happened. Perhaps her heart needed a little time to heal as well.

"Oh, no. We saved Christmas for you. You've got to come," Katy insisted. "If you don't feel like driving, Kurt and Bob can meet you . . ."

"I'm fine. Really I am, it's just that . . ."

"You've got to come. We won't believe you're really safe until we see you for ourselves," Cameron came on the line and tearfully added her appeal. "Kurt said if you're not here by tomorrow, he's coming after you." Reluctantly Kendra agreed to continue her trip.

When she got off the phone, she made one more call. Sheriff Hatcher had said her bishop had called every day. He'd added that her home ward had held a fast for her the day before Christmas and she wanted them to know she was safe.

After hanging up the phone, she stared around the hospital corridor, not really seeing the bedraggled holiday garland and wilting poinsettias with which someone had attempted to add a little cheer to the medical facility. Feeling lost and unsure of what she should do, she wandered aimlessly down a corridor. Her car was back in Darcy. As was her purse. She didn't even have money to call a cab. She'd had to call collect to reach Katy.

"Ms. Emerson." She looked up to see a woman dressed in a sheriff's department uniform coming toward her. "I thought you might need this." She held up Kendra's purse. Kendra moved quickly toward the deputy and accepted the bag with a smile of gratitude. Surely getting her purse back was the first step toward returning to normal life.

"Your car is in the hospital parking lot," the officer smiled again and held out her keys. "You can be on your way as soon as you like, though I need to make certain of where you can be reached. The county attorney may want you to return to testify."

"That won't be a problem," Kendra assured the deputy.

The officer carefully recorded her home and work addresses and telephone numbers, as well as Katy's phone number.

"Thank you for looking after my purse and for bringing my car," she told the woman. "Now I just need to return to Darcy to pay the mechanic, then I'll be on my way."

"Oh, the mechanic won't accept payment. He said to tell you it's on the house and to have a merry Christmas," the deputy informed her.

"Oh, but . . ." she attempted to protest.

"It's all over town what you did for little David Rolando. The mechanic's wife is David's Primary teacher. There's no way he'll let you pay for repairing that tire," the officer assured her. "There won't be any problem with coming back for the trial, will there?"

"No, I'll come," she agreed, then added, "It sounds as though there will definitely be a trial. Has there been any word yet? Have those men been arrested?" She wanted to ask if Chase were safe, but she didn't.

"Yes, they've been arrested. No shots were fired; the men gave up when they realized they had no other option. They're being transported to the county seat and will be in jail before much longer. You needn't worry about them anymore." She smiled reassuringly.

"Did Mr. Kirkham return to Darcy with the sheriff?" she couldn't resist asking.

"No, the sheriff took his statement at the ranch, so he could stay there and take care of his stock." Changing the subject, she added, "I'm sorry your visit to our town caused you to miss Christmas."

Oh, but I didn't miss Christmas, she wanted to protest. *I had the very "bestest" Christmas ever.*

"Kendra!" David ran down the hall to where she stood talking to the female deputy. His leggings and the well-padded look of Chase's thermals under his pants were gone. His parents followed, looking apologetic.

"We're through here," the woman officer laughed. "She's free to go anytime she likes."

I don't want to go at all, her heart cried.

"Are you going away?" David appeared disappointed.

"Yes, my sisters and their families are waiting for me in California. Remember, I told you about Katy and Cameron and my nephew and nieces?"

"Yes, but I want you to stay," David declared stoutly.

If he only knew how much she wanted to stay, she thought sadly. Aloud she said, "It's time to get on with my life. My sisters and their families are waiting for me."

"I don't want you to go," he said in a small voice, and she knew if she didn't distract him, they would soon both be crying. She'd cried enough, and she didn't want to leave David crying.

"Well, David," she said, hugging him one last time, "did the doctor check all your toes to make sure you didn't freeze one?"

"And my ears and my nose! He said I'm a lucky little boy, but I'm not, 'cause they said you were going away." He stuck out a petulant bottom lip and refused to be distracted.

"I have to go, David, but we can still be friends. I could write to you, and when the bad men's trial is held, I'll come back for a few days," she promised.

"But I want you to stay," he persisted.

She held him close, then blinked back tears as she stood. She forced herself to smile. "Just think, in a little while you'll be home. It'll be Christmas all over again when you see what Santa brought you."

"Did Santa Claus bring me a train?" Hope lit his face as he turned to ask his parents. Before Guy could hide the stricken look on his face, Kendra knew the train wasn't waiting for David. She wished she hadn't said anything to remind him of his earlier Christmas dreams. She'd only meant to take his mind off her departure.

"Honey . . ." Vicki touched her son and Kendra bit her lip, knowing how difficult the young mother found it to disappoint her son. "Santa Claus doesn't have enough trains for every good little boy. Perhaps it will be your turn next year."

A look of sadness crept across David's face, but he didn't cry or protest. Kendra suspected he wasn't unfamiliar with disappointment. She'd noticed earlier that Vicki's coat was shabby and Guy's pants were threadbare. From David's guileless chatter the past few days, she knew Guy was out of work and that Vicki was worried about her elderly father in Denver. A wave of sadness passed over her as she considered the miserable Christmas this struggling young couple must have endured.

"There are quite a few surprises under the tree waiting for you to open them," Guy spoke jovially, trying to lighten the mood. He didn't fool Kendra. She saw the regret in his eyes and knew how much he dreaded disappointing this son who was lost, then found.

Kendra lightly touched Vicki's shoulder and asked her to accompany her down to the desk to checkout. Once out of earshot she asked, "Would you give me your address? I'd like to send David a postcard occasionally. I grew quite attached to him while we were together."

"Of course," Vicki took the paper and pen Kendra pulled from her purse and scribbled quickly. "I don't know what to say," she spoke quickly as she handed the paper back to Kendra. "I want to thank you for taking care of David. In my mind are all these terrible pictures of what might have happened to David if he'd been alone. He's my son, and I love him, but I know he's stubborn and can create a lot of noise and disruption when he gets upset. His sister, Becca, worried constantly that he'd make his captors angry, and they'd do something terrible to him to make him be quiet. I think you saved his life."

"He saved mine, too." She clasped Vicki's thin hand between hers. "I had made up my mind those men would have to kill me to get me into that van, but when I realized they were holding David, too, my focus changed to one of protecting him. Out there on the high desert; lost and cold, I would have given up without him. Through all that happened, his sweet, persistent faith in the message of the Savior's birth sustained me."

Vicki wiped tears from her eyes. "I'm sorry," she apologized. "I've turned into a watering pot since all this started."

"It's all right." Kendra hugged the other woman. "You have a very special son and you have a right to be a little emotional right now."

"Excuse me, ma'am," a voice interrupted. "Would you pose for a few pictures with the Rolando boy?" She looked up to see a young man with a camera. He quickly identified himself as a reporter for the local paper.

"Go ahead," the nurse at the desk urged. "He'll be through asking questions and give you a chance to be out of here before reporters from the city arrive. He'll write a good story, too."

She agreed to his request and the Rolandos gave their permission for David to be photographed, then she answered a few questions. She let David do most of the talking. When the reporter finished, she prepared to leave before any other reporters discovered her whereabouts.

Vicki turned to Kendra and the two women embraced before Kendra walked away. She turned back once to wave to David. He ran after her and held out his hand. There on the palm of his little hand was a small grubby lamb. "You don't have any sheeps, so you keep him," he said, thrusting out his lip, and Kendra knew two things. First, that giving away one of his lambs was about the hardest thing the little boy had done since the moment he'd been abducted, and second, that she would break his heart if she refused to accept his precious gift. Slowly she reached for the tiny offering. Taking a clean handkerchief from her purse she carefully wrapped it around the small figure. Lovingly she placed it in her pocket, knowing she would cherish forever this small link with Chase and David.

"Thank you," she whispered. Quickly she kissed his cheek and hurried out the door before she could lose her ability to hold back the tears. Looking back at the hospital doors for one last glimpse of the child she'd learned to love, she saw him, standing with his nose pressed to the glass, watching her as she drove away. Tears streamed down her cheeks and she made no effort to wipe them away. She couldn't see well and the glass was between them, but she suspected David was crying, too.

Kendra meant to find the interstate and leave town immediately, but when she reached the freeway entrance, she drove right past it. There was something she had to do. As she approached Darcy she noted that it didn't look much different than it had the night she'd found herself stranded there waiting for a tire to be repaired. She passed the service station. Next to it was a boarded-up building with faded letters above the door proclaiming a business that had gone the way of so many once-thriving small-town businesses. There was the bank, and across the street was Decker's Department store. There was an ample number of parking spots in front of the store. Pulling into one, she shut off her engine and grabbed her purse.

Once she reached the sidewalk, she stared at the large plate glass window for several minutes. Someone had replaced the window and the two trains still raced through the tiny village. Some of the trees looked a little worse for wear and there were small chips in some of the ceramic roofs, but the trains rushed on. Memories crowded in of the times when she'd stood with her hand in her father's watching trains like these and the night she'd stood in the rain comparing the merits of the two trains with David. She shouldn't have had to grow up without a train and neither should David.

She hurried inside. "Excuse me, miss," she spoke to the first clerk she saw, a fiftyish woman with a bouffant hairstyle that had long ago gone out of style. "I'd like to buy the red train in the window."

The woman looked startled, but she smiled and bustled toward the window. Kendra suspected the little store didn't get the crowds of after-Christmas shoppers she was accustomed to seeing in the malls in Salt Lake.

She watched the clerk carefully remove the pieces from the window and place them in a box. Each length of track and the little bridge were separated, then added to the box as well. Impulsively Kendra added a train station and the clerk contributed a package of plastic trees.

"I'd like it gift wrapped, please," she told the woman.

"Birthday?" the clerk asked as she automatically reached for a length of blue birthday wrap.

"No, definitely Christmas," she responded with a smile. The clerk paused to look at her, then her smile widened. "You're that lady, the one who was kidnapped with the little Rolando boy!"

Kendra smiled, but she neither acknowledged nor disputed the clerk's statement. The woman continued to smile as she reached for shiny red foil paper. With great care she wrapped the box holding the train and stuck the biggest gold bow she could find on the top. All the while she worked, she kept up a running commentary on how worried everyone had been and what a relief it was that everything had turned out so well.

"My grandson plays with Becca, that's little David's sister, and I can tell you that child has been just sick with worry. She's a little worrier anyway, awfully serious for her age, if you know what I mean. Anyway, she's been just miserable, blaming herself for not watching the little scamp closer." She paused to give the bow a slight tug, making certain it was secure.

Kendra had never even seen Becca, but she felt she knew her. David had talked about her, revealing a great deal and she suspected David's pleasure in his train would be dimmed if his sister didn't get her wish as well. Remembering David had said his sister was looking at the Sports Barbies when he'd gotten bored and wandered outside for a better view of the trains, she went in search of a Barbie doll with her own athletic wardrobe for Becca and when she found her, had the doll wrapped too. The clerk chattered cheerfully about the mess they'd had to clean up after their display window had been shattered and how thankful they were that little David had escaped and that the security guard was getting well.

After handing the salesclerk a bill to tip the deliveryman if he could get the presents to the Rolando house within a half hour, she turned away.

"Oh, Miss?" The clerk called after her. "I know for a fact the Rolandos never lock their door. I'll just have Matthew—he's my son—take these things right inside and leave them under the tree. "That poor family. They were so upset Christmas morning, they didn't even open their presents. Quite a few folks have been slipping a little something under that tree all day today."

Though she felt her heart was breaking, Kendra felt a kind of peace, too. David would be all right. People in this little town cared about him and his family. She reached for the door and pushed it open.

"Don't you worry, none, dear," the clerk called after her. "You just have a good drive to California. "I'll take care of everything."

Feeling like she might break down and beg to stay if she lingered another minute, she hurried to her car. As she backed out of the parking spot and turned the car toward California, she wondered who she could beg to allow her to stay. The clerk would think she was crazy. The Rolandos didn't need her and neither did Chase. She had to remember her life was ahead, not behind her.

CHAPTER 23

Roscoe leaned against his owner's leg demonstrating more affection than Chase had ever known the old dog to display. His hand sank into the thick fur on the animal's head and together they watched the helicopters lift off. He'd been tempted to go with them, to see Kendra one more time, but his sheep needed to be fed, and unless he missed his guess, there was an old ewe who would be dropping twins before the new year. Good Old Glory, she always jumped the gun.

"I missed you, Roscoe." He patted the dog's head. The animal had no way of knowing how relieved Chase had been when the old dog had come creeping out from under the hay wagon to greet him when he'd arrived with the sheriff's men. He crouched down beside the dog and rubbed the dog's head between his hands in an affectionate gesture. "But I was glad I had one friend here looking out for my woolies." The dog whined as though asking a question, and Chase chuckled. "You miss Rags, don't you, boy?" He smiled remembering how disdainful the old dog had been when he'd first brought the pup home from the Peters' ranch. Rags had been quick and anxious to please. At first, she'd seemed to annoy the older sheep dog with every move she made, but gradually the older dog had accepted the younger one, and Chase credited Roscoe more than he did his own skill, for turning Rags into the remarkable stock dog she'd become.

"You're not the only one missing someone," he admitted to the dog what he'd had trouble admitting to himself. "I miss a certain lady, too. Your lady will be back in a few days, but I likely won't ever see Kendra again."

Slowly he and the dog walked through the barn, finding a little damage, but nothing he couldn't fix in a few days. He'd already checked on his sheep, but once again he stepped outside to examine them more closely. The house was next. He'd been putting that off. The barns were hard enough, but he wouldn't be able to step inside the house without thinking of Kendra.

He supposed he'd never know what had happened on his ranch while he was gone or why one of the men had shot Rags. His sheep were fine, though the ones penned in the barn appeared a little nervous. The damage to the barn indicated a skirmish between the trespassers and the dogs. He could only surmise that when the strangers had entered their domain, the dogs had interpreted their presence as a threat to the sheep. They may have attacked the intruders and the men had retaliated.

As he saw to his animals and replaced a board that had been broken out of the side of his barn, he found himself listening for Kendra's musical laughter and David's incessant questions. He smiled sadly when he found David's angel on a ledge next to Old Glory's pen. He thought about taking it with him to the house, then decided to leave it where David had placed it.

When he finally went inside his house, his heart sank. Where there should have been warm memories of an unforgettable Christmas, there was only mud and debris. He took offense for Kendra's sake at the muddy tracks across the floor she'd kept spotless during her short stay. The cupboards and refrigerator had been ransacked with no trace left of the cookies and pies she'd baked. Dishes that once held salads and vegetables were piled haphazardly on every surface.

He looked around the dirty kitchen and thought of how he'd looked forward to that Christmas dinner more than any other meal he could remember in his life. He was a passable cook himself if he stuck to basic stuff, but Kendra's cooking was the best he'd ever tasted. It wasn't just the food; it was her, he admitted. Sitting across from her at the table made everything taste better. At least those miserable grinches, as David called the robbers, hadn't got any of the fudge. Between David and himself, they'd eaten all of that themselves.

His chest tightened and anger exploded as he viewed the

Christmas tree sprawled on its side with Kendra's origami birds and David's stars crushed beneath careless heel marks. If he weren't a grown man, that sight alone would make him want to sit down and bawl. Instead he reached out to stand the tree back in its place. As he lifted the heavy trunk, he spotted the stable and the little figures he'd carved for David. Stooping to gather them up, he discovered they were undamaged. Carefully he placed them on the mantel, which hadn't been disturbed. As he did, he wondered if he were being a bit melodramatic to imagine that David's tree had somehow saved the boy's single Christmas present.

Methodically he picked up the trampeled birds and stars. He smoothed them the best he could and placed them in a careful pile on a table. The floor needed sweeping and dishes should be returned to the kitchen. It occurred to him that just as the toppled tree had kept the little stable safe, perhaps Kendra's cooking had protected the three of them, too. Those men hadn't expected to be stranded, far from food and supplies. They were probably ravenously hungry when they'd stumbled on the house and found it filled with Kendra's good cooking. Just the thought of those men eating Kendra's pumpkin pies, the mashed potatoes with gravy, and the Waldorf salad he'd glimpsed in the refrigerator raised his hackles. They'd probably gorged themselves, and in their greed delayed coming after him and their former hostages, giving them the needed precious time to make their escape.

Muddy tracks led to the bedrooms. The thieves had obviously availed themselves of the beds, and the drawers hanging open with their contents spilling on the floor told him the trio had searched his home for valuables and helped themselves to his clothes. Since he didn't have anything of great monetary value other than his land and his sheep, he knew their search had been fruitless. Objects like the diamond ring he'd given Carol years ago and his mother's gold brooch were still in a safe deposit box back in Phoenix. He'd never found a need for expensive trinkets on his remote sheep ranch.

It took him most of the night to restore his house to order. When at last he finished scrubbing floors and washing bedding, he sank into the comfortable chair beside the fireplace. He leaned back and pictures of Kendra filled his mind. He saw her kneading bread, stirring fudge, rocking David, and patting the woolly heads of his sheep.

He heard her laughter as she flung snow his way, and he saw her face relaxed in sleep with dark circles beneath her eyes. He closed his eyes and saw the wonder in hers when he kissed her.

With a groan he rose to his feet and leaned wearily against the fireplace mantel. He should have asked her to stay, but this was no life for a woman. Women needed malls and pretty clothes, parties, and things like that. He'd actually known Kendra less than a week, but something deep in his soul told him he would miss her forever. Gripping his hands together he leaned his head against the rough stone and prayed. *Father,* he pleaded. *Keep her safe, and help me to know what to do. Please give me the strength to be happy with my sheep and my ranch again. My dreams of a family died with Carol and our baby, but Kendra and David taught me to want again. Now I can't stop thinking about Kendra and how it would be if she were part of my life, too.*

He stood still for long minutes after he finished praying. As from a long distance he heard the wind blowing and heard the rustling sound of rain striking the window. Slowly, moving as silently as Rags and Roscoe, peace stole into his heart. He opened his eyes, and there inches from his nose, the sock Kendra had hung for him, still dangled from the fireplace undisturbed. In all the chaos the intruders had made of his house, one small thing, last touched by Kendra, was undisturbed. He reached to touch it, to touch something she had touched, and found a lump in its toe. He reached inside to pull out a small tinfoil wrapped package. Opening it, he found a morsel of fudge, and suddenly he wanted to laugh or cry. He wanted to hug Kendra. Somehow she, with more than a little help from David, had taught him to believe once more in hope and joy. This last small reminder of the most memorable Christmas of his life, seemed to whisper there could be other Christmases.

Suddenly, he sobered. Kendra had told him she lived in Salt Lake, but he didn't know her address and Salt Lake was a good-sized city. He didn't know how long it might take to find her, and lambing season was about to begin. He couldn't leave the ranch to go looking for her.

She would likely have to testify at the trial. He'd probably see her then, and if he still felt the same . . . but he didn't want to wait that long. Sometimes lawyers managed to put off their clients' trials for months, maybe even years. Discouragement weighed him down until he remembered the sheriff would have her address. Sheriff Hatcher would have to know how to contact her.

His euphoria was short-lived. Until he got his bridge rebuilt, he had no way to get to town. Even when he got the bridge rebuilt, his old truck might not make it that far. Why hadn't he replaced that truck when it first started acting up? He could certainly afford to. He'd spent some money building his house when he first came here, but since then he'd spent little.

If the truck wouldn't run, he'd get to town if he had to walk, he suddenly determined. But what about his sheep? He couldn't go off and leave them alone for several days, even after lambing season was over. By the time he could leave the ranch or find a way to get Ted to send her a message for him, it might be too late. He couldn't even be sure she'd be interested once she got back to the city. He pondered the question far into the night, then did what he should have done in the first place. He knelt and explained his problem to his Heavenly Father, concluding with a request that if it was the Lord's will that he and Kendra should be together, He would show them the way that they might be reunited.

CHAPTER 24

Huddling together on the back seat of the car, Becca and David whispered and giggled together. It was a pretty good indication of how much the children had missed each other Vicki thought. Instead of fighting as the two often did when they were both in the car, Becca listened in raptured awe while David told her about Chase Kirkham's sheep. From the corner of her eye she saw him pull something from his pocket to show his sister. Turning her head for a better view, she saw two carved dogs, each about two inches tall.

"They're so cute!" Becca reached out to touch them.

"I got this, too." David proudly produced a small doll.

"It's a baby! Let me hold it. Please!" She begged to hold the tiny figure in her hand and David generously handed it to her.

"It's Baby Jesus," he informed her importantly.

"Where did you get it?" Becca asked as she cradled the wooden infant in the palm of her hand.

"Chase made it. He made lots of stuff for me for Christmas. And Kendra made candy. We walked in the snow, and I picked out a big Christmas tree bush. Chase chopped it down and me and Kendra made stars and birds for decorations. I helped him feed his sheepies 'cause he said he needed a helper. Taking care of sheepies is fun, but Chase said it's hard work when he has to do it all by himself." He seemed to consider for a minute, then he took the baby back and gave Becca the small donkey.

"Chase has a horse, not a donkey," he explained to his sister. "It's at Brother Peters' barn because it's going to have a baby. He said I could see it after the baby horse gets borned."

"I want to see it, too," Becca said.

"I'll ask him," David responded confidently.

Vicki wiped a tear from her cheek. How could she ever thank Chase Kirkham and Kendra Emerson for all they had done to make Christmas special for David? She wished there had been time to ask Kendra more about those days when her son had been missing.

Almost as though they were afraid to lose physical contact with one another, they all four held hands as they made their way up the walk to the house. Guy pushed the door open, then stopped in astonishment. A mountain of packages littered the floor beneath the Christmas tree, and stacks of covered dishes cluttered the kitchen table and filled the little house with enticing aromas. A wave of appreciation for the people in their small ward filled his heart; they had worried and prayed with his family through the entire ordeal. Now they were silently sharing their joy.

"Is it still Christmas?" David gasped as he looked around at the unopened packages beneath the tree.

"I think so," Vicki laughed. Her eyes were on her son, not the heap of gifts. Getting David back was the best gift she'd ever received.

"Can we open them?" Becca squealed. The child who had listlessly ignored her gifts the day before had disappeared completely. She rushed to the tree and began separating the gifts into stacks for herself and David. There were even a few with Vicki's and Guy's names on them.

"Go right ahead," Guy encouraged them both, and because today felt more like Christmas than the previous day had, he stepped to the tape player and inserted a Christmas tape. In seconds the strains of Christmas carols filled the little house. He took Vicki's hand and sat beside her on the sofa to watch the children dive into the pile of gifts. Neither he nor Vicki felt much interest in opening the gifts with their names on them. Watching the children was enough.

Soon Christmas wrap littered the floor and filled every corner. The stacks of books and toys beside the children grew at a tremendous rate until at last, David reached for a large red package. At the same time his sister picked up a glittering green foil package, wrapped with exquisite care. While Becca carefully picked at the tape, reluctant to tear the pretty paper, David grasped the red foil and ripped. In seconds a large cardboard box sat on the floor before him. He lifted the lid to stare in shock.

"What is it, David?" Guy started toward him.

Almost reverently he lifted the bright red engine from the box. The look of rapture on the little boy's face brought a lump to Guy's throat. He wished he'd been the one to fulfill his son's dream. The thought was petty, and he dismissed it abruptly. He was just glad someone had given David the train. With sudden insight he knew who had done so. He turned to Vicki, a silent question in his eyes.

He found his wife smiling through tears as she watched Becca fit a tiny tennis racket in a doll's small hand. Becca's eyes glowed with wonder, and once again he found himself swallowing and taking a deep breath before he could speak.

"Kendra Emerson," he whispered huskily, so only Vicki could hear. She nodded her head in agreement.

"She asked for our address. She said she wanted to write to David," Vicki mouthed back.

"We owe that woman a lot," Guy spoke thoughtfully. "Probably more than we'll ever know."

"I wish Kendra could see it," David said. "She likes trains, but she had to go to California. What's this car for?" He held up a train car for his dad to see.

"That's a box car," Guy explained. "Box cars are used for hauling lots of things for long distances."

"Rags and Roscoe could ride in it." He proceeded to put his toy dogs inside the little rail car, then pulled them out and set them in an open car. "They can see better," he explained. He looked thoughtful for moment, then spoke with a touch of sadness. "Chase made lots of sheep and king guys with camels. I wish I could give them a ride on my new train."

"Let's go get them," Becca suggested.

"Can't," David informed her as he connected sections of track. "Chase hasn't got any bridges anymore." He paused then added with a note of hope. "Brother Peters gots an airplane. He could take us."

"We'll find a way," Guy promised. "But not today. Tomorrow, I'll have a talk with Ted Peters."

After space had been cleared to spread out the train track and David had given Barbie and the carved dogs a dozen rides, they moved to the kitchen where they sampled and nibbled until no one could hold even one more piece of pie.

"I never got two Christmases before," David announced happily as he licked the back of his fork before setting it back on his plate. Looking sad for a moment, he added, "Kendra made pies, but we didn't get to eat them. Do you think those mean guys ate them? I bet they did," he answered his own question with a scowl. Then his expression turned sympathetic. "Chase will be sad. He really wanted to eat Kendra's pie; he said she was the bestest cook in the whole world. Maybe we could save him a piece of ours?" He looked hopefully toward his mother.

"As soon as we can figure out a way to get it to him, I'll bake him a whole pie of his own," Vicki promised. Baking a pie would be a terribly inadequate thank you for all Chase had done to shelter and protect her son. She'd be happy to keep him supplied with pies for the rest of his life!

"I think he'd like it best if Kendra baked it, but she's gone away to California." He looked pensive for a moment, then he laughed. "She said it doesn't ever snow at that place in California where her nieces and nephew live, but Santa's sleigh is magic so they get presents anyway."

"You received nice presents," Vicki reminded him, "and we had more rain than snow."

"Kendra said getting a happy heart is the best present. I got a happy heart two times." He jumped from his chair to run to his mother's side where he threw his arms around her and hugged her tightly. She hugged him back, unable to put into words the happiness in her heart.

That night as they knelt for family prayers they took turns expressing their gratitude for David's safe return while he seemed surprised that everyone had worried so much about him. "I was okay the whole time," he assured his mother. "Kendra carried me when I got tired and on the scary bridge. Chase didn't let anybody hurt us."

When the children were tucked in bed, Guy smiled to see Becca holding her doll in the crook of her arm just as he'd expected, but it was the two wooden dogs and the little carved baby that held the place of honor on David's pillow. He had a hunch David's first

Christmas celebration had been much more pleasant than theirs had been. At least it had started out that way. He had a strong feeling David had been crossing that "really scary bridge" about the time Vicki had awakened from a nightmare in which she'd seen him in danger. Feelings of love and gratitude brought a lump to his throat.

At last he returned to the living room to find Vicki staring pensively at the Christmas tree. She looked tired, yet almost radiant from some inner light.

"Whenever people talk of the Christmas they remember best, I'll always think of this one," she murmured softly, and he noticed she held the small, red train engine in her hand. "Kendra said David had only gone outside to see the trains better, and that they had just turned to come inside to find us when the window was shot out."

"The sheriff said they would have both died out there on the desert if Chase Kirkham's truck hadn't stalled," Guy added.

"Close as I can tell, Chase and Kendra did everything possible to protect David and give him a nice Christmas," Vicki continued to speak. "Of all the things I imagined David was going through, it never once occurred to me that two good people were taking care of him."

"Not only Chase and Kendra," Guy continued thoughtfully. "He had some heavenly help, too. With all he went through he could have easily been traumatized. Instead he seems to have some keener insight into the real meaning of Christmas."

"You're right. He talks about Chase's barn and livestock as though they were part of the Christmas story. And he's certainly attached to those little figures Chase gave him. He's even named the dogs." Vicki leaned her head against her husband's shoulder. "I think I've gained a new insight about Christmas and especially about giving, too. As I've pieced together what Kendra told me and the events David has talked about, I suspect there were many times David could have been killed or injured. If he'd been alone out there on the desert, or if Chase's truck hadn't stalled, if those horrible men had discovered Chase's house sooner, or if something had gone wrong on that bridge that obviously frightened him, I shudder to think what might have happened. I'll always believe our prayers and the faith of our ward family had something to do with his survival."

"I believe that, too," Guy told her.

"It's funny, but before David was kidnapped, I resented anyone giving us anything. My pride saw helpful gestures as charity. Now all I feel is gratitude for so many people's love and generosity. Almost everyone in our ward family not only contributed time, food and gifts, but they shared their faith and prayers. I've never felt so loved before, either by God or by other people," she concluded.

Guy held her for a long time and she experienced a closeness that brought another level of joy to her heart. They still faced a lot of problems, but a quiet warm assurance filled her mind. They would be all right. They had each other.

When Guy spoke it was to return to the little carved animals David so obviously loved. "Those little wooden dogs he carries around make me wish we could give him a real puppy. A boy his age ought to have a dog." Guy finished on a sigh, telling her his thoughts had turned to their precarious financial situation.

"There won't be room for a dog when we move back to Denver." Vicki's voice couldn't hide the sorrow she knew the move would bring them all. "And speaking of Denver, I'd better call Dad. I should have done it hours ago. He'll be worrying until I do."

"Go ahead," Guy released her so she could make the call. He settled on the sofa and found himself going over in his head all the things David had told him about his unexpected adventure. It was hard getting past the anger that boiled to the surface each time he thought of the men who had stolen his son, then left him to die in a winter storm on the desert. But no matter what their intentions had been, David hadn't been injured, and in time he would forgive them. There was no room in his heart to cling to hatred and anger.

Gradually his thoughts drifted to Chase Kirkham. He'd always considered Kirkham a little strange. He lived like a hermit on a remote ranch out in the hills with his sheep. He only came to town once or twice a month to pick up groceries and whatever supplies he needed for his ranch. He camped just outside of town over night, then went to church the next morning before heading back out into the desert. He usually only made it to sacrament meeting, though he'd been staying for priesthood meeting more often the past few months.

He'd heard a lot of speculation about the scars on the man's face and hands, but no one seemed to know just what his story was. From what David had said, he'd guess the boy hadn't even noticed the scars. Kirkham had been awfully good to David, and without his quick thinking to get them off the ranch and destroy the bridge behind them, he feared both David and that Miss Emerson would have likely wound up dead. He had a lot to thank Chase Kirkham for. There was a great deal he needed to thank God for as well.

Something else the boy had said stuck in his mind. Chase needed a helper. He wondered if the man really was looking for someone to help with his sheep, or if those had only been kind words to make a little boy feel wanted and needed. David had obviously loved everything about Kirkham's sheep ranch. He couldn't blame him. He, too, loved this open land with its endless miles of brush, jagged hills, and deep washes set against a backdrop of stark, boulder-strewn mountains. He didn't relish leaving it to return to the city.

He looked up when Vicki walked back into the room. She looked troubled, so he reached for her hand and drew her down beside him.

"Has something happened? Is your father all right?" he asked.

"He's fine, though he broke down and cried when I told him about David. He said he'd been fasting for his safe return. Of course, I cried again, too," she admitted. "The problem is, he's completely over the broken hip and getting around fine, but because of his age the doctor doesn't want him going back to living alone. All these months in a convalescent center have drained his savings, and he can't afford to rent an apartment again. He'll be released in a few weeks, and he has nowhere to go. He wants to come live with us."

"He knows I'm out of work, doesn't he?" It hurt for Guy to ask the question. "You know I've no objection to him living with us. I've always thought highly of him and would enjoy having him around. The kids would, too, but . . ."

"I know. I explained all that. I thought he might go to my brother in Florida, but he said Daniel's company is sending him to South America for eighteen months. He begged to be allowed to just come live in the trailer. He said if he had a place to stay, he could get by on his social security checks and maybe even help us a little."

"The pitiful little bit of social security he gets won't go far. He spent most of his life trying to take care of his father's small farm and drawing minimum wages on the side to get by, so he only gets minimal payments. Anyway, I've been thinking we might have to move into the trailer ourselves when the rent comes due next month," Guy said as he shook his head and wondered what to do. Vicki's father was a good man, who had worked hard all his life to take care of his family, and he certainly deserved their care now. They couldn't turn away the old man, but how was he going to support one more person?

"Guy, I told him we'd work something out. David's return was a miracle. His life was at stake, and this problem isn't nearly as terrible as the prospect of losing David. All problems seem smaller than what we've just gone through. Somehow, I know we can work it out. No problem can be so awful as losing part of our family." Vicki spoke with an earnestness that made him ashamed of his own doubts. They'd find a way. Besides, he had an idea.

CHAPTER 25

The miles passed with Kendra nearly oblivious to the scenery. She stopped for gas and something to eat at a truck stop and found herself shivering in her disreputable-looking coat.

"Is there someplace I could purchase a coat?" she asked the cashier who took her credit card.

"I dunno," the girl looked at her with a dubious expression on her face. "We only have the kind of jackets truck drivers like, but you can look." She waved her toward the far corner of the small store.

The choice was small and tended toward leather or something that looked like leather and bright nylon jackets. Kendra finally selected a bright blue one with the logo of some trucking company on the back and a stitched truck where the left breast pocket would be on a more formal coat. Her arrival at her sister's house wouldn't be the fashion statement she once expected to make, but at least she'd be warm.

In Los Angeles she stopped again to hastily finish her Christmas shopping, then drove on to the beach community where Katy and Bob had purchased a home overlooking the ocean two years ago. The sun was shining and a warm breeze brought the tangy smell of the ocean inside the car. She'd long since shed her trucker's jacket. She turned into the driveway and brought the car to a halt. Before she could open her door, she heard her name called.

"Kendra!"

"Aunt Kendra!" Her sisters, their husbands, and three children ran to meet her and engulf her in hugs.

"Are you all right?" Katy gasped through her tears.

"We were so worried," Cameron echoed.

"Did they hurt you?" Bob's eyes showed genuine concern, while Kurt vowed they'd "talk" later.

"I'm fine." She laughed as she returned their hugs.

It didn't take long for her brothers-in-law to carry her luggage and the gifts she'd brought into the house. The children ran in excited circles, constantly under foot, until Kendra started handing out packages. While the children played with their new toys, Kendra opened the gifts her sisters had saved for her. Amid exclamations of delight and a lot of happy laughter, Kendra acknowledged she'd missed her sisters. *But not the way you miss Chase*, a sneaky little voice whispered in the back of her head, making it impossible not to compare this Christmas celebration with the one she'd just spent with Chase and David.

The afternoon flew by so quickly it was bedtime before she had time to stop and think again. She slept the sleep of the exhausted and awoke to sunshine pouring through the window. She knew immediately she was alone. No small boy snuggled against her side and no tall cowboy waited in the kitchen. Bleak loneliness filled her heart. How could she continue on with her solitary life? Were those few joyous days all she would ever have of being part of a family again?

Cameron arrived shortly after noon and it soon became apparent her sisters were planning an extravagant dinner party. It wasn't until she'd finished dressing for the party that she discovered a doctor friend of Kurt's had been invited to be her escort for the evening.

Kendra stared at Katy in astonishment. "You set me up with a blind date?"

"It's not exactly a date." Cameron came to Katy's aid. "He's a very nice man, and we just thought we'd introduce you and see what happens."

"Nothing is going to happen," Kendra spoke evenly. This was a new twist. Her sisters had never played matchmaker before. "I don't want to meet your Dr. Chambers," she told them.

"Come on, Kendra. It's just for dinner, and we'll be here, too," Katy implored.

"Besides it's too late to back out. He'll be here in twenty minutes." Cameron practically gloated as she delivered the *coup d'etat.*

Kendra sighed in defeat. Coming to California had been a mistake. Her sisters and their families had been wonderfully kind. They'd done everything imaginable to make her visit special and let her know how much they'd feared for her safety. It irritated her though, that she couldn't make them understand that being stuck on a sheep ranch sixty miles from the closest highway hadn't been the ordeal they imagined it had been.

Katy and Cameron had let her know right from the start that they were planning an elegant Christmas dinner to make up for the one she'd missed. They'd even bought her a beautiful, much too expensive dress that made her eyes look more blue than gray. But not even a new dress and an elaborately decorated dining room or the wonderful aromas drifting from the kitchen could generate any excitement in her heart. She couldn't imagine any dinner that would suit her more than the roast-filled rolls and fudge, washed down with fruit juice that she'd shared with Chase and David on Christmas Day. And she certainly didn't feel any enthusiasm for meeting any man who wasn't Chase, no matter how wealthy and important he might be.

Dr. Brent Chambers turned out to be a handsome man with a charming sense of humor, and he seemed perfectly at ease at Katy's dinner table. He was in his early forties and really quite attractive. He glanced at her admiringly several times during the evening, leaving her no doubt he was interested. Strange, just a week ago, she would have been pleased and flattered by his attention, but now she couldn't help comparing him to her cowboy. Though polished and better looking than Chase, Brent somehow didn't measure up in her eyes.

Picking up an empty breadbasket, she carried it to the kitchen for a refill. Cameron followed her.

"Give him a chance," Cameron whispered as she refilled a pitcher of sparkling punch.

"What do you mean?" Kendra whispered back. "I'm being polite, I laugh at his jokes, I talk, I've even listened to him recount his adventures in South America where he does volunteer service among indigent tribes."

"You know what I mean! Most of the time you're a thousand miles away."

"I'm tired. I told you I wasn't ready for this," Kendra defended herself.

"I'm sorry, Kendra. Katy and I don't mean to nag; we just want you to be happy. We wouldn't have the life we do if you hadn't made so many sacrifices for us. We both met our husbands while going to school, and we were only able to go to BYU because you worked so hard to pay our tuition and insisted we take seminary and keep our grades up in high school." Cameron threw her arms around her sister for a quick hug. "When those horrible men kidnapped you, we weren't only afraid of what they might do to you, but we felt so guilty. Because you've given us so much, you've missed out on all of the things that make our lives happy. We can't stand for you to be all alone after all you've done for us. Besides if you hadn't been alone in that horrid little town, those men would never have taken you. Please, please, just try."

"Okay," Kendra sighed. "I'll try." *Whatever that means,* she added under her breath.

She returned to the table, forcing herself to concentrate on Brent. He really was entertaining. She found herself genuinely enjoying his sense of humor, and she found his humanitarian service easy to admire. She wondered fleetingly why he was still single. He certainly seemed to have all the attributes that attracted women. She wished she could be one of those women. Falling for Brent should be so simple, but for her something vital was lacking, even though she didn't know what that something was. Each time she looked at him her mind conjured up a man with a scar crinkling one side of his face and a Stetson pulled low, almost obscuring eyes that spoke to her as though they had a voice of their own. She had to forget Chase, she reminded herself. He had been kind and generous, but he was content with his solitary life. He'd given no hint that he was interested in sharing his life with her or any other woman. Besides she could just imagine Katy's and Cameron's reactions if they suspected she cared anything for a man who ran a remote sheep ranch!

When Katy and Cameron began clearing the table, she jumped up to join them, only to have Katy suggest that she show Brent the beach behind the house. Her face flamed red. Why did her sisters have to choose now to blatantly push her toward a man who could only be as embarrassed as she felt? She stood awkwardly, uncertain of how to deal with her sisters' obvious manipulation, until Brent took her arm and propelled her toward the patio door. He reached for a shawl draped across a chair, just before stepping outside. Casually he placed it around her shoulders.

The night was cool, though nothing like the biting cold of a northern Nevada night. She couldn't help wondering if the sky was clear over Chase's ranch or if the rain still continued to fall.

Pointing out the path leading from Katy and Bob's back yard down a twisting path to the beach, she led the way. Brent didn't speak, and she couldn't think of anything to say. After a few minutes of walking in silence, Brent laced his fingers through the fingers of her left hand, and slowly swung their interlocked hands together as they walked across the damp sand. It should be so romantic, she thought—a moonlit beach, a handsome man, and faint music drifting from the homes above the beach. But she found herself wondering whether Chase's old ewe he kept in the barn, the one he called Old Glory, had delivered her lamb.

"I'm sorry Katy embarrassed you," Brent spoke after a few minutes. "If you don't want to be alone with me, I can take you back."

"It's not that," Kendra spoke in a low voice. "I think you're a very nice man; I just don't like being manipulated."

"They love you. I think you're very lucky to have sisters who care so much about you." She was probably being overly sensitive, but she thought she detected a hint of pain behind his words.

"Do you have sisters who would like to run your life?" she asked only half jokingly.

"Not sisters. No brothers either. I was an only child, but I always imagined it would be nice to have a brother or sister to take some of the heat." He smiled down at her.

"Aw, the Demanding Parent Syndrome," she said the words with a hint of laughter in her voice.

"You'd better believe it," he laughed back openly. "My old man had his heart set on me becoming a rocket scientist, and I could only muster enough brains to become a heart surgeon."

They laughed together and walked on companionably, discovering they enjoyed the same music and had read many of the same books. They shared glimpses of their childhoods, and she discovered he'd married young and his wife had left him when she discovered how demanding of his time medical school became. He'd joined the church four years ago after a six-month stint in Guatemala with a doctor from Primary Children's Medical Center in Salt Lake.

At last they stood on the sand, watching silver-edged waves roll smoothly toward them, to break apart mere feet from where they paused. The moon lit a golden path across the water. Never once had she imagined herself in such a romantic setting with a handsome, congenial man beside her. Perhaps her sisters were right. She should try. Her days with Chase and David had taught her one thing; she didn't want to live alone any more.

"Kendra," Brent touched her hand. "I'd like to see you again. There's a little theater I know that's doing a revival of *You Can't Take It with You.* I could get tickets for Friday if you'd like to come with me?"

She paused only a moment before saying, "Yes, I think I'd like that."

• • • • •

Kendra struck her hands together, joining the thunderous applause at the end of the play. It had been a good performance, at least the parts she'd actually watched. Her mind had a disconcerting tendency to stray to rain-drenched sagebrush and a man with rain-plastered hair, running and sliding toward her with a look of determination and fear on his face, a man who calmly chopped peppers and onions to add to eggs and ate fudge as hungrily as a small boy, a cowboy who raised sheep and carved exquisite nativity figures.

"It's not far to the restaurant where I made a reservation for dinner." Brent's voice brought her back to the present and she rose to her feet. He took her hand and led her through the crowd to where he'd parked his car. As he held the door for her, she slid inside, her hand brushing the rich leather. Immediately, her mind flashed to a cracked seat and a scratchy blanket that smelled of horses and dogs.

Making an effort to stay focused, she listened to Brent talk of his jungle clinic and the upscale city office where he split his time. He told her of the home he was thinking of buying in Monterey and commiserated when he spoke of being tired of apartment living. It didn't take long to recognize that for all his busy life, he was as lonely as she was.

After he took her back to Katy's home, Kendra lay in bed unable to sleep. Bob and Katy had still been up and had acted disappointed when Brent didn't accept their invitation to come in, but had brightened when Brent told Kendra as he was leaving, "I'll pick you up for church about a quarter to one."

She felt confused. Brent was everything she'd always thought she wanted in a man. He was a member of the Church, intelligent, attractive, kind, devoted to helping others, and he made her feel comfortable in his presence. He planned to buy a home only thirty minutes away from her sisters. Why didn't she feel more excited about his obvious interest in her?

A knock sounded at her door. Before she could answer, Katy called, "You're not asleep are you, Kendra?"

"No," she tried to keep a sigh out of her voice.

Katy opened the door and made herself comfortable on the side of Kendra's bed.

"I'm so glad you and Brent are getting along so well," Katy enthused. "Cameron and I have both been praying you would meet and marry someone really wonderful. When Kurt told us about Brent, we just knew you two were right for each other."

"I don't know, Katy." Kendra tried to stem her sister's enthusiasm. "Brent's very nice, but—"

"He's perfect!" Katy crowed. "He's not only a member of the Church, but he's as handsome as any Hollywood star. He dresses better than any other man I know, even nicer than Bob. And his practice is in Los Angeles, so if you marry him you'll be close enough so we can shop and do so many fun things together."

"Whoa, talk of marriage is rather premature," Kendra protested.

"Don't be silly; it's never too soon to think about marriage. Besides if you plan to have a baby or two, you don't have any time to waste." While Kendra spluttered helplessly, Katy hugged her sister and twirled toward the door. "I'll invite him to stay for supper after church tomorrow. Even though it's New Year's Eve, it's Sunday, so that lets out a real party," Katy rambled on. "I think a nice supper for just us three sisters and our men would be perfectly suitable." She waved airily and was gone.

So Brent is perfect? Perfect for whom? her mind asked of no one once her sister was out of sight. Suddenly she felt like a little girl again standing in a toy store watching the trains race around in circles, wanting the train, but knowing she'd get a doll.

Brent accepted Katy's invitation for supper after Church, and Kendra found herself annoyed by the lavish dishes her sisters set on the buffet. The food was delicious, but she would have preferred simpler fare. After dinner Katy and Cameron once more maneuvered Kendra into a moonlight stroll on the beach with the handsome doctor.

This time he led the way and when the path leveled out he walked beside her. She didn't protest when he caught her hand and held it as they drifted slowly along the beach.

At last he paused beside an old pier and turned her until she faced him. "I like you," he told her, and the corners of his eyes crinkled in a becoming way. "I like you a lot." He bent his head until his lips just touched hers. She backed away as though she'd been burned.

"Sorry," he said, his tone sincere, but not hiding his dismay at her reaction.

"I'm sorry, too," she ducked her head, feeling foolish. She'd overreacted.

"Too soon?" he arched a brow.

"No, I don't know. It doesn't feel right," she practically stammered.

"We could keep trying until I get it right," he teased, and she felt her face flame.

"I'm sorry," he said again. "My ego is working overtime. I've known from the moment Katy introduced us that you didn't really see me. You've only been going through the motions because your sisters would be hurt if you didn't. There's someone else, and why you're not with him is what has been puzzling me since the first evening we met."

"Oh, dear," Kendra covered her face with her hands. "You really are a nice man, and I didn't mean to . . ."

"What? Lead me on?" Brent winked and picked up her hand again. "I don't think you did. I've enjoyed the time we've spent together, and quite frankly, I expected that first evening to be dull, and was pleasantly surprised to find it otherwise. I've taken blatant advantage of a sympathetic ear ever since then."

"I wish I could . . . like you . . . that way. It would be so much simpler. I mean I do like you, but . . ." He laid a finger across her lips.

"Say no more. We shall agree to be friends, and nothing more." He walked a few more steps, leading her by the hand. When he spoke again, it was to ask, "So who is this mysterious man who has captured your heart, but is foolish enough to let you go off to strange places without him?"

She hesitated answering. She had no claim on Chase and telling someone else of her foolish heart's vain imaginings could possibly shatter her fragile dream. Yet something about Brent's gentle teasing urged her on. "We really haven't known each other very long," she stammered, suspecting she wasn't making a lot of sense. "You know I was kidnapped off the street in a small Nevada town on my way here. There was a man who rescued me." Hesitantly she told him about the man she'd mistakenly assumed to be a cowboy. "I don't think he feels the same way about me that I do about . . . Oh, it wouldn't work out anyway. Katy and Cameron shudder every time I mention him. Cameron says she can't even imagine being stuck for five days in such an awful place with no one but a man who raises sheep. Katy said—" She stopped with an almost childish gasp of delight.

"Oh look!" She pointed to a cove just ahead of them. Boats bobbing on the water near the wharf looked like decorated Christmas trees. A few moved in a delightful sway of color across the dark water. Fireworks exploded in the sky.

"Happy New Year!" Brent whispered softly and for a moment she thought he was going to kiss her again, but he didn't.

"David would love this!" she exclaimed unthinkingly.

"David? Is that your mysterious, absent lover's name?" Brent murmured in her ear.

"Goodness no! David is the little boy who was kidnapped with me. He's only five." She launched into the tale of how David came into her life, and inadvertently found herself telling him more about Chase than she intended. When she finished, Brent looked at her pensively. After a moment he spoke. "You're quite a woman. I could envy your sheepherder."

"Chase isn't a sheepherder! He's a rancher!" Kendra hotly defended Chase's status.

"He herds sheep, doesn't he?" Brent's eyes sparkled with mischief, and she found herself joining in his laughter.

"Actually it's his dogs that herd the sheep," she laughed.

"Sorry again," he said at last. "Your sheep rancher is a lucky man."

When she looked hesitant, he tucked her arm in the crook of his elbow and turned to start the trek back. His laughter was gone, and he spoke in an unexpectedly serious tone. At once she knew his words held great personal meaning. "Don't relegate him to a lovely memory. Go after him. Once I loved a special woman, but she came from a different culture, she wasn't well educated, and by our terms she was terribly young. I was afraid she'd be unhappy in my world, and I knew I couldn't live in hers. I thought the only noble thing to do was give her up. I walked away, thinking I was saving us both from years of heartache and embarrassment. For ten years I've been lonely and afraid of life. I've concentrated on my career, and I've made a lot of money, but I've never forgotten her, though I lost touch with her. Ten months ago I found her again."

"Was she happy to see you?" Kendra asked timidly.

He gave a short bark of laughter. "She hates me. In fact she called me 'a stupid pig.' And you know she's right. I don't know about the 'pig' part, but I certainly was stupid. My 'poor little peasant' worked her way through medical school and is now a top pediatric surgeon in her country. I let what my friends and colleagues might think of our relationship keep me from loving her. Her mother—a tough old bird if I ever saw one—was with her when I saw her and she said her daughter hates me because I stole her child-bearing years."

"You what?" Kendra stopped to stare at the man who walked beside her and talked so nonchalantly about his lost love.

"Honest, that's what she said. Where she lives, women marry young and give birth to half a dozen children long before women here finish going to school."

"Was that the daughter's real reason, or the one her mother gave?" Kendra asked.

"Do you think that's why she called me a stupid pig? Because I believed her mother?" Brent quirked an eyebrow as though he were considering a new possibility.

"Her mother probably wants to be a grandmother and she blames you because her daughter fell in love with you. Choosing not to marry someone else, she went to school and became a doctor instead of having the home and children her mother thought she should have," Kendra speculated.

"I hadn't looked at it like that," he mused.

"I doubt the daughter regrets going to school and becoming a doctor," Kendra added.

"Do you think she might be happier working with other people's children than having a family of her own?" There was a touch of alarm in his voice.

"How old is this woman?" Kendra demanded to know.

"Probably about fifty, but she doesn't look a day over ninety," Brent responded, deliberately misunderstanding her.

"No, the girl, the pediatric surgeon." She almost stomped her foot. He knew perfectly well she wasn't asking about the girl's mother.

"Must be close to thirty by now, at least twenty-seven or eight." He smiled, and she nearly hit him.

"Thirty isn't too old for babies, so unless you're making this whole story up, you should catch the next plane to whatever backwoods country she practices in and marry her." She surprised herself with the vehemence of her advice.

"Do you think there's a chance she still loves me?" he asked suddenly serious.

"Of course, she still loves you," Kendra responded. He grinned and wrapped his arm around her shoulders in a brotherly gesture.

"And you, my dear lady, need to learn a thing or two about sheep," he told her. "To begin with, the smelly creatures have a penchant for turning maternal the way lemmings jump into the sea. Once one gives birth, they will all jump onto the band wagon in a frenzied rush to turn your sheep rancher into a nonstop, around-the-clock midwife. And this is just the time of year the madness begins. It'll be months before he comes up for air, so unless you don't wish to see him until summer, you'd better jump on your own plane." Suddenly he was serious again. "I made a regrettable mistake when I quietly backed away because I thought the obstacles were insurmountable. We could have worked everything out if I'd had the courage to try. I should have told Maria how I felt, and we should have decided together what to do about our feelings. Don't make the same mistake I did." He finished on an imploring note.

If only it were that simple. It wasn't in her nature to boldly pursue a man. But Chase wasn't just any man. Brent's words swirled around in her head. He'd ended his romance because he'd assumed Maria wouldn't fit into his lifestyle, but he hadn't given her a chance to make that choice for herself. Was she letting Katy's and Cameron's view of what her life should be, keep her from going after what she really wanted? She'd never told her mother she wanted a train. Her sisters didn't know she hated "dry clean only" dresses, pantyhose, and high heels. She'd always accepted without argument that her mother and sisters knew what a woman should want from life, then she'd quietly resented them for expecting her to be just like them. Over the years she'd adopted a more formal manner of dress than she really felt comfortable with because she knew it was expected of a woman in her profession. She'd learned to ignore her own tastes and desires in favor of what her sisters would choose or what she believed was expected of her. But it didn't mean she loved her sisters any less if she chose a different life from theirs. They would always share the important things—love of each other and the gospel.

Suddenly she knew what she wanted and it didn't include a house in Malibu or shopping trips with her sisters. Just this once she was going to do something wild, something *she* wanted to do.

"Come on." She took Brent's arm and began leading him back the way they'd come. "We both have to be up early in the morning. You have a ticket to buy, and I have a late Christmas present to send."

CHAPTER 26

After almost a week of cleaning up and repairing his house and barn, Chase realized it was New Year's Eve. He sat in his chair listening to the radio and feeling dissatisfied with his life. Another year was ending and a new one beginning, but he didn't feel the surge of hope and excitement with which he'd once faced each new year, nor did he feel the indifference with which he'd faced each one for the past fifteen years. Was it just because he was older, or was there more to it than that?

His mood hadn't been the best since Kendra and David had gone. At first he'd blamed it on the lack of opportunity they'd had to really say good-bye, but that didn't quite cover it. He'd probably feel the same if they'd had all the time in the world for a nice leisurely good-bye. The truth was, he finally admitted to himself, he was lonely. Not just plain lonely. He was lonely for Kendra. Sometimes he thought about going to Salt Lake and looking her up after the lambing was over, but then he'd think about her being a city woman and figure he'd just be wasting his time.

The wind picked up and he could hear ice rattling against his windows. The new year was coming in with a raging blizzard. When the news program went off the air, he picked up his scriptures and tried to read for a while, but his thoughts kept returning to Kendra. He wondered where she was and what she was doing tonight. He drifted to sleep, then woke up still thinking of her as the announcer on the radio wished everyone a happy new year.

He did something he hadn't done since last summer. Getting up off his chair, he went to his bedroom to pray aloud. He couldn't tell

Kendra, and Roscoe didn't seem too interested, but he had to tell someone how he felt about the woman who had unexpectedly spent Christmas in his home. And he wanted to ask Heavenly Father to watch over her and help her to be happy.

New Year's Day he awoke to nearly a foot of snow and more still coming. For two days he struggled through knee-deep snow to take feed to his sheep and to keep their water tanks free of ice. Finally on the third afternoon, the skies cleared and a warm wind began to blow, leaving puddles in its wake. By nightfall, he dragged his weary body back to the house for a few hours sleep. Unless he missed his guess, he wouldn't get an uninterrupted night's sleep. Glory's plaintive bleating warned her time was near. He fell asleep to the sound of water dripping from the eaves of his house.

He slept for a few hours, then bundled up for a trip to the barn. He'd been right about Glory and with the dawn two small, wet lambs, one after another, drew their first breaths and sidled up to their mother for their first warm breakfast. When he felt everything was under control, he started for the house, only to be drawn back by the frantic antics of a young ewe. He decided he'd better get her inside the barn.

Chase slapped the side of his pants and Roscoe moved to the right. It was the young ewe's first lamb, and she was being recalcitrant about moving into the barn. Her agitation seemed contagious and soon the whole herd was stirring restlessly. At first the ewe seemed to consider confronting the dog, but Roscoe would have none of it. In minutes with a little direction from the savvy dog, she finally edged toward the pen where Chase held open the gate. Once she was inside Chase closed the gate panel and inspected her carefully. She was one of Old Glory's offspring and she looked like she was going to take after her mother by giving birth early. It wouldn't be many hours before a third lamb would be sheltering in the barn.

He hoped another ewe giving birth wasn't a sign lambing season was about to begin. Old Glory's lambs always seemed to do well, but most lambs who arrived early had a hard time, and if the weather forecast he'd heard on the radio earlier this morning was right, they were in for another blizzard tonight. The puddles dotting his yard would turn to ice and be hidden beneath a new layer of snow.

As he stood, he caught sight of the little angel David had left on a ledge over the soon-to-be mother's pen. He'd looked at it quite often since he'd found it there, and each time he decided to leave it where the boy had placed it. If David thought his stable ought to have an angel, it was okay with him. He turned toward the door and stopped at the sight of a figure blocking the light. His muscles tensed before he recognized Guy Rolando standing in the doorway outlined by the early morning light. Rags had arrived as well and stood a few feet away happily rubbing her head against Roscoe's neck. The old dog seemed more than happy to have his partner back.

"Brother Kirkham?" The younger man spoke hesitantly, then his words gushed forth as though he were racing the clock to get them all said. "I hope you don't mind, but something David said led me to believe you might be hiring. I haven't had a lot of experience with sheep, but I'm willing to work hard, and I do know something about growing hay and building things."

"How did you get here?" Chase stared at him in astonishment.

"Ted Peters is my home teacher. He stopped by last night to make sure we were all right. I mentioned that a package had come for you from Miss Emerson. I needed to get it to you, and I was also hoping to be able to talk to you about a job. He offered me a lift to within a mile of your sheep bridge. This morning I rode out with him, and he set me up with a pile of boards, a hammer, and some nails. The dog came along, too. Ted said she was yours, and that if I'd just follow her she'd lead me right to you."

"You repaired the sheep bridge?" Chase asked incredulously.

"Well, yes. It looked like the only way to get across. I didn't get the rail fixed, but I could do that easily enough another time." There was a hopeful lift, almost a question mark, at the end of his sentence.

"Come on to the house, and we'll discuss it." Chase led the way, stopping briefly to pat Rags before he left the barn. Once inside the house he offered Guy breakfast. While the two men ate, Chase's thoughts kept straying to the package from Kendra the other man had mentioned though he didn't see any sign of it.

"I had a good job up until October," Guy was saying. "When the feed yards west of town closed, I was laid off. I'd hoped to find work around here, but I haven't had much luck. My family likes it here and we would really like to stay if we can." He ended again on a hopeful note.

"I'm a long way from town out here." Chase spoke of what he thought might be a problem. Admittedly, he'd thought a time or two about hiring someone to help out, but he hadn't gotten around to seriously considering what would be involved. A reluctance to share his solitude had been the main stumbling block. Now he discovered that no longer mattered. In fact, he really didn't want to be alone anymore, and his ranch really had reached the point where there was too much work for one person to handle alone. Possibilities began to stir in his mind, only to be quashed when he remembered Guy's family.

"I have been thinking of hiring a man to help out, but you've got kids. How would they get back and forth to school?" He found himself exploring the possibility in spite of his reservations.

"Ted's kids and a couple of his hands' kids are taught at home by his foreman's wife until they're old enough for high school. She's an accredited teacher and works closely with the local school district. They're just fifteen miles away, and Ted said Becca and David would be welcome there. Until your bridge is repaired or if the weather's bad, Vicki can help them with their homework and see that they don't get behind. Once your bridge is fixed, she could drive them over and pick them up, so I wouldn't have to take time off."

"What about church? Don't you teach the Elders Quorum class on Sundays?" Chase continued his questions.

"Just on the fourth Sunday and Vicki helps in the Primary, but we don't mind driving that far once a week." Guy responded.

It was sixty miles to the highway and another seven or eight into town, but suddenly that distance didn't seem as insurmountable as it once had to Chase. If he had a dependable truck, it wouldn't be bad at all.

"Sometimes even with the bridge where it belongs, the roads or weather keeps me from making it into town," he pointed out in an attempt to be fair.

"I know, and Church is important to us, so those times we couldn't make it, we'd have to hold our own meeting and have lessons for our kids." Guy seemed to have thought his offer through, Chase mused.

"What about housing? Have you got that figured out, too?" He felt a growing excitement, which he carefully hid. If the Rolando family moved to the ranch, he could see David every day and watch him grow to be a man. Even more important, he could leave the ranch for a few days once lambing was over. He could head for Salt Lake to look up Kendra. Was Guy Rolando the answer to the prayers he'd been offering for more than a week?

"We have a trailer we lived in when we were following the oil drilling rigs," Guy answered the question Chase had asked aloud. "It's small, and it needs a little fixing up, but it would do. We can't afford to pay rent anymore, so we were planning to move into it next month anyway. Vicki's father is coming to live with us soon. It'll be a little crowded, but if you'll let us move it out here, it'll work out fine." Guy's face reddened and Chase suspected the man was having a difficult time speaking of his financial troubles.

"That might not be necessary," Chase responded thoughtfully. "On the other side of my hayfields, there's a rock house that needs a little modernizing. I'll provide the materials if you do the work in your spare time. It only has a couple of bedrooms, but if you're handy with tools, you should be able to fit another couple of bedrooms into the attic. I lived there when I first bought this place, and I only installed rudimentary plumbing because I didn't want to put too much into that house when I was planning to build a new one here. The bank robbers holed up there for a few days, and I don't know what kind of shape they left it in."

Guy's face lit up. "I don't mind fixing it up. In fact, I'd enjoy doing it."

"Okay," Chase grinned. "It's a deal. How soon can you start?"

They discussed salary and spoke of the work involved. Chase invited Guy to move into his spare bedroom until the bridge was finished and Guy could find time to make the old rock house habitable. They shook hands and agreed Guy would start in a couple of days, as soon as he had a chance to tell his wife his news and pick up some supplies and building materials for both the house and the bridge. Chase wrote out a letter to Bishop Samuelson, who owned the hardware store, authorizing Guy to charge the needed materials to Chase's account.

"Oh, I nearly forgot." Guy paused, before putting his coat back on. He pulled a brightly wrapped Christmas present from his coat pocket and handed it to Chase. "This came for you yesterday afternoon. Sister Decker brought it over. She said it was from Kendra Emerson." Chase took the package, turning it over thoughtfully in his hands. The shiny gold paper seemed to whisper of happy secrets and of a woman who was never far from his thoughts.

"Thanks," he spoke from his heart, making little effort to conceal the excitement that seemed to radiate from the package to his fingertips. "I have something here that belongs to David, too. Let me get it." Reluctantly he set down the package and reached for the wooden figures that still sat on his mantel. He placed them in a bag, then handed the bag to Guy.

"Tell him the stable was too big to go in your pocket, and that I'll keep it here until he comes out here to live." Chase smiled as the plastic bag disappeared inside Guy's shabby coat.

"Thank you, Brother Kirkham. I can't tell you what this means . . . That Miss Emerson gave David the train he had his heart set on . . . now a job . . ." Guy struggled to control the emotion that threatened to leave him speechless.

Chase suddenly remembered Guy would have a long hike back to Ted's house where he'd presumably left his car. "How are you getting back to Darcy once you cross the sheep bridge?" he asked.

"Ted said Tracy and a couple of his hands would be checking the herd down that way around three this afternoon, and he'd tell them to watch for me. If I'm going to meet up with them, I'd best be on my way."

"Yes, there's a storm coming in. You'll want to be across the bridge before it arrives," Chase added.

Chase watched Guy until he was out of sight. He felt good about hiring the man. Through David he knew more of Guy's integrity than the man could begin to guess. It would be good to have the little family about the place. A warm feeling filled his chest. He thought about checking on the young ewe in the barn, then decided there was no hurry. He couldn't wait to see what Kendra had sent him.

Carrying the package to his chair, he sat down and fingered the crushed ribbon on top of the gift. How long had it been since he'd gotten a Christmas present—not counting the shirts and socks Lucy sent him every December? With care he pulled off the tape and smoothed the paper as he pulled it aside. He stared at the box, not comprehending for several seconds, then a slow grin spread across his face.

A telephone! She'd given him one of those little digital phones, a smaller model than the ones Ted and Tracy hauled around, but nevertheless, it was a telephone. Tentatively he touched the on button and his grin widened when the dial tone let him know she'd had it activated for him. "Now if I just knew her number!"

A slip of paper caught his eye. He unfolded it and laughed aloud. The paper had four telephone numbers labeled *Home, Work, Katy,* and *Cameron.* A brief sentence said she'd be at Katy's until January fifth. He glanced at the calendar and breathed a sigh of relief. Today was only the fourth. He leaned back, closed his eyes, and smiled in anticipation. Then anxiously, before he lost his nerve, he leaned forward and tapped in Katy's number. As the number began to ring, panic struck, and he nearly hung up. Fortunately someone answered before he could push the off button.

"Uh, may I speak to Kendra Emerson?" He found himself almost stammering.

"Okay," a very young voice agreed before bellowing, "Aunt Kendra! It's for you."

He fidgeted nervously as he waited for what seemed a long time, although it was no more than a minute.

"Hello," Kendra spoke tentatively, and Chase's heart went into overdrive. For precious seconds he couldn't speak. "Chase? Is that you, Chase?" He heard the hope in her voice and suddenly felt more courageous.

Over the miles that separated them he heard the same loneliness and tentative longing he carried deep inside his own lonely being. It freed his tongue, and he spoke. "Merry Christmas, Kendra." Some would say Christmas was past, but deep in his soul he knew that for him Christmas was just beginning.

"Chase!" Something in the way she said his name warmed him to his toes. He thanked her for the phone, and she told him she'd had good roads to follow all the way to Los Angeles. They went on to talk between bursts of static about the mess he'd found when he'd arrived home, and he assured her that Roscoe was fine when she asked, and that Rags was home now, too.

"I hired someone, not only to help with the lambing," he told her. "But I think he'll be a lot of help with getting the bridge rebuilt and doing the haying next summer." She shared his enthusiasm when he told her about Guy's visit.

"I think they've been having a hard time," she told him. "I talked to Vicki quite a bit before I left the hospital where the sheriff insisted David and I had to be checked. I'm convinced they're good people and they'll work hard to prove themselves. I know David will be delighted to live on the ranch with your dogs and the 'sheepies.'" His laughter joined hers as they both thought of David and remembered his enthusiasm for everything on the ranch.

"Glory had twins," he told her. "And before the day is over I suspect she'll have a grandchild, too."

"I wish I could see them," Kendra said wistfully.

"You'll be driving back to Salt Lake in a few days, won't you?" he asked, suddenly gripping the little phone tighter than necessary.

"Yes," she answered, and he wondered if she felt the same excitement he felt growing inside him. "I was going to start back tomorrow, but the weather forecast is for snow over the pass, so I thought I'd wait a couple of days."

"The bridge won't be finished by then, but with Guy here, I could leave the ranch long enough to meet you in Darcy for a few hours on Saturday." To spend a few hours with Kendra, he'd walk the whole way if he had to, but he was pretty sure Ted would loan him a vehicle once he reached his neighbor's ranch house. They made plans to meet and with reluctance he finally clicked the button to end the call. He whistled all the way to the barn to check on the young ewe.

CHAPTER 27

It was early Saturday morning when Chase arrived in Darcy. He was driving the big four-wheel-drive pickup truck he'd purchased by phone two days earlier. Guy had taken delivery of it for him the previous day, and Chase had made arrangements with Ted Peters to park it on his range as close to the sheep bridge as they could drive it until the other bridge was completed.

Nervously Chase parked in front of Decker's and looked at his watch. It would be several hours before Kendra arrived, so he busied himself at the lumberyard and the hardware store while he waited. The telephone office was his next stop. The small wireless phone was great, but sometimes the signal was mostly static. He figured it was time to make arrangements for a line to be run to the ranch or to invest in a heavy-duty portable. He should have done it years ago, but until recently he hadn't particularly cared about talking to anyone.

Shortly past noon he saw a small blue car turn onto Main Street. He had no idea what kind of car Kendra drove, but somehow he knew she was behind the wheel of that particular car and it wasn't just the Utah plates that gave her away. Standing beside his truck and watching her pull in next to him, Chase noticed his hands felt clammy. She stepped out of the car, and he stood frozen to the spot. Wearing faded jeans, hiking boots, and a bulky, blue nylon jacket with the picture of a truck stitched over her heart, she looked wonderful. The wind blew a strand of satiny brown hair across her eyes and she pushed it away with one hand, leaving him unable to string two coherent words together. Every word he'd rehearsed saying to her flew out of his head. She spoke first.

"Hello, Chase." The words were hesitant as though she were unsure of her welcome. Her hesitancy galvanized him into action.

"Kendra." He stepped forward, intending to take her hand, and somehow found his arms wrapping themselves around her. He bent until his cheek pressed against hers. It was soft and warm and sent an arrow of heat straight to his heart.

She backed up, blushing and laughing, and he wondered if he'd been too forward. Main Street was a pretty public place to hug a woman.

"I'm glad you came," he whispered.

"I am, too," she whispered back. Suddenly he felt like tossing his Stetson in the air and whooping with joy.

"Come on." He reached for her hand. "Let's go over to Carla's Diner for lunch, then we'd better stop to see David for a few minutes. And there are a few things we need to talk about."

The moment they stepped inside the diner, he knew he'd made a mistake. There would be no opportunity to talk. The whole town seemed to be present and bent on meeting Kendra. One person after another stopped at their table to thank her for her part in rescuing David Rolando. He couldn't even buy her dinner. Carla Munroe, the café's proprietor and chief waitress, insisted both of their meals were on the house.

Leaning back against the plastic-covered booth bench, he watched Kendra nibble on a piece of chicken then timidly smile at two elderly ladies who stopped to meet her. He'd seen them around before. Their hair was white and they generally clung to each other as though one would fall without the support of the other. The worst part was they were well-known as the town's most formidable busybodies. He stood politely when they stopped, and they both ignored him. They introduced themselves to Kendra as Sarah and Rose Elliot, widowed sisters-in-law, who had lived on neighboring ranches as children, married brothers, then had eventually decided to share a house in town after both their respective husbands had passed on. Kendra seemed a little taken aback at the disclosure of so much personal information upon first meeting the women, but she nodded sympathetically. He stood awkwardly for several minutes, then decided since they weren't paying any attention to him anyway, he might as well sit down and eat his dinner before it got cold.

"Young David told us how you saved him from those robbers," Sarah remarked in a loud voice.

"Oh, I didn't save him," Kendra protested modestly. "I only took care of him after they let us go."

"Same thing," Rose ended Kendra's protest.

"Now don't you go getting the idea this town is wild," Sarah warned.

"We never had a shooting or kidnapping before this," Rose added with a sniff.

"We're so glad you've come back. It'd be a shame if those rowdies scared you off before you had a chance to get used to us. 'Bout time young Kirkham got married. Don't believe in putting off marriage the way young folks do these days." Sarah went on. Kendra's face flamed red and Chase choked on the soft drink he'd been about to swallow.

"Come along, dear," Rose shouted to Sarah. "Best we leave these young folks alone to do their courtin'." She took Sarah's arm and the two tottered toward the door, leaving Chase and Kendra unable to even look at each other.

"I see you've met the sisters," a voice cut through their embarrassed silence. Chase looked up to see Bishop Samuelson. Quickly he introduced Kendra.

"They mean well," the bishop said, his gaze following the two elderly women as they reached the door.

"They're priceless," Kendra sputtered, then broke into full-scale laughter. Seeing her reaction, Chase began to laugh, too. At least Kendra hadn't been so upset by small town nosiness that she couldn't wait to escape.

"It's a pleasure to meet you at last," the bishop finally said to Kendra. "I've certainly heard a lot about you, and I'm glad you stopped in again on your way home."

Her eyes met Chase's and they both quickly looked away. The bishop chuckled before turning his attention to Chase. "How'd you manage to get away this close to lambing season?"

"Guy Rolando has started working for me. He's staying with the sheep tonight so I can be in town today. I'll head back out to the ranch right after church tomorrow," Chase explained.

"I'm glad you plan to stay for church. How about stopping by my office right after priesthood meeting?" Bishop Samuelson asked. "I promise I won't keep you too long," he added.

When Guy nodded in agreement, the bishop smiled at both of them. When he seemed about to leave, he looked back at them with a sparkle of mischief in his eyes. "You know Sarah and Rose aren't as batty as some folks think. Actually their advice is pretty good." He grinned and walked away.

Giving up on any chance of a quiet lunch, Chase left a generous tip on the table, since Carla wouldn't let him pay for their lunches, and hurried Kendra out of the restaurant.

On the ride to the Rolando home, Chase asked Kendra about her vacation in California, and she told him about her nieces and nephew and about the boats and fireworks on New Year's Eve, but she didn't mention Brent. Not that he was a secret. In fact, some day she hoped she could tell Chase the part he'd played in encouraging her to throw out her sisters' plans and act on her own dreams. Besides she was much more interested in hearing about the sheep and learning how Rags' wound had healed than talking about anything that had occurred in California.

At the Rolando home, David met her with a squeal of excitement. He hugged her, then tugged on her hand to lead her to see his train. She paused only long enough to say hello to Vicki and meet Becca before sprawling on the floor beside David to watch his sheep speed around the track, firmly packed in the red train's coal cars. The time flew by too quickly and it was soon time to say good-bye again.

"Guess what!" David gripped her hand tightly as he escorted her to Chase's truck.

"What?" she laughed down at his excited face.

"I'm going to go live on Chase's ranch. All of us—Daddy and Mom. Becca too. Why don't you come with us?"

If only he knew how much she wished she could be there with them. Instead of telling him so, she smiled and said, "I have a job in Salt Lake. I have to be back at work Monday morning."

"Please come," the boy pleaded. Chase didn't say anything, and she didn't know what to say.

"Perhaps I can visit sometime," she whispered and hurriedly climbed in the truck through the door Chase held open for her.

He didn't say anything on the drive back to Decker's department store where she'd left her car. Her hopes plummeted with each block they drove. She'd been so excited to come. She wished with all her heart that she, like David, was returning to the ranch, but Chase had said nothing about wanting her to stay or even come back for a visit.

When he parked his truck beside her car, he made no move to open the door. She sat quietly twisting her hands in her lap, wishing he would say something.

"I guess I'd better go," she finally managed.

"It's a long drive," he seemed to agree, but made no move to open the truck door. Feeling awkward, she debated whether she should simply open her own door and say good-bye to Chase and all her foolish hopes or continue to sit until he made some move. Only the memory of the peace that had filled her heart when she'd prayed about contacting Chase again kept her from reaching for the door handle.

Another minute or two passed before Chase shifted nervously in his seat. He had to say something. He couldn't let Kendra leave without telling her he wanted to see her again. Time had passed so quickly, and there had never seemed to be the right time to talk about exploring a future together.

"Lambing season has started," he finally blurted out. "It'll be in full swing through February and March."

She seemed to understand what he was trying to say. "You'll be awfully busy," she agreed.

Encouraged, he went on. "I won't be able to get to Salt Lake until after that. But if it's all right with you, I'd like to . . . that is . . . if you want me to . . . I'd like to go to Salt Lake and . . . uh, see you again." To his mortification, he was stammering like a boy asking for his first date.

"I'd like that very much," she whispered shyly. Her smile lit up dark corners he didn't even know he had and made him wonder how he'd last clear until April.

• • • • •

Sunday morning he sat through all three meetings and felt a spiritual awareness that seemed full of hope, and for the first time since he'd been a kid he bore his testimony during sacrament meeting. Priesthood meeting brought an unexpected camaraderie he hadn't known he'd needed. There was some joking and teasing about his unexpected house guest's return to Darcy the previous day, but he found he didn't mind, that in fact there was a welcoming element of friendship to the remarks.

Steeling his courage to knock on Bishop Samuelson's door, he tried not to worry, but he couldn't quite escape feeling like a small boy sent to the principal's office. He lost that feeling when the bishop opened the door and immediately embraced him warmly and invited him to sit down. Without quite knowing how it happened, he found himself telling Bishop Samuelson about Carol and Jesse and the long slow road that had led him back to the Church. He told him, too, about those days with Kendra and David and his budding hope for a future with Kendra.

"Sister Emerson struck me as a woman who won't settle for less than a temple marriage," the bishop remarked. "If things work out between the two of you, you'll have to be prepared to take that step."

"I wouldn't want anything else either this time," Chase answered. He'd known without ever discussing the matter that Kendra was a forever kind of woman.

"Good, I don't see any problem then," the bishop smiled. "It appears there aren't any serious obstacles you have to overcome, but your church attendance could be better."

"I know, and Guy and I have been talking about that. It will be hard for us to get to church regularly during lambing season, but we hope to take turns, barring an emergency. He brought me some books and has been helping me set up a study program at home, like teenagers who miss out on the opportunity to take seminary study."

"I have a couple of books here you might like to borrow." Bishop Samuelson rummaged through a cabinet behind his desk, then handed Chase two books, one about temples and one about preparing for a temple marriage.

He left the bishop's office filled with renewed anticipation and a sense of purpose, something that had been missing in his life for a long time. Next he stopped at the Rolando house to pick up a few things Vicki had said she wanted to send out to the ranch for Guy, then he turned toward home.

On his way to town the day before, Chase had stopped to replace the wire on the sheep bridge. Now crossing it, he remembered the strange experience that had occurred that afternoon two weeks ago on the bridge. He stopped in the middle of the bridge and looked up at the sky, then bowed his head. He'd prayed for help more times during that Christmas Day than he'd ever prayed for anything before in his life. Now he thanked his Heavenly Father, not only for sparing him and his charges, but for bringing Kendra into his life. Warmth eased into his heart, assuring him the way would be opened for them to be together.

He wished Kendra could have broken her drive by spending the night at the ranch, but her little car wouldn't have made it as far as the bridge on the weather-roughened road, even if he still had a bridge, and it would never survive the trek through Ted's hay fields to the sheep camp where they'd sheltered on Christmas night and where he'd just parked his new truck. He'd had to put the truck in four-wheel drive to make it. He wouldn't want her to have to take the long hike he'd already taken, nor the long one still ahead of him to make it to his house.

He had only known Kendra a short time, but already he knew he didn't like the prospect of being separated from her. He thought of Guy staying at the ranch while his wife and kids were still in town. Guy wouldn't make it into town to see his family often during the next few months, and Chase found he didn't like the thought of Vicki and Guy being apart. They should be together, just like he and Kendra should be together. He felt a sudden urgency to hurry the replacement of the main bridge.

That night he called Kendra to make certain she'd gotten safely home and to tell her about his talk with the bishop. The next night she called him to talk about her first day back at work. After that it seemed the most natural thing in the world to share a nightly telephone conversation. Their calls became the highlight of his life. His telephone bill would be astronomical, but he didn't care. He'd pay it cheerfully for the privilege of discussing each day's events with Kendra.

Over the next few weeks Guy proved to be a fast learner as a trickle of lambs filled the pens in the barns, and the two men spent every spare minute working on the bridge. On days when the ranch work was lighter and Guy wasn't needed to work with the sheep, he hiked down to the rock house to get it ready for his family. Chase made arrangements to install a gas-powered generator to provide power until arrangements could be made to extend the power line from Chase's house and barns to the rock house.

As January drew to a close, the bridge took shape, this time with steel girders to anchor it in place. The two men tacitly agreed that only the sturdiest bridge would do for Vicki to cross each day with the children on her way to the Peters' ranch. In his mind Chase pictured Kendra crossing that bridge, too, and he wanted only the best for her.

Guy mentioned to Ted Peters at church one Sunday that the bridge was almost complete and work had proceeded so quickly on the old rock house, he'd be ready to move his family into it in a few days, or as soon as a vehicle could travel between the two houses.

"I don't care if the house is ready or not, or if we have to carry our furniture and boxes on our backs," Vicki had whispered. "I'm ready to move. I don't like being apart so much." He didn't like it either. It was the most they'd been apart since they'd gotten married, and after nearly losing David, he wanted his family to be together.

"It won't be long," he promised as much to comfort himself as her.

The next day as he helped Chase hammer the last of the planks in place, they both heard a deep rumble and looked up to see Ted approaching with a Caterpillar on the back of his biggest hay truck.

"I hope you built that bridge good and sturdy," Ted called as he moved steadily toward it.

"It'll hold," Chase called back, and Guy felt a surge of pride as the big truck with its heavy cargo rumbled across the bridge he and Chase had built.

"All right, where do you want that road?" Ted asked him, and Chase pointed to a row of stakes between the river and the cedars. As Guy looked to where Chase pointed, he was filled with a sense of anticipation. He'd had no idea Chase planned to build a road so soon.

It took most of the week to cut the road and he lost track of the number of trucks that arrived to spread a layer of gravel along the longer lane leading to the rock house and the shorter one leading to

Chase's house. When the job was finished, Guy helped Ted and Chase load the Caterpillar back on the truck and as he snapped the last chain in place, he looked up to see Chase and Ted talking together. A broad smile lit Chase's face, and as the truck rumbled back across the new bridge, Chase walked over to him and handed him his cell phone.

"You'd better call the fuel company and make certain they can deliver fuel for your heater tomorrow," he said. "Then call Vicki and tell her to get packed. I want them out here Friday because Saturday I'm flying to Salt Lake with Ted. You can use my truck to move, and Ted said he'd get some of the elders to help."

• • • • •

Vicki awoke to the sound of muffled giggles. She glanced toward the uncurtained window and groaned. The blackness of night had only turned to a lighter shade of gray. It couldn't possibly be considered morning yet. A glance at her watch confirmed it was almost six. She considered burrowing back beneath the covers, then a slow smile slid across her face and she leaped from bed. She felt a moment's shock as her feet hit the cold linoleum floor and she hurried to find her slippers. Today was the first day of their new life and she didn't want to waste a minute of it.

Wending her way through packing boxes to the kitchen, she found Guy and the kids sitting at the table with an open box of cold cereal between them. Becca and David didn't seem to be any the worse for spending the night in sleeping bags on the living room floor. Their bedrooms weren't finished yet, but Guy had promised to work on them every spare minute he could.

She was surprised to see her father at the table, too. He'd arrived a week ago, looking fragile and frail, yet he'd pitched in and insisted on helping them move to Chase's ranch the day before. He should be resting, instead of getting up before dawn, she thought. She shouldn't have let him do so much yesterday, but he'd seemed so happy to be helping that she hadn't said anything. She wondered if he'd had trouble sleeping in the new house.

"Good morning," she called softly.

"Morning, honey," her father smiled.

"Hi, Mom," the kids chorused while Guy stood and came around the table to give her a quick kiss.

"Sorry," he murmured. "We didn't mean to wake you. You worked so hard yesterday, we thought you'd sleep until noon."

"I didn't work any harder than you did." She smiled back at him. The previous day had been difficult and exhausting and today she definitely had a few aching muscles, but she was glad to be awake. She had a house to organize and a whole new world to explore.

"That isn't much of a breakfast for a bunch of ranch hands." She looked disapprovingly at the box of cold cereal on the table.

"We like it." David grinned and dug his spoon into his bowl.

"The stove doesn't work, so we couldn't cook oatmeal," Becca informed her and Vicki noticed her daughter didn't appear particularly disappointed.

"I meant to tell you about that." Guy looked guilty as he explained. "Until the power company installs our line, we won't be able to use the stove. It takes a 220 line and the generator only gives us a 120. That means just lights and small appliances. It'll only be for a few weeks."

"I could fix pancakes in the electric fry pan," she offered. "Cold cereal won't stay with you very long, and you'll be working out in the cold."

"I'll be fine," he assured her as he pulled out a chair for her to join them. "You can have a warm supper waiting when I get back."

"I want to go with you," David told his father. "I want to help."

"Not today." Guy reached over to ruffle his son's hair. "Chase will be gone all day, and I'll be awfully busy. Besides your mother needs help getting all of our things unpacked and put where they belong."

"Where am I going to put my toys?" He looked around, noticing for the first time the obvious lack of space.

"You'll have to leave most of them in a box for a while," Vicki told him.

"I'll build you some shelves in your room for your toys," Guy told him. "But I probably won't have time until after all the lambs are born."

"I want to see the lambs again," Becca stated. She'd been enthralled with the little ones she'd visited for a few minutes when they'd first arrived the day before.

"I didn't know Chase had another house," David announced. He jumped up from the table and ran to look out the window. "I like it!"

I like it, too, Vicki thought. Looking around the snug kitchen, she thought how a little over a month ago she'd been feeling sorry for herself because Guy was out of work, the washer had broken, and they had no money for Christmas. This Christmas had turned out to be the most wonderful Christmas of her life, though it came a day late. She still didn't have a washing machine, but Chase had offered the use of his until she and Guy could arrange to buy one.

This house is old, she mused as she looked at the high ceilings and old-fashioned cupboards, but the rock walls will keep us warm this winter and cool next summer. *Already it feels more like home than anywhere else ever has. It isn't big enough for five people, but helping Guy turn the attic into bedrooms will give Dad something useful to do.* She could see where a sun room or family room could be added next to the kitchen. *In a few months I'll plant a garden.* Her excitement grew as she pictured fresh tomatoes and corn. Her heart felt light with the anticipation of all the things she and her family planned for this house.

Sunlight sent tentative fingers of light into the room, catching David framed in the deep window embrasure, and she sobered thinking of those dark days when she didn't know if she would ever see him again in this life. David's disappearance had taught her people matter most. It had also strengthened her faith in God. Somehow He had taken the darkest days of her life and turned them into a prelude to her greatest joy. Her family was together now, with both David and her father where she could watch over them. Guy would be home each night, they could stay in this open country they loved, and they would raise their children to feel secure in both their parents' and their Heavenly Father's love.

CHAPTER 28

Chase was awfully quiet, Kendra thought as she drove down the Bangerter Highway with him in the passenger seat. They'd soon be to Airport II, where he was to meet Ted Peters for the ride back to the Peters' ranch. This was the third time he'd caught a ride with his neighbor for the trip to Salt Lake. Each time Chase's short visit ended, she found it harder than the time before to watch the little plane take off, heading west and leaving her behind.

Turning west on 6200 South, she inched along in bumper-to-bumper traffic on the too-narrow street. Suddenly Chase pointed to a church parking lot on the south side of the street.

"Pull over here," he said. Startled, she put on her turn signal and waited for an opening to make a left-hand turn. It would be difficult to get back on the road, but she didn't care. Stopping to share a few last minutes together would be worth it.

The moment she shut off the engine, she was surprised to find Chase suddenly wrenching open his door. He stalked around to her side of the car and opened her door. Puzzled she stepped out.

"Let's go for a walk," Chase said and led her across the parking lot to an area that was probably a nice little park in the summer time, but right now the grass was brown and the trees looked dead. A chill breeze blew from the Oquirrh Mountains, rattling a nearby leafless shrub. It wasn't exactly the kind of day one normally chose for taking a walk. Chase frowned and continued on to where a closed bower provided a scant amount of shelter on one side. With one hand, Kendra snugged her coat tighter against her throat. It seemed much colder than when they'd strolled through Temple Square and walked to the new Assembly Hall earlier in the day.

He placed his hands on her shoulders. Turning her to face him, he scowled and she drew a shaky breath. Chase had acted nervous since he'd arrived shortly before noon and had hardly eaten when they'd stopped at the Olive Garden for lunch. She wondered if he were trying to find a way to tell her he wouldn't be coming again. He'd come to mean so much to her, she couldn't bear it if he decided not to see her anymore.

"Kendra, this has got to stop. I can't keep running off this time of year to come to Salt Lake." His words left her wanting to scream in protest, but he quickly went on as though he'd finally found the words he'd been struggling with all day. "Each time we say good-bye, it feels like I'm near dying. I want to marry you and take you back with me. Is there any chance you could put up with me and come to live in the middle of nowhere with me as my wife?"

Speechless, she stared at him until the light began to dim in his eyes, sending her into a near panic. She certainly didn't mean to appear reluctant, when in fact, he was offering her exactly her most cherished dream. Finally she found her voice, "Oh, yes, Chase. I want that more than anything." She threw herself in his arms, laughing and crying.

He held her in a crushing bear hug and she knew she wasn't the only one trembling with emotion. "Are you sure you don't mind giving up your career and all those city things women like to do?" Chase asked, a note of concern in his voice.

"No, I don't mind at all." If only he knew how little she cared about those "city things"! She stood on her toes to reach his mouth and assure him she found other things more important than her career.

They hugged each other until Chase suddenly remembered he had a plane to catch.

"Honey, I don't have a ring for you. There hasn't been time to . . ."

"It doesn't matter," she interrupted him.

"It does matter," he protested. "We'll pick one out the next time I can get away for a day." He kissed her again. "We'd better go now. I don't want to keep Ted waiting." His actions belied his words as he bent to kiss her once more.

A few minutes later at the airport, they told Ted their news. He congratulated them but didn't appear the least bit surprised. He smiled broadly as he congratulated them.

"When's the big day?" he asked.

They looked at each other blankly, then Chase grinned. "The sooner, the better as far as I'm concerned. You pick any day you want," he told Kendra. "But I guess you'd better pick a date after lambing season is over and after we've both had time to make appointments with our bishops."

"I'll call the temple in the morning to see what days are available," she whispered to Chase before the two men boarded the plane.

Ted ducked his head to enter the plane, then stopped, nearly causing Chase to run into him. "Hey, Kendra," he called. "Aren't you an accountant?" When she nodded, he shouted back, "If you get bored counting sheep, come on over to my place. I've got a few cows that need counting. I've been looking for an accountant for years." Chuckling, he ducked his head and disappeared inside the plane without waiting for a response. Chase gave her one last long look, then disappeared, too.

• • • • •

"You can't be serious!" Katy wailed as she stopped her pacing to face Kendra. "Cameron and I have discussed this thoroughly, and we just can't let you do it."

"Can't let me?" Kendra laughed. "Who's the big sister here?"

"You are," Katy bit her lip. "But you haven't been yourself since that awful incident at Christmas. I know you have reason to be grateful to that sheepherder for rescuing you, but you don't need to marry him."

"Katy, he's not a sheepherder, he's a rancher. And I'm not marrying him out of gratitude; I'm marrying him because I love him." Kendra tried to be patient, but she'd been annoyed ever since Katy had arrived to try to talk her out of getting married. It seemed she and Cameron had decided one of them needed to talk some sense into their big sister, and Katy had been elected.

"Oh, Kenny," Katy started to cry and reverted to the nickname she'd given Kendra when she was a child. "Why couldn't you fall in love with Dr. Chambers? You were so perfect together."

Kendra walked to her sister's side and placed an arm around her. "Brent is a good man, but I don't love him, and he doesn't love me. When you get to know Chase, you'll see he's a wonderful man. Why can't you just be happy for me?"

"How can I be happy about having my sister, who has always been a second mother to me, go live in some remote place full of sagebrush and sheep and snakes? I won't see you anymore. You won't be able to shop or go to concerts or do anything fun. And you'll be wasted on a man who smells like sheep and doesn't know the difference between tin plates and Mama's good china," Katy sobbed.

Kendra struggled not to laugh. "Sit down in that chair," she said sternly to Katy while pointing at a comfortable velvet-covered rocking chair she planned to take with her to Nevada. Sulkily Katy sat.

"I want you to listen," Kendra continued in her best big sister voice. "You're confusing a modern sheep ranch with the Australian outback or the wild west of the nineteenth century. Chase has a modern house with all the modern conveniences, including a microwave and a jetted tub. He bathes every day and his table manners are as fine as anyone's. More important, he's a decent, loving individual who makes me happy. He's also an elder, worthy to take me to the temple. His ranch is remote, but I don't care. I love the fresh air, being able to see forever, being around his animals, and most of all, him. I've never liked to shop, and I'd much sooner relax in front of the fireplace and listen to a concert on a compact disc than get dressed up for a concert. We can travel and shop if we choose to—just not during the busiest times at the ranch."

"But we had it all planned," Katy continued to protest.

"You and Cameron had it all planned," Kendra corrected.

"We only want what is best for you," her sister asserted.

"Remember when you told me you and Bob were getting married, and I said you were too young? You reminded me you were all grown up, and you could do what you wanted. Now I'm telling you the same thing. I'm all grown up and I'm going to marry Chase. You were right then, and so am I right now." She smiled, trying to make peace with her sister.

Shakily Katy returned her smile. "Okay, I don't like it, but if you insist on living where there isn't even a Nordstrom's, we don't have any time to waste. We need to start shopping. You're going to need a wedding dress, a flannel nighty, and a complete outback trousseau."

"It's a deal," Kendra laughed, reaching for her sister to hug her. "Let me grab my checkbook and we're on our way!"

That evening as Kendra curled up on the sofa with the telephone in her hand to talk to Chase, she told him about her sister's visit and their whirlwind shopping trip. They laughed together, then he told her he'd had a visitor that day, too.

"Guy and I both were in the barn when we heard a vehicle pull up outside. Guy went to check and in a few minutes he came back with a tall blond man, dressed like he was headed for church, only he was carrying a fancy brief case. He asked to speak to me alone, so I took him to the house."

"Surely a salesman didn't track you down clear out at the ranch?" Kendra laughed.

"No, he wasn't a salesman. At first I thought he might be a lawyer for those crooks that caused you so much trouble, but it didn't take him long to let me know he was your brother-in-law and he was looking out for your interests."

"You're kidding! Kurt came to see you?" Kendra straightened in her seat and made no attempt to restrain her indignation. Katy was one thing, but her brother-in-law had no business playing big brother.

"Yeah, it seems your brothers-in-law are as concerned as your sisters that you might be making a big mistake. Kurt drew the short straw and came to confront the dragon in his lair," Chase drawled.

"He had no right!" Kendra sputtered.

"Yes, I think he did," Chase disagreed. "Your family loves you, and I can understand their concern. They don't know me or anything about the life we'll be living. I think maybe it was a good thing he came."

"Kurt is a good man, but he can be rather pompous and a bit overbearing," Kendra admitted reluctantly.

"I figured that out right quick," Chase chuckled. "But we parted on pretty good terms. I think I convinced him you won't be disappearing into some uncharted wilderness."

"And he knows I won't change my mind?" she asked.

"He knows I won't change my mind," Chase corrected. Kendra thought how she would have loved to witness that meeting between Kurt, who saw himself as the head of the family, and Chase, two strong-willed men with slightly outdated notions about taking care of the women they loved.

CHAPTER 29

Today was the day! A shiver of happiness launched Kendra out of bed and into the shower. All while she dressed she found herself thinking, *In a few hours I will become Mrs. Chase Kirkham! Kendra Kirkham!* The name sounded wonderful! She wanted to pinch herself to be certain she wasn't dreaming. She'd given up dreams of marrying a long time ago. Now she was not only getting married, but she was marrying the most wonderful man in the world!

But when she attempted to brush her hair and apply her usual light makeup, nothing seemed to look right. She kept trying, even though she knew Katy would redo it the first opportunity she found. After her fourth try, she finally gave up. In exasperation she put away her lipstick. Her hands shook so badly, she knew she'd never get it straight!

Finishing her preparations with a burst of nervous energy, she gathered her luggage near the door and moved the plastic bag holding her wedding dress from the closet. Her sisters and their husbands would be here soon. They were in rooms further down the hall in the same hotel where Kendra had spent her last night as a single woman. Yesterday they had helped her pack all her belongings in the back of Chase's pickup, and she'd returned her apartment key to her landlord. She'd felt a little tug of sadness to leave her cozy apartment, but the feeling hadn't lasted long. Her apartment had served her well, but she was ready to move on. She could hardly wait to share Chase's home. Along with shopping for a trousseau, she'd picked out curtains for the kitchen, a room that already held some of her most precious memories.

Looking around, she discovered there was nothing more to do, but pace a path in the carpet. She was ready and her family wouldn't arrive for twenty more minutes. No, there was one more thing she must do. Sinking to her knees beside the bed, she opened her heart in a prayer of gratitude to her Heavenly Father. As she prayed, peace filled her heart. A quiet certainty filled her soul, assuring her that meeting Chase had been no chance encounter. The Lord had seen the righteous desires of their hearts and brought them together. When they spoke their vows this morning in God's holy temple, it would be with His complete approval.

• • • • •

Tulips and pansies, damp from a brief early morning shower, lined the walk, lending an air of festivity to the April morning as Chase hurried toward the temple. Beside him his sister's heels tapped a rapid staccato, and he slowed a bit to make keeping pace with him easier. Slowing his steps was difficult. He wanted to run, maybe even shout. It was a glorious morning and he was on his way to meet his bride. He supposed he should be nervous; he certainly had been the day of his first wedding. He'd been so scared, he'd thought of jumping in his car and leaving town. No hesitation or doubts plagued him this morning, however. He knew with all of his heart and soul that he wanted to marry Kendra, today, in this special place.

He paused a moment to stare up at the spires glistening in the early morning sunshine. He'd entered that building for the first time only the day before, and today he was filled with anticipation for his return.

"I'm happy for you," Lucy spoke. "I'm glad you found Kendra. I only met her yesterday, but I feel almost like I've always known her." She paused a moment, then went on. "I know you're big and tough and perfectly capable of leading your own life. Still I've worried about you and prayed you'd meet someone you could be as happy with as I've been all these years with Kevin. You probably think Kendra is the answer to your prayers, but in a way she's the answer to mine, too."

"You were praying for a wife for me?" Chase raised an eyebrow at his sister's statement.

"In a way," she admitted calmly. "I think what I prayed the hardest for was for you to love, and be loved, again. I think marrying

Kendra in this sacred place will finally bring you peace. I'm still praying that one day we can have Mom and Dad sealed to each other and the two of us to them, becoming the family I think we always should have been."

"Do you think Mom would want that?" Chase knew he sounded skeptical, but though his father was a member, his mother had never been baptized. She had attended church with her husband and children occasionally, but had never expressed a desire to join the Church.

"Mom was never the problem," Lucy quietly informed him. "I think she would have been baptized if Dad had ever indicated it mattered to him. He only attended church when it was convenient, and he never gave any indication that it was particularly important to him. Before he died, he regretted that a great deal."

They were at the door now. Chase showed his recommend to one of the men dressed in white at the first desk and watched as his name was checked off on a list, before he and Lucy were directed to an area to wait for Kendra to arrive. Lucy's husband, Kevin, joined them a few minutes later, puffing from his jog from the parking lot where he'd left his car. Chase found conversation impossible as his attention drifted to the sliding glass doors each time they opened.

They didn't have to wait long. Some sense alerted him to Kendra's presence seconds before the doors slid soundlessly open. Their eyes met and he knew how essential she was to his eternal happiness. She was his family, his forever. Softly he spoke to Lucy without taking his eyes off Kendra, "If you'll take care of the paperwork and set a date, we'll meet you at whatever temple you choose, any day you like. I think I'm just beginning to understand how important it is for families to be together forever. In fact, Kendra suggested a few weeks ago that I should have Carol and Jesse sealed to me. I don't know if Carol will accept that, but I mean to give them that choice. Mom and Dad should have that choice, too."

Kendra stepped to his side and he bent to lightly brush her mouth with his, then they were lost in a happy swirl of activity. They were interviewed and produced their marriage license, then rushed off to dress for the ceremony. At every turn, Kendra found a sweet elderly lady in white directing her to where she should be. Her sisters fussed with her hair, smoothing into place the simple, heavy satin dress she had chosen. Other brides, much younger brides, dressed in lacy, frothy gowns filled the brides' room, and as she joined them to view herself in the floor-to-ceiling mirrors, she felt just as lovely.

Chase's eyes confirmed that feeling when she sat beside him in the celestial room for a few precious private moments before proceeding to the sealing room where their families waited. A few minutes later Chase took her hand as they knelt at the altar, and joy filled her heart. Chase spoke his responses firmly and she followed with no hesitation. Warmth and peace enfolded her. Words she hadn't even known she'd memorized flooded her soul, *Be still and know I am God and that with me all things are possible.*

CHAPTER 30

Rain fell in a gentle patter against the windshield as Chase drove his king cab pickup truck toward the new bridge. Kendra leaned forward to see better. The bridge was wide and smooth, hardly making a sound, as they crossed. Beneath them water frothed and churned with the enthusiasm of spring runoff, but there was nothing frightening about it as there had been the last time she had come this way.

To their left she picked out the stand of cedar trees where she and Chase had found a Christmas tree for David. A new road forked to the left, leading, she knew, to the old rock house that had become the Rolando home. Chase took his hand from the wheel and squeezed hers gently. She knew he was remembering, too.

"The potholes are gone," she laughed as the new truck purred smoothly up the hill.

"I had them filled with gravel, but they'll be back," he assured her. They rounded a corner and pulled to a stop in front of the house. Neither one spoke or moved. Slowly Kendra looked around. Everything was the same, yet so different. A nearly black mountain towered behind the ranch buildings, but somehow it didn't look so forbidding. Green pastures and hayfields spread across gentle slopes, and the hills were dotted with sheep. Lambs played beside their mothers. In the corral beside the barn, a spindly-legged colt cavorted beside its mother. A sharp bark drew her attention, and she looked toward the barn to see Roscoe trotting toward the truck. Behind him pranced Rags, followed by three staggering puppies.

"Oh, Chase, they're so cute." She hurriedly exited the truck and stooped to pick up one of the puppies. Rags licked her face and

Roscoe stood back, wagging his tail in obvious paternal pride.

Chase hunkered down beside Kendra, and the remaining puppies immediately crawled over his boots. "I think old Roscoe got a little lonely when Rags followed us across the sheep bridge that night." He grinned before adding, "He wasn't the only one that got lonely."

Kendra smiled and leaned toward her brand-new husband. He reached out a hand to cup her cheek, and her eyes closed.

"Hurry up, you guys!" a voice shouted from behind them. Kendra turned to see David standing in the doorway of the house. Feeling slightly flustered, she set the puppy back on the ground before turning to face him.

Chase's arm came around her waist and they walked slowly through the misty rain toward the house. When she would have hurried forward to embrace David, Chase swept her up in his arms to carry her across the threshold to a chorus of clapping hands and cheers. When he set her on her feet, David catapulted toward her. Next she received a hug from Vicki and a hearty handshake from Guy. Vicki pushed a suddenly shy Becca forward to meet her again, then introduced her to a smiling, older gentleman Kendra understood was the children's grandfather.

She took a deep breath and the tang of cedar filled her lungs. Then she saw it. A huge cedar tree filled the front window. It was decorated with silver stars and colored paper chains. A few of her own origami birds, looking a little sad for wear, graced some of the branches. Beneath the tree was a little wooden stable, where a slightly grubby infant rested on a manger of real straw, surrounded by sheep and dogs, three wise men with their camels, a couple of angels, and a reunited Joseph and Mary.

Kendra opened her purse and groped for the lamb David had given her that long-ago winter day. Carefully she knelt to place the little figure back with its flock, and David beamed his approval.

"Everybody's here now," he exclaimed as he knelt beside her. She couldn't speak, but she felt Chase's hand on her shoulder and knew he understood.

"We couldn't come to your wedding party," David announced, and she smiled at him through the wet mist that covered her eyes. "We tended the sheep so Chase could go."

"Thank you," she whispered back. "I'm glad Chase could come."

Everyone laughed, but David went on, "Chase said Christmas was really in the spring, and that the Baby Jesus was born about the same time as the baby lambs, so I told Mom we should have a Christmas party for you 'cause Christmas is the bestest."

Chase raised her to her feet and somewhere in the background she heard David saying something about pumpkin pie and fudge, but all she really heard was Chase murmuring, "the very bestest," just before he kissed her.

ABOUT THE AUTHOR

Jennie Hansen is a well-recognized name in LDS romantic fiction, with several successful best-sellers to her credit, including *Run Away Home, Some Sweet Day,* and most recently, *The River Path.* A circulation specialist at the Salt Lake City Library, Jennie has also worked as a newspaper reporter and editor. She has served in all of the ward auxiliaries as well as in a stake Primary presidency and as Stake Inservice Leader. Before serving in her current calling as the ward Teacher Improvement Coordinator, Jennie served as the education counselor in her ward Relief Society.

She and her husband, Boyd, make their home in Salt Lake County. They are the proud parents of ten children now that their four daughters and one son have married. To their delight they now also have five grandchildren.

Jennie writes from a firm belief in our Savior's love for all of his children. She believes that love is an integral part of relationships between a man and a woman, between family members, and in lasting friendships.

Jennie welcomes readers' comments. You can write to her in care of Covenant Communications, P.O. Box 416, American Fork, Utah 84003-0416.